A DRAGON'S GUIDE TO KILLING GODS (AND OTHER LIES)

LEAH R CUTTER

Reviews
It's true. Reviews help me sell more books. If you've enjoyed this story, please consider leaving a review of it on your favorite site.

Come someplace new...
Are you a traveler? Do you enjoy exploring strange new worlds, new cultures, new people? Sign up for my newsletter and I'll start you on your travels with a free copy of my book, *The Island Sampler*.

http://www.LeahCutter.com/newsletter/

Buy More!
Did you know that you can buy directly from the Knotted Road Press website?

https://www.knottedroadpress.com/shop/

ALSO BY LEAH R CUTTER

Epic Fantasy Series

The Fallen Elves

Ruins of the Gods

Stairs of the Gods

Cities of the Gods

Graves of the Gods

Houses of the Dead

Houses Divided

Houses Fallen

Houses Reborn

Forgotten Gods

A Wind Blown Torment

A Stone Strewn Clash

A Sea Washed Victory

The Tanesh Empire Trilogy

The Glass Magician

The Desert Heart

The Ghost Dog

Urban/Contemporary Fantasy Series

The Shadow Wars Trilogy

The Raven and the Dancing Tiger

The Guardian Hound

War Among the Crocodiles

The Cassie Stories

Poisoned Pearls

Tainted Waters

Spoiled Harvest

Bloodied Ice

The Witch's Progress

Circle of Air

Circle of Fire

Circle of Water

Circle of Earth

Seattle Trolls

The Changeling Troll

The Princess Troll

The Fairy-Bridge Troll

The Troll-Demon War

The Troll-Human War

The Troll-Troll War

The Clockwork Fairy Kingdom

The Clockwork Fairy Kingdom

The Maker, the Teacher, and the Monster

The Dwarven Wars

The Chronicles of Franklin

Franklin Versus The Popcorn Thief

Franklin Versus The Soul Thief

Franklin Versus The Child Thief

Science Fiction

The Long Run

Project Nemesis

Project Nyx

Project Tisiphone

Project Persephone

War of the Allied Worlds

The Labors of Darius Linard

Huli Intergalactic: Science/Space Fantasy

Origins

The Strawberry Girl

Mysteries

The Purloined Letter Opener

The Tell Tale Heart Pin

Dancer in Darkness

Trophy Hunters

The Alvin Goodfellow Case Files

The Rabbit Mysteries

The Shredded Veil Mysteries

Mystery, Crime, and Mayhem

CONTENTS

HERE THERE BE DRAGONS

THE FINDING OF THE FOUNDLING

ORLA HAS TWO DADDIES

A WIZARD IN TIME

A RECIPE FOR WAR

EPILOGUE

HERE THERE BE DRAGONS

IN THE BEGINNING...

The great god Ulthir was lonely.

He was the epitome of loneliness sitting by himself on the top of his mountain. He exuded solitude from every pore of his being. Nothing else existed except for Ulthir, his mountain, and the stars above him. Since he was the only one who existed, he *defined* loneliness at that point, at the start of everything.

Because Ulthir didn't have a mother, let alone a grandmother, he didn't have someone to smack him upside the head and tell him to *do* something about his loneliness. He was the great god Ulthir! He could do whatever he liked. He didn't need anyone to tell him anything.

So it took him longer than he wanted to eventually come to the conclusion that maybe he should create something to alleviate that pesky loneliness of his. (Some of the tales of the Before Times state that it took him eons. He adamantly denies that it took him *that* long.)

(Perhaps a single eon. Not several.)

Like all proper mountains, snow capped the top of Ulthir's. One day, when he was *not* just feeling sorry for himself and moping like a god half his age, Ulthir gave a great (not self-pitying) sigh. He might have been laying down on the snow instead of sitting in his proper seat at the time.

The snow reacted to the great expulsion of his breath, dancing up and swirling a little before it settled back down again.

Ulthir blinked, startled.

That was *new*.

Something else in all the universe had just moved, not just Ulthir.

So he blew again, delighting in how the snow swirled up for a moment then settled back down again.

However, even the great god Ulthir grew tired of forever blowing and sighing. There had to be something else he could do. Plus, he was cold lying flat on his stomach on the snow. Not very comfy at all.

At one point, Ulthir had blown so hard he was dizzy when he sat up. That made him stick his hands in the snow and raise them up, watching the snow gently fall from his fingers, a dazzling white stream against the cold black sky.

Some of the snow melted on his bare fingers, forming into ice crystals.

When he blew those off, they twirled a bit before settling back down again.

It didn't take long for Ulthir to figure out not just how to form ice crystals, but proper tops. They followed the same crystalline structure as the snow, with sharp points on the top and bottom, while the sides were flat planes that slightly bulged in the center.

When Ulthir set his tops to spin, for the first time, there was laughter in the universe. It echoed across the cold stars, making Ulthir's great seat on the mountain tremble. When the laughter sunk down into the shadows of the snow, Ulthir felt it taking root, sending tendrils down, beneath his domain.

He didn't pay attention to what was below, not at first. Some of the writings of the Before Times claim that was the beginnings of the world of men. Ulthir wouldn't deny that might be the case, though he'd like to think that creating a world took more forethought, even for a god such as he.

For a while (not even a single eon) Ulthir delighted in watching his crystal tops dance before his seat. They frequently kicked up the snow that lay there, their sharp points digging through the cold white fluff.

Eventually, the tops got all the way down, through the snow, and into the black earth that lay underneath.

Ulthir may have been disturbed and cursed a bit when he saw the flecks of black on his clean crystal tops. However, after he stopped one set of twirling tops to clean them off, the next set promptly got dirty.

He was stuck again, instead of forever blowing snow to watch it dance, now he was forever blowing dirt off spinning tops to clean them.

How did the universe get so messy? Particularly when there were still so few things in it?

There were some questions not even the great god Ulthir could answer.

Still, Ulthir was intrigued by the dirt. Maybe he could do something with it.

Again, after a *short* while (nowhere near even a decade, or so Ulthir swears) the great god started experimenting with making dirt tops. He invented clay—dirt that hardened with just a little heat applied—then set those tops to dance beside the pure crystal forms.

It got him thinking about what else he could create out of clay.

It didn't take him too long to create a form that resembled his own. But this wasn't a simple top that he could just set spinning. No, it needed more.

He tried using ice inside the clay creature, but that didn't work. So instead, he took the cold winds that blew on the mountains to give the creature breath. Then he took the fire of life, turned that into blood, and filled the creature with it.

However, the clay creature just lay there, inert.

Ulthir may have sworn at it. A bit.

It wasn't until he exposed his creation to the bright light of day that the creature stirred and began to move.

Ulthir named him Eomar because it sounded like a good name. It could mean whatever he wanted it to, so Eomar became the first man, the first dancer, the first, well, everything.

Ulthir set Eomar to dance among his crystal and clay tops. But Eomar was clumsy, and sometimes stepped on the tops, breaking them. Plus, Eomar wasn't tireless, unlike his other creations. When the light receded, Eomar needed to rest.

Plus, Eomar seemed to have inherited his creator's loneliness. Not that he was copying Ulthir when he gave great sighs and moans. Ulthir had never sounded as pitiful as that. Really.

So Ulthir made Eomar a mate, named Eowin. She, at least, was a lot more graceful and didn't step on things or break them. Many nights, after she tucked her husband in, she came to look at the stars with Ulthir for a while before she rested.

Light seemed entranced with Eowin. Ulthir would sometimes see her dancing alone, with just the stars as her companions. She was more practical than either Ulthir or Eomar as well, and so, instead of complaining about how empty everything was, or how alone the three of them were, she went ahead and did something about it.

The light that loved Eowin so much made her fertile. Both Ulthir and Eomar were a little befuddled by that, but Eowin easily bore her children, one after another. Hundreds, then thousands of them.

It was getting a little crowded on Ulthir's mountain. And as much as he loved the company, sometimes, he still needed time alone. (Everyone needs a little "me" time, right?)

About that time, Maloneal came into being—whether borne by Eowin, created by Ulthir, or birthed by the stars has never been precisely determined. Different tales tell different origins of the trickster. Perhaps all three played a role. Or perhaps Maloneal simple assumed himself into being. (Ulthir wouldn't put it past that arrogant twit.)

Maloneal wanted to leave Ulthir's mountain. The words, "This mountain isn't big enough for the two of us," were spoken, maybe in anger or perhaps in jest.

After many adventures, Maloneal eventually led Eowin along with her children on a daring escape, taking them into the green fields of the world that had grown below, showing them how to sow wheat, hunt the creatures who lived there, as well as build sturdy shelters.

Ulthir was fit to be tied. He huffed and stomped angrily across the top of his mountain. Even his crystal tops no longer brought him joy.

He may have gone a little overboard at that time, nearly destroying all his creations, first through flood, then through fire. He'll acknowledge that his reaction was a bit excessive. He's a big enough god to admit that perhaps, *maybe*, he went slightly crazy at the time.

However, Ulthir also discovered that when left on their own, Eowin's children were *fascinating* to watch. Much better than plain tops. Though he still kept a few of those out of sentimental value, continually dancing at the foot of his great seat on the mountain, he spent most of his time looking below.

Eowin left the earth and came back up the mountain to be with Ulthir, though she tended to only come out after the sun had set, to spend time with him under the stars, looking out over the cold expanse of snow, down onto the hills and valley far below.

Eomar stayed with their children on the world below. In time, he fashioned a few of his own: the lesser, local gods, who people could use to communicate with Ulthir and Eowin. They lived where Eomar placed them, haunting mountains, rivers, glens, forests, and even occasionally, cities.

Maloneal came and went, depending on his mercurial mood.

After the local gods and goddesses were established, he may have then decided to show off a little (I know, I can tell, you're all shocked, shocked I say) when he siphoned off a bit of that divine essence and brought magic to people.

Mostly, Ulthir ignored those on the world below, or so he'd claim. He'd deny that he's old too, though he's been there, up on his mountain, since the beginning of time. It is more and more difficult for people to prompt him into action. Possibly because he claims not to be lonely anymore: so many people to watch, little stories to follow, small lives to live to the fullest. And he has Eowin who still dances for him sometimes, when the stars align and the moon is just right.

It is possible though, to get through to Ulthir, to get him to grant a boon.

This is the tale of one such hero who makes that attempt. And it didn't take him eons to do it, either.

KILLIAN

Killian woke with a start, his blood on fire.

It was strange, really, for him to be sweating and so warm. Though it was only the start of fall, the nights already had a bite to them, as evidenced in white clouds breathed out by his army once the sun set, tent sides stiff with frost, and heavy piles of furs on his cot.

Except that Killian didn't feel any furs weighing him down. Had he kicked them off in his sleep? He remembered pulling them up and dropping off quickly, even with the huge battle coming in the morn.

It took him a moment to realize that something *else* held him down. Firmly. So firmly, in fact, that he couldn't sit up. Couldn't lift his head to look down his body. Was barely blinking. Couldn't move.

Yet, he was breathing. Wasn't he?

Or was that part of why it felt like his blood was on fire? Because his lungs burned without air?

It was only then, over the crackling roar of the blood in his veins, that Killian heard the chanting in a foreign, snaky tongue. Lots of hisses there, long drawn out vowels and very few clicks of "K"s or "T"s. (Killian couldn't help but remember when he'd expressed interest in learning a language other than Common, how one of his tutors had exclaimed that all them "furine" words would be the death of him. Had the man been prescient?)

Killian couldn't turn his head to look, but he would bet that there was a wizard standing by his left shoulder, reading from some ancient tome and casting a spell over him.

Why someone would do such a thing wasn't even a question.

Killian was the chosen one. All his life, he'd been favored by the Twins of Fate. He was destined to lead the armies of King Rodwell to victory over their sworn enemy, King Harald. Of course, his enemy would try to do something as underhanded as destroy him, the champion.

Though sending a wizard meant that they not only wanted to kill Killian, but to disfigure him, discredit him, or discombobulate him and his troops somehow.

But how?

Above Killian's head all he could see was the unbleached material of his tent, lit with an unnatural yellowish-green glow. He couldn't make out what was happening to him. Though he tried, he found he couldn't even close his eyes now that he'd managed to open them.

That was when his arms fell off.

It was so disorienting.

He could still feel them, lying there on either side of his long, muscular torso. He couldn't move them, couldn't wiggle his disconnected fingers, couldn't try to lift a hand to see if maybe it could attach the other arm to his shoulders.

He waited a few moments to see if maybe his legs would fall off as well. But no, they appeared to be fusing together into a solid whole. Soon, he was one long torso, or maybe just a head with a body.

His eyes changed at that point. He felt them retreat into his head while his snout pushed out. Colors faded and scents increased. Though he couldn't see the damned spell caster, he could now smell the peaty smoke that clung to his wool cloak, the bitter scent of the spell, even the faint traces of the mustard and ham the asshole had had for dinner.

What was Killian turning into? Long snout, solid body…

Was this damned wizard turning him into a snake?

As soon as the thought occurred to him, Killian felt himself start to shrink.

He feared he wasn't being turned into some majestic or frightening snake, or even something poisonous. No, probably a common garter snake that could easily be smacked with a club or skewered with a sword. Hell, possibly even thrown into a pot and boiled alive.

Killian had to escape. Had to stop this wizard somehow. Had to reverse, or possibly change, this spell. He had an army to lead. A battle to win. A war to end.

What would his brothers- and sisters-in-arms think of him, transformed as such?

Killian had been lucky his entire life. He swore he'd felt the sticky fingers of fate prodding him along frequently. He'd never fought them, never sought a different path for himself, but just gone along and done what he felt had been required of him.

After all, if the fates and the gods had taken that much interest in him, surely that meant he was destined to do important things?

Not to be ignobly trampled underfoot.

As the dimensions of Killian's world shifted, growing smaller moment by moment, he called for help as loudly as he could in his mind. He pleaded with the Twins of Fate to notice his predicament. He howled loudly to any and every god he could think of—Temulous the god of thunder, Acronomi the god of snow, Heloki the goddess of rain, and even Hilthadul the little local goddess of white rabbits—screaming how unfair it all was, how he deserved better, how he *must* survive this.

In short, he despaired as mightily as any hero dying on a battlefield, their assured victory stolen from them at the last moment.

No matter how often Killian thought about what happened next, he was never really certain.

It didn't feel as though the sticky fingers of the Twins pushed at him. He never had the impression of some sort of intervention.

Maybe the wizard messed up the spell at that point. Maybe instead of eye of newt he'd used eye of pigeon or some other inferior ingredient.

Or maybe Killian, for once, took hold of his own fate instead of merrily going along with whatever the gods intended for him, by yelling and pleading about how this needed to stop.

He heard the turning of a page as the wizard continued reading from his tome, casting his spell.

The air in the tent *whooshed* suddenly, as if someone had opened the front flap and a gust had blown through.

Killian felt the change immediately. Instead of shrinking, he started to grow. Rapidly. His snout pushed out. He could see the edges of it, out past his eyes, something yellow-greenish in color. Were those huge nostrils at the end of it? And did he have whiskers now, drooping down off his chin?

Then his arms reattached themselves. That was very weird. He didn't really have shoulders anymore, so they kind of stuck themselves to the front of his torso. They felt weak and spindly after being disconnected from his body for so long.

Something else was growing out of his back, almost directly opposite his arms. They hurt being folded and compressed underneath him, growing more uncomfortable as his increasing weight pressed down on them.

Killian found that the spell holding him in place was loosening. Was that because of the change? Was it only meant to contain someone of a certain size, a size that Killian had just a few moments ago surpassed? Or was it because the shape of him was no longer so snake-like?

Moving his eyes carefully (because he couldn't turn his head fully, not yet) Killian was able to look to the side.

There *was* a wizard standing there. Killian actually felt relief at seeing him. Though this was a nightmare, at least he wasn't imagining it. There really was someone next to his cot holding a big book in his gnarled hands that he was reading from.

He looked just as ordinary as Killian had assumed, wearing a sensible beige shirt and gray trousers under a heavy, purple cloak, instead of evil-wizard garb, like black silk robes with lightning bolts embroidered across the chest. His greasy gray hair tumbled down to his shoulders, in need of a good wash and probably a trim. Dark eyes bore into the page, fortunately not noticing that something had gone awry.

Had been aiming for worm, and gotten wyrm instead?

The wizard looked well fed, so money wasn't the only motivating factor here. (What did one pay a wizard to get him to turn a champion into a snake? Had he asked for King Harald's daughter in marriage? Killian had heard rumors of a new suitor eager to prove himself. Killian had assumed the newest suitor would use the field of battle to test his mettle, not, well, *this*.)

A great crack suddenly sounded in the small space.

The cot that had been supporting Killian broke, dumping him flat onto the floor.

Killian found he could move his jaw. A great forked tongue snaked out and curled back in his mouth without him thinking about it.

Interesting. The number of scents he now tasted/smelled had trebled.

He didn't know what all of them meant. But he thought he sensed a certain scent of triumph from the wizard, along with the fact that the man was younger than Killian had originally believed—just prematurely gray.

The wizard looked up at the crack, abruptly losing his place.

As the words ran dry, Killian found his strength flooding back into him.

His greatly increased strength.

He surged up from the floor, intending to shout at the man.

No words came out.

His snout really wasn't meant to form such sounds. He had fangs, not teeth.

Killian found himself coughing, as if the words choked his throat and needed to be cleared.

A hissing stream of black gunk flew out of his mouth unexpectedly, landing directly on the wizard's face.

Killian immediately tried to apologize. That had been rather rude of him, even if the wizard had been in the process of turning him into...whatever.

However, it turned out that Killian hadn't coughed up gunk. Or merely gunk.

Given the man's immediate screams, the sizzling of his skin, as well as the way he dropped his spell book to clutch at his face, Killian had to assume that he'd spat out some sort of acid.

At first, Killian was horrified. That wasn't the way he ever wanted to kill someone. Even someone as evil as this wizard.

Later, he did find himself mostly okay with it, given what the wizard had been doing to him.

Fortunately, or perhaps unfortunately, the wizard's screams alerted the guard who'd been standing outside at the front of the tent, oblivious to what was going on inside. The solider ducked his head inside, looking to see what was the matter.

"By Ulthir's great balls!" the man swore. "A dragon! He's attacked Killian!"

It took Killian a moment to piece together what the guard saw.

There was a person lying on the ground, his face eaten away by acid. He'd be difficult to recognize.

And a great beast, namely, *him*, just sitting here.

A mute creature, who couldn't speak and explain to the guard that he'd made a mistake.

More soldiers rushed in. Killian knew it was time to beat a hasty retreat. He did *not* want to kill, or even accidentally injure, any of these good fighters.

They had no such compunction, racing straight toward him with swords drawn.

Killian thought quickly. He turned and spat at the side of the tent, weakening the tough fabric with acid.

Then he burst through the side, his wings automatically unfurling and taking him up into the air while those good men of his hurled spears and shot arrows at his rapidly retreating back.

At least Killian learned at that time that his hide was armored. Most everything thrown at him clanged off harmlessly.

Only his wings were vulnerable, and he didn't discover that until after he'd flown away, landed, and tried to fold them back down again, only to find an uncomfortable arrow stuck between the webbing of one, while the other bore a horrible gash.

However, now that he'd gotten away, the only thing he could think about was how to get back. How to convince his men that he was not the enemy.

How could he still lead them in battle, even after he was no longer, well, *himself?*

THE FICKLE FINGERS
OF FATE

There are many stories told about the Twins of Fate. They almost always start with humble beginnings, such as an old woodswoman—let's call her Nell—who greatly desired children but she and her husband didn't have any for years.

No one is certain what exactly changed the tide of their life. Prayers to a local god? Some miraculous herb? Promises better left unsaid? No one is quite certain.

Nell will have you know she didn't do anything unnatural to get pregnant, thank you very much. Those children were conceived and borne the usual way.

However, even from the start, there was nothing natural about them.

Except their names. Stories have altered them, of course, making them fancier or prettier or giving them extra meaning. But Nell originally called them Erin and Sara, partly because she liked the names, but mainly because one was her mother's name and the other was her mother-in-law's.

The twins didn't look like their parents, who were plain and ordinary. The girls were both strikingly beautiful, like changelings who'd been left behind by one of the local goddesses. Any who saw them were arrested by their beauty, so much so that Nell tended to put scarves over their heads anytime they made the long journey into the nearest town, hiding their faces so they could walk around the market and not be bothered.

They weren't born as bald as normal babies. No, straight out of the womb they both had long hair. Given any chance, one sister's hair would tangle with the other's.

Watching tendrils of hair creep toward one another and bind together was one of Nell's first hints that her children weren't normal.

Another indication that something was different was her children's coloring. Erin's skin was as white as newly fallen snow, while her hair was as black as the sky above Ulthir's mountain. Sara, on the other hand, was born with a natural tan, her skin almost golden in color and turning a dark brown whenever she was out in the sun, even for the shortest amount of time. Her hair was so blonde it looked white, particularly when entangled with her sister's.

Who was older, and who was younger? That's a secret that only Nell knows, and she's not telling.

The babies didn't have the chubby cheeks that normal children did. Instead, they were long and skinny. Nell did what she could to put more meat on them, feeding them venison stew with hearty vegetables, roasted pork shoulder with crispy skin, and as much porridge as the girls could stomach.

Didn't help.

They grew tall, taller than their parents, in short order. They were mostly good girls. Of course, there were tears now and again, skinned knees and early bedtimes without supper. But there was also laughter with the four of them crowded around the kitchen table, rolling dice and playing games of chance.

By the time Sara, the golden-skinned one, was ten, she started being able to predict what the exact roll of the dice would be. There was no cheating involved, despite the mounting accusations. Sara just knew.

Just as Erin, the one colored so starkly, started to know the history of things. She could touch an object in the small cabin and tell Nell who'd made it, when, and why. As well as what the object had been used for recently. (Nell started keeping them out of her and her husband's bedroom after that, in an effort to keep Erin away from their bed. There were things children shouldn't know about their parents, though she suspected they knew anyway.)

When the twins were about twelve, Nell came upon them in a small clearing in the forest, playing a game that they'd obviously been playing for some time now.

Later, she learned that they called the game, "Make the frog jump."

The girls stood in the sunny meadow, back to back, their hair all entangled, the breeze blowing softly, tickling the edges of the grass. They kept their arms outstretched to their sides. Despite it looking somewhat awkward, they grasped each other's hands, fingers intertwined tightly as they spun around, like one of Ulthir's tops.

"You see him?" Sara asked.

See who? Nell wanted to know, but she didn't ask. She merely stood and watched her girls work some sort of magic. (Though none of the close relations were wizards, there were rumors about what exactly Great-Grandmother Elisa could do with a little snow, as well as that weird cousin who no one talked about and his strange ways with birds and bats.)

Both of the girls had their eyes closed as they spun. When they abruptly stopped, the girls both looked in the same direction, as if someone were standing to the side of them, as clear as day.

Maybe Nell *did* see the shadow of a person standing there, given the intensity of the girls' stare. However, the image flickered off and on, like wind-blown trees with dappled sunlight underneath.

(Though Nell loved her daughters very dearly, they also sometimes, *maybe,* might have spooked her a little.)

"What's he done?" Sara asked. She sounded more clinical than curious, as if they were actually discussing a frog and not a person.

"He's been begging his wife to go visit her mother. So that *he* can spend some time with his mistress," Erin said. She, at least, sounded less detached, as though the story she was viewing had some interest to her.

Not much, though.

"Ah," Sara said. "And if we encourage her to go see her mother, maybe she meets up with her old lover, the one from before her husband. She just needs a little push."

"Exactly," Erin said with a grin.

One of the pairs of hands of the twins started to glow, as if a sliver of the sun had embedded itself between their entangled fingers.

Before Nell could step out from under the trees, the light flared so brightly she had to shield her eyes. When it faded, her girls still stood in the center of the clearing, both of them wearing a self-satisfied smirk.

"What do you think you're doing?" Nell asked as she crossed over to them.

"Nothing, Mama!" they said in a chorus as they stepped apart.

Though they now faced her, locks of their hair were still intertwined, showing just how closely they'd been standing.

Nell sighed as she took in the sight of her girls. She could see it now, though it'd always been there, that *otherness* that filled her children. They were night and day, darkness and light, past and future.

Despite the normality of their birth, they were different, too different, to stay in the woods with her and her husband.

They needed training, and not at some fancy magic school that neither her or her husband could afford.

And though it broke her heart, Nell had to do what was right for her children.

"Come," Nell told Erin and Sara. "It's time for us to go visit the Lady."

The girls looked at each other, then Sara shrugged. "Always was a possibility," she said.

"I thought you didn't like the Lady," Erin said, peering closely at her mother.

"Like is not the same as respect," Nell said. "And besides, we get along fine. Particularly when I bring along some of that apple scrumpy of your father's."

"Hmmm," was all Erin said, though she still looked puzzled.

Seemed that even when her darling daughter poked, she couldn't always see a person's past.

Particularly when that person happened to be a local goddess.

Nell packed a small bag for the girls, stood stoically as they said their goodbyes to their father, then marched them out of the house for the last time.

It didn't really matter which direction Nell went, which of the well-worn paths through the trees that she followed. She just had to keep her intent clear in her mind, where it was she wanted to end up. Despite any misgivings, Nell knew where they needed to go.

So Nell led them up the familiar path, heading toward the same clearing where she'd found the girls earlier that day.

Except that when they stepped out from under the trees, the meadow was completely different.

Instead of being a small, flat field filled with grass and flowers, busy bees buzzing between them with birds cheering them on from the sidelines, now a large oak stood in the center of it. Nell wasn't certain what the phase of the moon currently was, but in the clearing, the full moon was caught in the branches of the tree.

As soon as Nell's feet touched the silvered grass, the Lady walked out of the tree. She was tall and slender like the twins, her hair as red as the leaves of the maples during the fall. A soft coat of bark covered her skin, greener in the summer and more gray come winter. Her eyes were the color of pale pine wood, large and round in her long sharp face.

What Nell told the Lady, and what the Lady said in reply, is up for interpretation. Was the Lady happy for the company? Resentful of having two teens thrust on her? Eager to shape their power? Angry at how undisciplined they were?

That's all up to the teller of the tale.

For ours, a couple of rounds of scrumpy might have been involved, the girls also getting a small sip. In the end, Nell left the girls behind, backing away slowly from the grand tree, blowing kisses to her children, giving a deep bow to the Lady, before stolidly turning and marching into the woods, tears blinding her as she went back to small house in the woods where only the remembered echoes of laughter remained.

As for the girls, some legends proclaim they stayed with the Lady. Her tree shot up, growing taller than all those around it, the top branches brushing the sky and tangling with the stars. The twins worked from there, following and guiding people along their path.

Other tales say that the Lady took them to Ulthir, up on his high mountain perch, so that they could see all the lands and work their magic there.

Still others say that the girls only stayed with the Lady for a short while, before finding their own cave in a nearby hill. Locked away from the light, they lived on the dreams they sought, the lives they changed, the merry dances they led.

As for Nell, well, she and her husband continued leading ordinary lives that were possibly softer and sweeter now, as luck now always landed in their laps and anything they turned their hands to led to gold.

But their stories are for another day.

KILLIAN

Killian spent the next hour trying to talk, to get his new mouth to form words. He could hear what he was trying to say in his head, but he couldn't force the sentences through his snout.

All that came out was more of that dripping acid. It was kind of disgusting. At least it would do the job of protecting him from an attacker. He actually had a pretty good range with the acid, able to spit it ten yards, easily. No decent accuracy—that would only come with practice.

He stayed in a clearing far from the coming battlefield, spitting and swearing (at least in his head) while slithering from one side to the other. (Oh, how he missed being able to pace!)

His body was now about twenty feet long, from snout to tail. Between six to seven of those feet seemed to be his "upright" section. He was much broader now than he'd been as a man, and perhaps three times as big around. His arms were shorter and weaker than before, and his fingers had grown long and spindly. He doubted that he could even pick up the great sword that had once been an extension of himself.

Despite there only being a sliver of the moon lighting the

clearing, he could see. His night vision had improved greatly and he wasn't likely to trip over a root, even under the trees.

However, his vision lacked details. While he could see the trunks, he couldn't make out the bark. He knew that he wouldn't be able to see the rings of a bullseye from ten yards away.

Instead of skin, he was now covered with fine scales that worked like armor. He couldn't really see the color—he only later learned that his back was a dull, greenish-brown, while his belly was a greenish-yellow, the same color as the light that had surrounded the wizard's spell.

Not the worst colors for a dragon, but certainly not awe-inspiring.

As Killian slither-paced, he kept asking himself what was he going to do now? He had to get back to his soldiers, those men and women who were dependent on him to lead them into battle come morning.

Though he was still learning what all the scents were that his newly improved nose (and tongue) brought to him, he thought it was still late at night. He couldn't smell the dawn in the air.

When had the wizard shown up? Had Killian actually fallen asleep so early and so easily because he'd been bespelled? Thinking back on it, that might have been the case. Though there were occasionally nights before a battle when he slept well and deeply, generally, he slept tense and was awake half the night, still determined to be brilliant regardless.

How had the wizard gotten into his tent? How many of Killian's guards had the wizard subdued in order to reach him? (Killian didn't learn until much later that the wizard hadn't had to kill anyone. He'd merely bribed one of the cooks with fresh meat to get himself let into the camp, then had hidden himself. Though Killian had known that an army marches on its stomach, he hadn't realized just how easily disgruntled cooks were.)

Eventually, Killian decided that he had to fly back to the camp, to see whether or not he could convince his people that he was, in fact, him.

There wasn't time to try to reverse the spell. Maybe later Killian could find someone to do that, though at this point, he wasn't sure if he was ever going to trust any sort of magic user within fifty yards of him.

Killian heaved himself into the air...and nearly fell flat on his snout.

What?

He'd certainly been able to fly earlier. Then again, that had been an act of desperation. He unfolded the great, leathery wings from his back and heaved himself up again.

At least this time he was prepared for the sudden return to earth.

What was going on? Why couldn't he fly now?

After much longer than Killian wanted to admit, he finally figured out what the trick was: he couldn't think about flying. At all. Flying was a natural thing for a dragon to do. He didn't even need his wings. All he had to do was just assume that he was airborne, and he would be.

When he overthought it, he nearly impaled himself on the trees below.

So while consciously not thinking, Killian slowly flew himself back to the camp. He smelled it long before he saw it; the smoke from the wood fires, the meaty scent of people, the sheep-like smell of the woolen fabric of the tents, the cold metal scent of the weapons and armor that many of his fighters armed themselves with. He also heard the camp rustling in the night, like a quiet windstorm in the trees up ahead. When he focused, he could make out snatches of conversation.

He flew over his old tent—the side still rent and violated. His leaders had gathered together there. At least they appeared to have realized that it wasn't him who had been lying there, but that damned wizard. Who was, indeed, dead. Killed by acid.

Served him right.

A part of Killian wanted to land, but something still cautioned him to wait.

Was he afraid his guard would turn on him again?

No, something else was unsettling. (Beside the fact that he was now a *dragon* and unable to speak.)

Killian took another turn over the camp, letting his nose lead him.

There. To the side.

The camp was on top of a large ridge, on the southern side of the battlefield. The front of the hill sloped more-or-less gently down onto the cleared area. The back of it was a craggy cliff, steep with many boulders.

Not unassailable, but not an easy climb, either.

Killian hadn't bothered flying over his enemy's camp, though he would get to that soon enough, to see what he could learn.

For now, something was still disturbing him about his own camp.

There, on the far side. Killian smelled something he could only at this time describe as being *off*.

It wasn't the scent of the dead.

No, these were the living. And they did not smell like his guard or his soldiers. These people had a spicier odor, somehow. Maybe the peat they used in their winter fires was wetter, or the wool they used for their cloaks had been dyed using different dyes.

It took Killian a third turn to spot them.

A long line of men slowly climbing the ridge behind his own camp, where his own guards wouldn't see them.

King Harald obviously wasn't planning on waiting until morning before starting the battle. Plus, all the commanders were up here.

He probably figured they'd be in a panic because Killian would be dead, or disappeared, a snake slithering away into the night.

Damn it! But how could Killian tell the others? Warn them of the coming soldiers?

Certainly, he could attack the group, but some might still slip through. These weren't regular fighters, he could tell, but more like trained assassins.

Killian folded his wings and willed himself to land in front of his old tent.

He mostly stuck the landing. Might have skidded a few feet and come down harder than he expected.

At least the sound of his long body hitting the earth brought all the leaders who'd been inside his tent out.

Killian tried to greet them, but only a muted, "Arrrggggh!" came out.

Plus some acid, which he thoughtfully spat out to the side.

"It's him! It's the dragon!" Asherly said, the leader of the guard.

"Are you Killian?" Moanithia asked. She led the archers, and in many ways, was the fiercest of all the leaders.

Killian nodded his head vigorously.

"Are you lying to us?" Gabija said. He was the leader of the berserkers, those shock troops who gathered at the front of the line and eagerly threw themselves at anyone who stood in their way.

Killian hadn't wanted to use them, given how crazy the berserkers were most of the time. They frequently turned on their own comrades once they ran out of enemies to kill. However, when Gabija said that he could lead them without the usual consequences, Killian had taken him up on it.

"No, I'm not lying to you," Killian tried to say, though it came out completely garbled. At least he was able to shake his head *no* at the same time.

"Why'd you ask it something like that?" Asherly said. "Of course it's going to deny that it's lying to us."

Gabija shrugged. "Wanted to see if it's an intelligent beasty, if it understood what we were saying. Sometimes my troops, well..."

Killian was suddenly *so glad* he'd accepted Gabija's group.

But before anyone could ask Killian any more questions, he needed to show them what he'd seen.

He turned and moved away from them, then looked back over his back. (He didn't really have shoulders anymore, just a solid torso. So he didn't just turn his head anymore. The upper half of his body rotated. It felt very odd.)

When no one followed him, Killian returned to the group. They were whispering at each other about whether or not they should trust him or not.

He cleared his throat—those whisperers were never going to hide their words from him, not with his enhanced abilities.

Unfortunately, clearing his throat meant spitting again, a long stream of acid that he hurled to the side before turning back to the gathered leaders.

They looked at him with what he assumed were various degrees of disgust on their faces. While he could see each person, the details were indistinct.

He'd have a much easier time recognizing people by scent rather than by face, now.

Killian slithered away again, looking back to see if at least someone would catch a clue and start to follow him.

"I'm gonna see what the beasty wants us to do," Gabija announced to the others, stepping forward.

Again, Killian thanked whatever god had prompted him to accept the berserkers as he led the way. They stopped a couple of times as Gabija picked up a few of his choice fighters to follow along.

When they reached the edge of the camp, Killian slithered away to the side so that Gabija could look over the edge.

Could the berserker even see the fighters? They were as clear as ants on snow to Killian at this point, given his enhanced ability to see at night.

But Gabija didn't merely rely on his eyes. He also lifted his head like a good guard dog and sniffed the air.

Killian noticed a couple of his fighters doing the same.

"There's fighters down there," one growled softly.

"And aren't they going to be in for a surprise?" Gabija said just as softly. "Thank you, beasty."

Killian gave a quiet snort. He wasn't some well-trained animal who'd just preformed a trick.

Hopefully, he could convince the others of his usefulness.

Even without words.

OUR DRAGONS ARE DIFFERENT

Eowin's children were not the only creatures to populate Ulthir's world. Other beings of power and myth also came to be: creatures like mischievous cave trolls, talking boars with silver eyes, paladin-like centaurs, and bears with fur made out of gold.

Admittedly, some of the beasts who people supposedly encountered aren't exactly as they have been described. Unicorns are merely flights of fancy, as are white does with golden eyes who beckon hunters to their deaths. (How else would you explain the demise of such great derring doers? Surely the fact that they'd drunk an entire season's worth of mead in a week and had wandered off a cliff had no bearing?)

Dragons, though, do exist.

How would such a creature come into being?

Well, when a mommy dragon and a daddy dragon love each other very much—

No, no, no! Nothing like that!

There are no such things as dragon eggs, or even baby dragons. Dragons are born fully formed and functionally adults when they are called into being.

So, given that, how would someone create such a creature?

One's need must be great. Greater than someone's desire for food or drink, or even for life. They must be desperate in that need, so driven that they forget to bathe or sleep. (The tales don't always go into how smelly these people are, but trust me, you wouldn't want to be in a closed room with one of them.) The times they are living through must be impossibly hard, difficult enough that every breath is a challenge. And they must be alone, with no one to turn to.

Must the Twins of Fate also be involved? Generally speaking, yes, though their contribution is much more difficult to ascertain.

Always, tales of dragons are interwoven with the tragedy of a person. Like Princess Kuokmok, who had a water dragon come to her, formed from her tears as she cried for the deaths of her entire family while sitting beside the waterfall at the end of the world. Or Little Irvine, who, after being chased by evil knights, got lost in the mines under the southern mountains for weeks, and formed an iron dragon to come to his rescue. Or even the wizard Soliki, who called an ice dragon into being after she buried the frozen dreams of her people in an ice cave.

Once the need is met, dragons usually revert back to their natural form, like the ice dragon who dissolved into a great pile of fluffy snow once Soliki was avenged. Very few stick around until they die of old age. Even Little Irvine's iron dragon crawled back into the mine after the boy had grown up and freed his people, the dragon's body supposedly turning into the greatest vein of ore anyone had ever found.

Tales of other dragons abound, of course, those who live long lives. But those reflect the needs of storytellers who want to spice up their tales, not the actual lives of dragons.

At least most of the time.

KILLIAN

While Gabija and Moanithia took care of their surprise visitors, Killian stayed with Asherly and the others.

It took a short while for Asherly to rig up a lantern and table outside (as Killian really was no longer tent-sized, and really didn't fit in any of the tents that they currently had set up).

Then, Asherly helpfully supplied pen, ink, and parchment. "Can you write?" he asked, looking hopeful.

Killian had no shoulders with which to shrug, so he ended up making a rocking motion with his hands.

Of course, Killian the man could write. Though his penmanship wouldn't have won any awards, it was generally clear enough to get his point across.

Could Killian the dragon force those scraggily arms of his to achieve some sort of legibility?

The answer, it turned out, was no.

First of all, the pen was too small. Though Killian would swear that his arms were smaller than they'd been, his hands had elongated, his fingers growing skeletally thin and scaly. He hadn't really paid attention to the long talons at the end of each digit before, but they were black and hard as steel. They also got in the way. The pen didn't look much bigger than a needle in his new hands, and try as he might, he just couldn't wield it.

At least Asherly was prepared for this, and brought out a hunk of charcoal that was fashioned into a cylinder. Killian could wrap his fingers around it and hold it in his fist like a child with a piece of chalk.

However, Killian was barely able to control his movements. He no longer had fine control over his limbs.

Not yet, at any rate.

Killian was prepared to work at regaining it, just as he was certain that at some point he'd figure out how to talk again.

The best he could do at this time was to grab a big stick—more like a tree limb—and draw in the dirt in front of the table.

First, Killian drew a circle, with a wobbly X in the center of it, to indicate where they were currently standing. Then he drew a second circle, to the north, where King Harald's troops were stationed.

It took some time—and it wasn't nearly as much fun as a game of charades normally was—but finally Asherly got the message that Killian was planning on flying over to the other camp to do some scouting.

He wasn't sure what he could report back, but Asherly seemed grateful for whatever Killian could tell him about their enemy.

That finally taken care of, Killian willed himself into the air again.

Not that he was feeling performance anxiety or anything, trying to take off in front of all his leaders. Or former leaders.

At least he only face-planted (snout-planted?) once before he managed to stop his busy thoughts and was able to fly up into the clear night.

It didn't help that a strong, acrid scent flowing from his leaders followed him above the tents—though he wasn't certain, he was starting to associate that smell with fear.

Killian flew up higher than he'd been before, trying to blend into the dark sky. His back was dark enough, but as far as he could tell, his belly was a lighter color. He wasn't about to try flying upside down, and tonight wasn't the time to experiment. (He learned later he couldn't.)

Darietta, the leader of the scouts had already taken count of the number of campfires burning at the far side of the battlefield. (She always insisted that her people were scouts and pretended to be offended when you called them by their true nature: spies.) Of course, as Darietta and the others assumed that King Harald's spies had come to count their campfires, they'd only allowed some of the troops fires despite the cold, in order to throw off the count.

As Killian circled the enemy camp he found that Darietta's count of fires was correct.

However, in terms of his nose, Killian counted more than twice the number of fighters than they'd estimated.

Where had King Harald gotten so many men? Who had he managed to work an alliance with? (Turned out to be some of the northernmost clans who'd been bribed with exaggerated stories of the wealth of King Rodwell's lands, which while of course were fertile, weren't that much better than King Harald's lands.)

These fighters were used to the cold, and so amassed at the back of the enemy camp, sleeping in the rough without tents or fires.

Killian didn't dare fly down closer to the enemy camp. Though the scales of his skin were pretty arrow-proof, his wings weren't. They still ached from where they'd been hurt earlier. He knew that they'd heal given time.

There was no time.

Killian did take a couple of turns across the enemy camp focusing on the other scents, mainly searching for that acrid smell of magic that he remembered from when he'd been transformed.

He found that odor at a couple of campfires, about the middle of the army, and marked those well.

He planned on coming back to those just before dawn, to see how well they dealt with a rain of acid.

Would serve them right for transforming him.

Killian still wasn't sure exactly why he'd been turned into a dragon. That surely couldn't have been the original wizard's intent. Who had twisted the spell? The Twins? Maloneal? The great god Ulthir? Or someone else?

Fewer of Killian's leaders were still awake by the time he returned to his camp. Darietta and Asherly came out of their tents when he arrived, both looking half-asleep.

After yet another game of not-so-fun charades, Killian was able to get across the number of men that King Harald had, as well as Killian's own plan to disrupt their spell casters. (King Rodwell hadn't bothered sending along any magic users with his army. He had a champion in the form of Killian. He didn't need magic to win this war. Killian was planning on having strong words, or at least lengthy charades, with the king about that after the battle.)

Asherly made plans for dealing with the extra forces, then yawned so widely Killian was afraid he'd split his face in two. Darietta appeared to be similarly sleepy.

Killian tried not to be too obvious about smelling the air around them, trying to learn that scent. He supposed he wasn't too subtle about it, though, as his tongue kept rolling out and tasting the air between the three of them.

Finally, he made shooing motions with his hands, sending them back to their tents to get some rest. He would stand guard for the rest of the night.

Killian felt surprisingly awake. He hoped that was just a side-effect of the magic of the transformation, and not that he was a night-creature now, who would want to sleep all through the day.

The camp settled down around him. Guards outside the tents of the leaders watched him suspiciously. Killian didn't mind. Better that they be overly cautious now, especially since King Harald had sent not one, but two surprise attacks that evening, before the battle even took place.

Killian spent the time focusing on what he could sense with his ears and his nose. While he could see better in the dark than he'd once been able to, the lack of details bothered him. For example, the edges of the tents around him were crisp, but he couldn't see the line where the flap closed.

By the time Killian smelled the dawn approaching, he was ready for the attack.

King Harald and his allies were going to regret what they'd done to him.

Killian would make sure of it.

THE STAR CHILD

Though there are many (many!) myths about the birth of Maloneal, the one he favors is the one where Eowin finds him buried in the snow on Ulthir's mountain. In these stories, he is already fully formed, not a child but a full-grown man, encased in ice.

Eowin carefully brushes the snow away from the frozen figure, discovering more and more about him as she clears away the wintry covering.

How white his hair is, despite tales that tell of him having brown, black, red, or even (ugh) no hair at all.

His eyes are closed as if in sleep, so she cannot see how silvery they shine, like the stars that occasionally peek out from the blackness above them.

His shoulders are broad, his hands and fingers long and well formed, leading to (absolutely correct!) speculation about other masculine parts being just as well endowed.

He has long legs, elegant toes and is perhaps just a touch flat-footed. That might have come from the shock of the landing, when this block of ice struck the mountain.

At first, Eowin cannot get to the sleeping figure. The ice is too thick, too stubborn, to easily give up its prize. Even in the brightest of sunlight, the covering around Maloneal will not yield.

Eowin tries to dance in front of the piece, thinking that might raise up the heat a bit more, particularly when she throws in some more, well, let's just call them provocative moves.

The ice ignores her, and the figure continues its slumber.

It is only when Eowin starts to sing that she hears the first cracking of the ice. It will not give way to loud songs, or brash notes. No, she has to coax the drops to form, inventing lullabies to sing for him. (Maloneal has always maintained that he heard Eowin singing before he came fully to his senses.)

Finally, the ice around the figure cracks and Maloneal takes his first breath in the full light, opening his silver eyes for the first time.

And no, at least according to Maloneal, the first thing Eowin says to him is *not* "Uh-oh."

She instead speaks warmly to him, calling him *son* and welcoming him warmly to their growing family.

No matter what that overgrown man-child Ulthir may say.

KILLIAN

Despite Killian's decision to make King Harald's troops pay for what had been done to him, he found his resolve wavering once the battle started.

Not against the spell casters, wizards, whatever it was that they called themselves. No, they'd deserved those first great streams of acid raining down on them.

But the rest of the fighters had no shield against him. They couldn't fight back against an enemy so high above them. They couldn't meet and face their foe.

It all left a bad taste in Killian's mouth, and no, that wasn't just the acid.

His own fighters preformed bravely. He was especially impressed with Gabija's berserkers. They seemed to be slightly less mindless than rumored, and actually coordinated their attacks, at least at the start. Eventually, the heat of the battle overtook them, then it was every fighter for him- or herself.

Moanithia's archers stood out as well. He hadn't realized that they had both long as well as short bows, so could pepper the opposing army both at the start and even as they charged closer. It was quite a clever strategy that fortunately, kept all eyes focused on the battlefield and not looking further up, where Killian flew overhead.

More than once he wished more than anything that he could tell Asherly where to send his troops. Killian had such a better view of the attacking armies. Though he couldn't see the faces of the people below, he could smell them, smell which ones were chugging along, just doing their jobs, which ones were fanatical about the killing, and more importantly, which ones were scared or desperate—which meant the ones most likely to break if hit with an opposing line of fighters.

The first time Killian tried to draw attention to such a group of fighters—seemed fear was contagious and this entire knot of people reeked of it—he nearly splatted onto the battlefield as he tried to do the dragon equivalent of an aerial somersault.

Fortunately, it appeared that Asherly had people watching Killian, looking for any sort of signal, as quite soon after Killian's acrobatics, a separate group of fighters barreled across the battlefield and into the people directly below where Killian was flying.

From then on, Killian focused on the fear. Sure, many of the fighters were scared. That was normal. If any of them appeared to have a little more, Killian might goad them with a few drops of acid to increase their dread. Death falling from the sky had that effect. Then he'd signal to Asherly and the enemy would soon find their fears of death well founded.

Killian knew that if he'd been on the ground, he wouldn't have realized when the turning point was approaching, when King Harald's troops were about to break apart, lose their formations and transform from a fighting force into a mob. Certainly he would have figured it out eventually. But as a dragon, flying high above the masses of people, Killian could spot it easily.

This was the only time during the battle when Killian fully used his acid, flying in lazy circles above the troops and killing indiscriminately.

The tide turned.

King Harald's troops broke. Some of the people fought on bravely, sticking to their ground.

Most of them, though, fled. Particularly those northernmost clans who later claimed that they heard the sound of the ice and snow mourning the loss of their lives.

Only after the soldiers had mopped up the survivors and messengers were sent to King Harald to come and work out a treaty did Killian land, up on the ridge where he'd spent the night outside the tents of the others.

Now, Killian was exhausted. As well as starving. But what did a dragon eat? How did they sleep? And how was he going to get himself transformed back into a man?

All questions that needed answers, some sooner than later.

However, Killian had again run out of time.

Asherly, Gabija, Moanithia, Darietta, and the others all came to meet with him among the tents.

And they brought soldiers. Lots of soldiers. Not too many of Gabija's berserkers—they were all sleeping off their battle-rush. But plenty of Moanithia's archers were there.

Killian looked at the soldiers amassed behind the leaders, then back at the leaders. He did that deliberately a few times, hoping that at least someone picked up on his question, namely, *what did they think they were doing*? He wasn't dangerous. Not to them. He'd proven himself during the battle, hadn't he?

Asherly finally stepped forward, the self-appointed leader of the group.

"So. While some of us believe that you might be Killian, transformed into a dragon—"

"You might not be," Darietta said, glaring at him.

Asherly shrugged.

"There's no real way to prove it, now, is there?" Gabija said, obviously trying to sound reasonable.

Killian raised his hands in frustration. What did he have to prove to these people that he was on their side? Hadn't he helped during the battle? He pointed to the battlefield where healers bearing stretchers were removing those people who would possibly recover, leaving the corpses to be cleared away later.

"Aye, the beasty did help some," Gabija continued. Then he fixed a hard glare at Killian. "But ye could have done more, don't ye think?"

Killian felt a momentary flash of guilt. Surely Gabija would understand that killing someone without them having a chance to fight back felt a little dishonorable?

"Then there's the part where you're now a dragon," Asherly said. "I know you helped out on the battlefield. But what are you going to do now? You can't go back to King Rodwell like that. You can't feast with the rest of the fighters. You can't even fit through the gates of the castle."

Killian sighed. Unfortunately, that caused a bit of acid to bubble up and spit out his snout.

He'd learned that his scales weren't hurt by the acid he spit.

Pretty much everything else that came into contact with it wasn't so lucky.

"And then there's that," Darietta said, sounding even more disgusted if that was possible.

Killian again huffed in frustration, but at least this time he didn't spit. Much. In the direction of Darietta. If any drops did fly that way, it was totally an accident.

"Ye might be clever enough to be a man," Gabija said. "But how long will that last? Will ye turn into a full beasty? Unable to think or reason?" He held up his hands. "Not that I have anything against those who are always in battle-lust. But they're also people. You're not."

As Killian couldn't see the details of their faces, couldn't tell what expressions they held, he deliberately flicked his tongue out at the group, gathering up all their smells.

A couple had a tinge of fear. Asherly appeared to at least have some regret.

The others...if he had to guess, he'd say they were determined to have their way.

Did they believe that there would be more spoils of war to divide if Killian wasn't there? It wasn't as if he could enjoy any new lands or titles that the king might bestow on him.

And they were right. There wasn't really a place for him, not now.

He'd helped. He'd told them of the surprise attacks, of the large number of fighters, pointed out the opposing army's weakest links.

There was a good chance that he helped turn the tide of the battle. That fewer good people on both sides had died because of him.

It wasn't enough.

Killian shook his head. Though he wanted to scream with rage that it wasn't right, it wasn't *fair*, he didn't have the words to fight them.

And he didn't want to fight them, to kill even more good people.

Too many had already died that day.

In many ways, himself included. Or at least Killian, the man.

Killian shook his great head in sorrow, then lifted himself up into the air on his first try (*yes!*), taking off above the trees and heading south, always south.

Eventually, Killian found a peak with suitable forest and farmable land surrounding it. He carved out that territory for his own, staying at the top of his mountain, while he waited, and waited, and waited, for *something* that would tell him why he lived.

All the stories agreed that dragons always had a purpose.

It turned out to be over two hundred years before he finally found his.

At least it didn't take him eons, unlike some gods who will remain nameless.

THE FINDING OF THE FOUNDLING

WIZARDS AND WITCHES AND SPELL CASTERS, OH MY!

Magic has always existed in the world. The trickster Maloneal saw to that at the beginning of things. I mean, why do the hard work of creating something lasting when you can cheat and pop it into being using magic? Or some such utter rubbish as that. (At least that was the argument Maloneal used to get people to start trying.)

Who can do magic? Pretty much anyone who sets their mind to it.

However, therein lies the rub.

The person needs to have the type of mind that can be set to doing magic. They must maintain a certain level of flexibility to their thoughts, to allow the impossible to become merely improbable. That's why tales abound of children being able to do magic, only to lose the ability as they age.

Still, a stubborn few retain their ability. They rely on props to guide their thoughts instead of merely wishing something to be so.

Then we get down to all the different types of magic users, and how to distinguish one from another.

Wizards tend to use great ancient tomes that contain all the knowledge and spells that one might ever need.

But then again, witches have spell books. And spell casters have entire libraries full of books that aid them in their casting.

Witches, though, use herbs and ingredients when they do magic. So do wizards, though they might not be as concerned as a witch about their herbs being sustainably sourced and organic. Some spell casters might not worry too much about ingredients, but many of them do.

Spell casters need to memorize long, involved spells and recite them out loud, sometimes taking days, in order to complete a particular piece of magic. Wizards tend not to take as long, and they may mumble their way through this bit or that. Witches also recite spells out loud, usually ones they've memorized, though they may improvise a bit more than the others.

All right, so perhaps there isn't as much difference between the three as the various practitioners might have you believe. Maybe they all do magic, and the same sort of magic—they just call it by different names.

Because names are important, and what you call yourself will frequently dictate who you are.

TALON

Of all the things from his old life as a person—as Killian, the Champion—Talon, the dragon, missed sunsets the most.

Sure, he could still see them. Watch as the brilliant ball of fire sunk down beneath the horizon. Could even get a pretty clear view of them when flying hundreds of feet from the earth.

But his dragon eyes just didn't have the ability to see colors, not like his human eyes had. Everything had a gray tinge to it, which washed out the brilliance of the orange and pink clouds, made the green of the forest below his mountain abode dim and dismal, even darkened the fields of flowers that bloomed every spring.

Talon had made plans to watch that night's sunset from high on his mountain peak. It was late spring and it had been raining for an entire week. Finally, though, the weather had cleared up, and Talon was determined to watch as much of the sunset as he could.

Until duty called.

Talon had been on his peak for a little over two hundred years. The land Talon claimed as his own, below his mountain, had slowly filled with farms, villages, and towns.

Talon had claimed the land by flying about three-quarters of a day out in different directions from his mountain. That was between three to five days travel for a person on foot, depending on weather and roads. In a grand circle around the peak he'd spit acid onto the ground, encircling his land. Over the decades, his border had sunk up to a foot deep in places.

On the side with his mountain in the center, Talon took care of everything and everyone. On the other side, he didn't.

He had eventually learned to speak. It turned out that the process was much like flying. He couldn't use his mouth, as it wasn't designed for words.

His thoughts could leak out, when he wasn't too stressed or worried, and others could pick them up.

Eventually, he was able to make deals with the people who moved onto his lands.

He divided his territory up into four quadrants, north- and southeast, as well as north- and southwest. Every year, each quadrant would supply him with one cow and two sheep.

That was enough food for him for half a year. (He ate a lot less than his size would have one believe.) The other six months, he'd hunt from his woods, capturing wily boars, bugling elk, or even shy deer.

It seemed fair to him.

Every house in his territory was equipped with a sealed bottle that contained a pendant impregnated with a particularly smelly oil.

Anytime someone opened one of those bottles, anywhere in his land, Talon would pick up the scent.

And come flying to the rescue.

Most of the time, he was too late to stop whatever had occurred. Very few managed to open the bottle then keep their lives out of the hands of the brigands or robbers who'd dared come into Talon's territory.

This meant that frequently, Talon wasn't a savior, but a righteous avenger.

Or a ruthless killer, depending on your side of things.

When that scent came that afternoon, Talon took off immediately. He easily judged it to be off by the border, based on the faintness of the smell.

Talon didn't feel the sticky fingers of fate—he hadn't felt them guide his choices since he'd become a dragon. However, he was still buoyed up by a fortunate tailwind, and so arrived at the farm much more quickly than he'd expected, while the sun was still above the horizon and the clouds just starting to pinken.

From far up in the air, Talon couldn't see the devastation that had been visited on the place.

He could smell it, though. The bodies hadn't been dead for long, but the odor was unmistakable.

What had been the name of this family? It took Talon awhile to remember. The McGillans, perhaps? Something like that. A young farmer and his wife. They'd brought his parents with them to help, though if Talon was remembering correctly, both of the older people had died over the winter.

There were still a couple of goats close to the farm, as well as a few chickens. The rest of the livestock had been rustled away.

Talon took his time before descending, gathering up as many of the scents as he could.

He would need to go hunting. Soon.

However, there was another scent that tickled his nose as he drew closer. He flicked his tongue out again and again, trying to track the elusive smell.

Was there still someone alive down there? A person, and not just an animal?

Talon landed gracefully, as he'd practiced that maneuver over the decades, if for no other reason than to appear more powerful to those in his care. (It really wouldn't do to snout-plant in front of his people. Though they might forgive him, he felt the need to be better than that.)

The body of the husband—Sean McGillan—was out in the field. He'd been away, out working, and had run back at the first sign of trouble, if Talon was reading the signs correctly. He nosed around the body. Two—no, three—brigands had been required to kill the man. Though Talon couldn't see Sean's face clearly, as his dragon sight wasn't good on details, the smell of the man's desperation still hung in the air.

The family dog lay dead next to the threshold of the house—a large mongrel with a shred of cloth still locked between its stubborn jaws. It had obviously given its life to protect those inside. Had possibly gained them those few moments necessary to break out the pendant so Talon would be warned.

He made a note to tell the neighbors about that so that they would properly take care of the pet.

The wife—Fiona McGillan—lay in the family room, stabbed in her belly. She still held a large knife and a dead man lay beside her.

Talon nodded in approval. Good for her for taking one out. That meant one fewer that he would have to hunt down and kill.

That elusive scent was stronger in here. Had the McGillans had any children? He didn't recall any, but possibly one had been born that winter and he just hadn't met the person yet.

Slowly, Talon made his way to the bedroom of the cottage. The big bed the couple slept on was pushed against one corner and a crib occupied the other side of the room.

They must have been doing well if they could afford a separate bed for their young. Most families slept with the baby in their bed until they grew older. Many just had a single family bed for years and years.

That soft scent, of milky breath and baby fat, still lived and breathed in this room. Though Talon couldn't see the child anywhere, he could smell it.

No, not it. Her.

There.

The mother had attached the baby to the underside of the crib, a touch of magic that Talon dismissed with a wave of one clawed hand while catching the baby with the other.

Mostly catching. Okay, so the kid might have fallen a little. Didn't hurt it.

Did startle the baby, and it predictably started wailing.

Seems it had been sleeping, probably another small spell that a desperate mother had used to keep her youngster alive.

Talon picked up the infant as carefully as he could, given that his claws were long and sharp and perhaps tore at the cloth swaddling the now kicking child.

As soon as he picked up the baby, bringing her close to his own scaled chest, she calmed.

Strange.

Her tears vanished as quickly as a spring rain and she gazed up at Talon with sharply focused eyes and a welcoming smile.

She even cooed at him.

Though it felt very awkward, Talon tucked the small child into the elbow of one arm. He held his other up, seeing if she could track his talons in the air.

She grabbed for his hand, tightly holding onto his pinky finger and waving it around without cutting herself on his claws. She kicked happily, once, twice, then appeared to settle down again. Her eyes closed and she dropped right back off to sleep, instantly doubling her weight—a type of magic that babies instinctively know.

Talon was surprised how she appeared to trust him. Even the people who'd known him for years still had an edge of fear about their scent. No one just accepted him as he was.

He stayed where he was for a moment, watching the baby sleep in his arms.

It was an amazing experience, something he'd never done before.

He may have cooed at her. A little.

Oh, how he wanted to keep her. To hold onto someone who

wasn't afraid, at least for a while. She'd probably learn fear as she grew older.

However, he knew she couldn't stay with him. How would he feed her, up at the top of his mountain? There would be no companions to play with, no brothers or sisters or cousins to love her.

Just Talon, and he knew that he wasn't enough. Had never been enough, not by himself.

So he slowly slithered backwards, out of the bedroom, through the main room, and out the door.

He'd take her to the neighbors. Tell them of the fate of her parents (and the dog). Then, he'd go hunting.

The brigands who'd killed the McGillans were going to pay.

TRICKY TRICKSTERS ARE TRICKY

Maloneal (MAL-o-neal) is kind of a put-together name that doesn't really fit with most of the other names given to the gods. It isn't a beautiful name, nor is it that easy to say.

Which fits its holder perfectly.

Only a few tales bother describing what Maloneal looks like. That's because even the people who were at whatever event occurred can't agree on his physical appearance.

Maloneal is a shapeshifter at heart and takes whatever form meets the occasion, whether that be male, female, beautiful, ugly, plain, striking, or something in between those extremes.

He will have you know that though he is *malleable*, he sticks with male human forms, thank you very much. None of that cavorting around like a horse and then giving birth. Any rumors to the contrary are just that—rumors. No, really. The entire genesis of satyrs is *not* on his head or due to a dalliance with a goat.

Filthy lies. All of it.

Like the Twins of Fate, Maloneal likes sticking his nose into other people's affairs, sometimes with disastrous results.

Never for him, though. He always comes out smelling like a rose.

It's for those other people, the little people, to put their lives back together, if they can.

What is his influence in this tale of ours? Was he partially responsible for Killian's transformation? Or for later events, soon to be unfolded?

That remains to be seen.

For now, just know that he's ever-present, like a sickly shadow, longing for the sunlight but unable to bear the heat.

TALON

After dropping off the baby at the neighbors, it didn't take Talon long to trace the scents of the robbers/murderers. They couldn't move quickly through the woods, not given the livestock they'd stolen.

This was good. Better to catch them in the countryside and not in some town.

Talon had come to an *arrangement* with most of the nearby towns that weren't in his territory. It only took a few occasions of knocking down the town's walls and destroying some of the buildings for the locals to learn that it just wasn't worth the bother of harboring brigands, no matter how much they offered to pay.

Now, when Talon showed up, the townspeople would shove any and all newcomers out of the gates. He only took those who were guilty, leaving the rest to possibly reconsider any plans they might have had for robbing people nearby.

This time, the brigands were still under the trees, a good mile or more from the nearest town. They'd stuck to the thicker part of the woods, possibly in the mistaken belief that since Talon couldn't see them from the sky, they'd be safe.

No one appeared to take into account that he could still *smell* them from many miles away. All eight of the ones who remained.

Talon waited until it was fully dark before he attacked.

His opponents needed light to see. He did not.

He spent some time circling their camp up above the trees, letting his nose map out the area.

The brigands had banked their fire as night approached. Given the amount of rope he smelled, he assumed that they'd built a loose enclosure made out of rope around the sheep and goats who'd accompanied them under the trees.

As darkness settled in, it felt to him as though only one of the brigands was awake and still on guard.

Very sloppy.

Talon landed some distance away (another perfectly graceful landing, thank you very much), then barreled through the trees toward the camp.

They would hear him coming as he raced through the underbrush.

They had about as much chance of stopping him as an unarmored foe against a well-aimed arrow.

Talon burst out of the trees and headed straight for the campfire, sliding over and crushing the coals.

It didn't really hurt, just stung a little.

And it destroyed his opponent's light source, blinding them.

Talon managed to stop his forward momentum before going too far, turning back to face his foes.

The nearest two fell screaming as acid blinded them.

That left six.

As Talon turned to the next, who'd been sleeping on the side of the fire, he felt something tickling his side.

The acrid smell of magic rose up.

A net fell heavily upon him, carried by magical winds, ensnaring his wings.

Crap.

Had this been their plan all along? Attack one of his farms so that they could get to *him*?

The net was woven out of magical rope, with good solid knots every three to four inches. It immediately drained Talon's strength from him. He couldn't even work up a good stream of acid to burn the thing away.

He bellowed loudly in dismay. Then he called out with his mind, *Why have you done this to me?*

Talon didn't speak, not really. He was able to direct his thoughts to people who were nearby. They could either speak back, or sometimes, just think words back to him.

"We have need of you," said the magic user (wizard, spell caster, witch, whatever it was that she called herself).

The others appeared to have recovered and approached him with their weapons drawn.

A small ball of light floated up, illuminating the area.

Talon kept his wings against his back and his arms down at his side as he tried to keep her talking.

People had made the mistake before of concentrating on a dragon's magic while not paying attention to his physical defenses.

There was a reason he'd taken the name *Talon*. And kept his claws sharper than any barber's razor.

With the mage distracted by talking to him, and just the tiny ball of light above, he could quietly start to work on the ropes.

In response to her statement, Talon snorted, then said, *Surely you're wise enough to know that I can't grant you immortality, or even longer life. Right?*

The scent of uncertainty wafted toward Talon, then her resolve hardened.

"So say you," she replied.

The other brigands fanned out, surrounding him.

Talon couldn't help but snort again. *Drinking my blood, eating my organs, or even making a paste of my bones won't preserve you. Which, ew. You know how gross that all sounds, right?*

This time, the magic user snorted with derision. "I've had worse. Some of the food we've had on the road has been…interesting."

Talon wanted to ask about how long they'd been traveling, but he'd get back to that. Hopefully.

Even if you manage to kill me, you know you can't preserve me, right? I'll dissolve when I die.

That was the thing about dragons. They all went back to their constituent parts when they passed.

In the best case scenario, Talon would become Killian again, as he had been, a young man with a full life ahead of him.

Chances were, though, Talon would become a two-hundred-year-old man, composed of dust and bones and not much else.

"We can sustain you," the woman said stubbornly. "Hold you near death but not let you cross over, until we get back to the coast."

Good luck with that.

There. Talon had sawed through one of the ropes holding the net together. The hole was big enough for him to stick his hand through. Now, he just needed to make it a little bigger.

Talon felt his life force being drained by the net. He let himself stoop over a bit more, partly play acting, partly because of the damned trees above his head, not allowing him to draw himself up to his full height.

Who taught you these spells? Someone on the coast, perhaps?

There weren't many powerful wizards close to Talon's territory. He possibly, *perhaps* had made it clear that he didn't like magic users, didn't trust them to not do something exactly like what had happened to him.

"That is not your concern," the magic user said.

I'm the one captured in your net. I think I should get to choose what I worry about.

Like how dark and gray the world was getting. How his eyesight was starting to fade. Even the scents he normally swam in were getting muddied.

But he'd sawed through another rope knot. One more to go...

"The great wizard has need of you," she said grudgingly.

Great wizard, eh? Sounds like a great wanker, sending others to do his work. Why doesn't he come and see me himself?

"Because you're so easy to lure out of your mountain, and have been easy to catch," the magic user said, her tone smug.

I wouldn't go counting your eggs before they're hatched.

That was the only warning Talon gave as he finished sawing through another rope knot.

With a motion that was as smooth as if he'd practiced it, Talon brought the hole he'd created up to his face, sticking his snout out.

He promptly spat a great gout of acid on the magic user.

She screamed as she fell back, clawing at her face.

She probably wasn't dead. Not yet.

Talon would make sure that her condition would change soon.

He could now use his acid to destroy the parts of the net that were in front of him, the rope quickly giving way.

The brigands surrounding him came charging forward. A hard metal sword clanged against Talon's right side, while a spear probed his back.

They probably knew that his wings were vulnerable, so Talon kept them folded up.

He wheeled around (again, a move that he might have practiced more than once) practically spinning in place on his tail so that his opponents were now all in front of him.

The net was still caught on his back—he'd probably have to extend his wings to get rid of it.

In the meanwhile, there were brigands to maim.

It didn't take long, now that Talon was mostly free of the net. The men and women fell to his acid attacks, unable to defend themselves, his own armored hide more than a match for their weapons.

When the battle was over, Talon paused, considering what to do next.

They'd been sent to attack him. To *take* him somewhere, back to the coast, which was more than a month's journey, even as a dragon flew.

The magic user had said something about a great wizard. He'd need the name of whatever idiot thought that Talon was an easy target.

Talon did *not* want to loot the bodies, to go through the pockets of the corpses and see what they were carrying. He'd rarely done so in the past. Just at the start, when he'd been building his hoard.

However, he needed more information, and that was enough to overpower his disgust.

The magic user wore a finely made silver pendant, a five-sided star with an open eye in the center of it. One of the fighters wore one as well, though it was bronze and not as well-made.

That was all that Talon could find of use on the bodies. He piled them up on one side, away from the livestock, and then spat great gouts of acid across them. It was very satisfying, watching the flesh and softer parts melt away until all that remained were bones.

Talon left those as they were, as a warning to the next group who were certain to come for him.

Then he made himself go through the brigands' bags.

There, at the bottom of the one that smelled like the magic user, he found a heavy leather purse filled with coins.

Not just local currency, but gold coins. A lot of them.

He sat holding it for a while, admiring the sparkle of the gold, before he got around to figuring out that it was from the kingdom of Alfaladon. (Okay, so maybe there was a little drooling as well, but not much. Really.)

Talon couldn't read the face of the coins, not with his eyes. But his fingertips were extraordinarily sensitive, and he'd taught himself to read the embossed or stamped surfaces of money.

Alfaladon was on the coast. West and south of Talon's peak.

Talon separated the coins into two piles—smaller currency into one, the gold and pendants into another.

He'd give the money in the pile of smaller currencies to the family who'd taken in the girl baby. And he'd tell them where the livestock were, so they might fetch home the critters who were still alive after spending a night in the forest with other predators present.

The gold was his. No one would begrudge a dragon his bright and shiny gold. He needed to do some research about the pendants, to see what sort of a group bore that mark. He had to learn all he could about the kingdom of Alfaladon, out on the coast.

As well as to put some thought into how to survive the attacks that were sure to come.

ORLA HAS TWO DADDIES

ORLA

Orla tried to be a good girl. She really did. She tried to sit quietly with Mama and do her stitching. The sitting room wasn't too stuffy— Mama did let Orla open the window to the fresh spring day, as it wasn't too chilly.

But it was dark and dank in there, the wood on the walls painted black, and Orla just wanted to be *outside* already.

Besides, Doreen, her closest sibling, who was thirteen (which meant five years older than Orla) felt the need to talk on and on and *on* about how icky the boys were in town, in particular the one who pulled her pigtails and laughed at her skirt.

Orla would have already punched him in the face. Or possibly someplace else, someplace that she knew she shouldn't. If she was really serious about not liking the boy.

Doreen, though, for all her talk, really didn't want to be left alone, or at least that was what Orla assumed. Da had taught her to watch people, because what they said wasn't always what they meant.

The eldest of the four sisters had already left the household, forming her own family with her new husband. She was ten years older than Orla, having turned eighteen over the winter. The next oldest was sixteen, and she was already betrothed and just waiting until the summer festival to be handfasted.

Orla didn't want to be married. Or to raise a family and have kids of her own. Children were a *lot* of work. She knew that from looking after her cousins.

She wanted to be a pirate. Or a bandit. But not a bad one, not like the ones Da chased. No, she wanted to be a *good* bandit, who helped people.

Orla kept looking out the window, up into the light blue sky. It was still chilly enough that the blue reflected the cold. It wouldn't grow a deep blue until summer.

"Would you pay attention?" Mama scolded. "Your stitches look like ant trails, wandering all over your cloth."

Orla sighed and looked down. Her stitches were never as neat as her mother's. Then again, Mama was a proper seamstress. People *paid* to have her do their stitching and put fancy embroidery on their clothes.

Someone would probably only pay Orla to stop stitching.

Orla was just so different than everyone in her adopted family. Her three sisters, Mama, as well as Papa were all tall, thin, and blond, while Orla had dark wavy hair and was short and stocky.

They did love her. Or at least tried to.

Finally, Orla heard the sound she'd been waiting for.

The sigh that wasn't a sigh, that wasn't spoken out loud.

It seeped in through the window, filling Orla with joy.

"Da's coming!" she exclaimed. She stood up, flung her stitching on her chair, and raced out the door.

She was vaguely aware of her mother calling her name while muttering and picking up the embroidery that had slid off the seat and onto the floor.

It didn't matter. Orla would make it up to Mama later.

Because right now, Da was coming.

Orla waited out in the courtyard in front of the house, the far-off dot in the sky resolving itself quickly as Da came flying down, barreling right toward her.

Orla knew not to flinch or to step backwards, no matter how quickly Da came racing up. It was a game they played.

Da would always stop in time.

As he did then, landing just a foot away from her.

Orla ran up to him and flung her arms around his scaly belly, holding him tightly against her. He always felt warm against her cheek, though slightly prickly at the same time, like fur that stood up on end. He smelled of acid and magic, as well as the cool winds he'd been racing through.

You came, Orla said with a happy sigh.

With everyone else, Orla spoke her words out loud. Only with Da could she just think them, knowing that not only would they be heard, the truth of her statements would always shine through.

Of course I did. You do know what day it is, don't you?

Orla nodded solemnly, rubbing her cheek up and down Da's yellowish scales. They were a little rough, and sliding her face across them was like lightly scratching her skin. She loved the feeling, loved how it made her skin feel energized. *It's the day you rescued me.*

A large hand gently touched her head, the fingers tracing through her loose hair.

Whenever Da was coming, Orla wore her hair down, just so he could do exactly what he was doing now. When she wore it in braids, sometimes his claws would get stuck and she never wanted to make Da feel bad.

Orla sighed again, content as a little fat kitten out in the sunshine. She wanted to stay like this forever, safe and loved.

It is your finding day, little one, Da said. He shifted his attention away from her, speaking in a more formal tone. *Good afternoon Madam Hayes. I take it all is well?*

With a sigh, Orla stepped back from Da. Mama had commented

more than once about how strange it was that Orla would hold on to a dragon that way.

He was her Da. She always felt safe with him.

Of course, she felt safe with Papa as well. However, Da was different. Special.

Hers.

She had to share Mama and Papa with her sisters and her cousins and aunts and uncles and everyone else in the large extended family.

The rest of the territory might all know Talon, but only she claimed him as Da. (She'd started using the name when she'd been young, and her tongue had gotten mixed up between Talon and dragon and so what came out was Da, or Dada. It made perfect sense to her, and it helped her distinguish between her human Papa and her dragon Dada.)

Even though Orla stopped hugging Da, she still grabbed hold of one of his clawed hands, wrapping her own hand around his long, bony pinky finger, avoiding the claw at the end by instinct.

It was only then that she realized he'd been holding something in his other hand. Probably a present for Mama, though maybe he would have something for her as well.

It was her finding day after all.

"All is well enough," Mama said with a sigh.

Funny, that was how she often sounded with Orla. Why would she be put out with Da? What had he done?

"I suppose you're still inclined to do this?" she asked.

"Do what?" Orla asked as she looked between Da and Mama.

I assure you she'll be perfectly safe.

Orla nodded. People could believe Da. He always spoke the truth.

Mama's mouth was set in a straight line of disappointment. But she merely nodded and said, "We'll see."

Orla looked between them again, still not certain what was going on.

Da lowered his great head—it was nearly as big as she was—and looked her directly in the eyes.

Orla loved Da's eyes. They were a bright yellow color that afternoon, though she'd seen them both paler as well as a deeper gold. They stared at her with a fire that soothed her nerves, made her warm and almost sleepy. It didn't matter to her that the pupil went up and down instead of being round. It was both alien as well as familiar.

(She'd been told that she was too young to remember Da finding her. She still did, though, those eyes filling her world and letting her know she was safe at last.)

I brought you something.

Da held out his other hand. He held two long leather straps with hoops riveted onto the edges. The straps went from his hand, which was above her head, all the way to the ground, maybe five or six feet long. They were both nearly as wide as her forearm. Great silver buckles hung from the ends.

"What are these?" Orla asked out loud, trying to be polite and include Mama in the conversation. While everyone could hear Talon's silent speech, no one except Da could hear Orla's.

Instead of saying anything, Da sent a picture to her mind.

The straps were wrapped around Da's torso, above and below his arms.

And Orla was holding onto them, on his back.

Blue sky spread above them, with white clouds underneath.

Orla gasped. "Really? Really?" She turned back to look at Mama. "Really?" She couldn't help but start to bounce with excitement.

She'd asked (okay, possibly begged and pleaded with) Da for a ride since *forever*. She'd always wanted to fly with him.

Mama had said that it was too dangerous, no matter how much Orla pointed out that Da would never *ever* hurt her.

Besides, he had magic and stuff. He'd catch her if she fell. She was certain of it.

She was as sure in her belief in him as in the sun rising every day.

"Really," Mama said dryly.

Orla didn't care how many embroideries she'd have to stitch to show her appreciation. She'd be able to do it while still thinking about flying. And her stitches would dart across the cloth like, like, hummingbirds, not meander like ants.

Mama helped fasten the first strap around Da's chest. She had to pick Orla up, though Orla knew that if she asked, Da would lower himself so she could climb up on her own.

She grabbed hold of the cleverly positioned handles sticking out of the edges of the strap, beaming.

Then Mama put on the second strap, not only around Da's body but also across Orla's ankles, attaching her securely.

"Not too far," Mama warned. "And not for too long."

Are you secure? Da asked.

Go! Go! Let's go! Let's fly!

Da gave a deep, rich chuckle that made her grin in return.

He leaped up.

And they were flying.

FEET, HOOFBEATS, AND WAGON TRAINS

For most people, travel involves walking from one place to the other. Possibly with a large rucksack carrying their essentials, or maybe it's just a small basket filled with baked goods for visiting a neighbor.

People who have a larger amount of things to carry and don't want to haul them around on their back turtle-like, may have a wheelbarrow that they can push or pull along a road. There are even some two wheeled carts that people harness themselves to and tug behind them.

Merchants traveling from one market to the next will have even larger carts. Ox are the animal of choice for pulling such vehicles. As a result, oxen have been carefully bred, the species differentiated, such that there are now small ox that aren't much bigger than a large billy goat, to huge creatures that are the size of sheds, their shoulders as tall as man's head.

Why are oxen used, and not horses, for such manual labor?

Simply this: oxen are stupid.

Sure, they can be stubborn and bad tempered. However, the aforementioned breeding has reduced their startle reflex to the point that if released into the wild, they would fall prey to the first carnivore that came hunting them, while their wild cousins would have already taken off for the hills.

On the other hand, horses are not only too smart for the job, they have an imagination. This makes them particularly horrible for carting anything around when magic is involved.

You see, a horse *knows* that magic is a bad thing. Terrible things happen to horses when they get around magic. That calming spell you just uttered? Horses *know* that after the calming comes the slaughtering, and they really, really need to get out of there, right now.

Fools still try to breed stupid horses, to see if they can create ones with less imagination. Then they're stuck with large dumb animals who are stubbornly certain that the magic is out to kill them but cannot be led away from it, given their lack of brains.

Horses in the wild have more of an affinity toward magic, and seem to be able to tell when magic is harmful versus not. However, they do tend to stick to areas that have less magic, plains where the magic has pooled around the edges instead of in the center. They are reported to actively avoid any place where magic has gathered in large swaths.

So oxen-drawn carts make up the wagon trains that stretch from one major town to the next during the summer when there are ongoing markets. Oxen may not be as fast as a horse, but they're sturdy and loyal and they don't mind a spell now and again.

As for flying, well, that remains a dream. Birds and bats fly, insects and butterflies, as well as the occasional dragon, but that's about it.

Magic users have never managed to enchant a pair of wings, a carpet, or a broom that could fly, or even create a flying machine.

One clever soul did come up with a floating spell. Could get himself up, between ten to twenty feet in the air and just hover there.

Couldn't move, though.

Threw down a rope and had a friend try to pull him along

through the air. This didn't work until the friend attached the rope to cart drawn by an ox. Then, the wizard could be dragged along behind the cart like so much refuse.

It was a type of flight. However, too many things made it impractical, the primary issue being the magic already existing in the land itself.

As explained before, magic doesn't exist like a single perfect layer of frosting spread evenly across the ground. So while being dragged along behind the cart, the wizard would hit a serious magical eddy and find himself shooting straight up into the air. (The spell he'd created needed a certain strength of magic where he'd first cast it, and now, in this new location, it was too strong.) Or they'd reach an area barren of magic, and the wizard would drop down and float just a few feet off the ground.

Someday, perhaps, wizards or spell casters or witches would figure out how to shoot across the skies like birds and bats. And dragons.

But for now, it remains a dream.

At least for most.

ORLA

Orla couldn't help but squeal a little as the town dropped beneath them.

We're flying! We're really flying!

Yes, and I promised your mother not to go too far.

This time.

She heard the snort with her ears.

This time.

She knew how a dragon bargained. Talon was very precise in his words and his agreements. She'd learned a lot from him, more than he'd ever appreciate, probably.

For now, the cold, clean air cleared away the dark dankness of the room she'd been sitting in before. Strange how the town looked like a patchwork quilt, all the houses crowded together, with spots of green where people had their house gardens, the brown canal that meandered close to the town wall.

No one could see her up here, flying with Da. Orla decided she didn't mind that at all.

It wasn't for them, this flight.

It was for her. For *them*.

Anyplace you'd like to go?

I want to see the house I was born in, Orla said without really thinking about it.

That's a little further away than your mother probably wants us to go.

But it's my finding day! We'll be remembering together. When you found me. And we found each other.

Orla wasn't sure what Da felt in response to that. He wasn't a person, and she could never really read his face, though she could tell sometimes when he was bothered by how stiffly his long whiskers stuck out from his snout. And mental speech didn't carry all of the emotions of the spoken word.

Yet, somehow, she could still tell that her words had an effect on him.

Probably a good effect, as he turned to the west, heading toward where she knew the original farmstead had been.

It didn't take them long to get there. Though there wasn't anything for Orla to do except to watch the ground speed by below, or to look at the clouds, she still loved every moment of it. The view beneath her changed, then changed again. It was so different than when walking or even riding in an ox-pulled cart.

She couldn't wait until all of it was as familiar to her as it was to Da, who'd flown over these parts for centuries, patrolling his borders, always on the lookout for brigands.

It would probably take a full day to walk all the way to the farmsteads from the town where Orla lived, but it hadn't taken much more than an hour before they arrived.

The family Orla had been raised with had moved five years before, when Orla had been three. She didn't really remember either the house she'd grown up in, or the house she'd been born in. She'd been told about it, how there were only three rooms, one for Mama and Papa, one for all the girls, then a larger area that was the living room/play area and also kitchen. They had an outhouse, and chickens and goats and for a year or so they'd had sheep as well.

There is your family's old place, Da told her as they started circling a farm.

The house looked so small, just a dot amidst all the green of the yard. It did have some nice fields around it.

But you didn't find me there, right?

Da nodded and headed further west. He started circling a much smaller house. It probably only had a single bedroom and a living room/kitchen.

That's it? Orla asked, excited to see the place though also maybe slightly disappointed. It looked...poor. The chickens had scratched up all the grass and there wasn't a garden, not really, just dirt surrounding the house.

That is the old farmstead.

Orla leaned closer and rested her cheek on Da's back, even though the scales on his back were much rougher than those on his belly. *I'm glad you found me.*

Da gave a rumble that resembled the loud purr of Mrs. Cafferty's orange cat.

After a few moments, Orla sat back up and looked around again.

Strange. Was that a large hedge just to the west, cutting off access to the fields and trees beyond it?

What's that? Orla said. She held the image of the hedge clearly in her mind.

Da nodded again and flew closer. *That's a fence I grew, to protect my people.*

Orla knew that Da sometimes did magic. He wasn't a spell caster, but he was a dragon. He had something of a magical spark, deep within him.

What's it made of?

Blackberry bramble, Da replied, sounding smug. *Well-behaved bramble. It can only grow in the circle I've made for it. Which makes it angry. While it may grudgingly give a few berries at the end of each summer, it has plenty of thorns, all year round. It takes a great deal of magic to cut a hole through it.*

What's it for? Orla asked, curious. She didn't recall there ever being any kind of fence around Da's lands before. There was just the mark, the deep groove that he'd created by spitting acid onto the ground for decades. Mama had told her about it.

To protect my people from attacks, Da said.

That's good, right?

It is. I like to keep my people safe.

But who protects you? Orla asked after they'd turned away and had started heading back toward town. She knew they'd gone farther than Mama would have liked. Hopefully she'd understand about where they'd gone. It was Orla's finding day, after all.

Da laughed, but it wasn't a nice laugh. It sounded almost like it hurt.

I protect me, Da assured her.

That isn't right, Orla said stubbornly. *If you get to protect us, then someone gets to protect you. That's the way it works.*

Does it? At least Da sounded truly amused now, and not so hollow.

It does, Orla said. *When I grow up,* I'll *be the one to protect you.*

Thank you, little one, but that won't be necessary.

Orla knew that Da wasn't telling the full truth. He needed someone to help him.

Right then and there, she decided to dedicate herself to the sword, to learning how to fight, so that Da didn't have to do all the work himself. She'd probably have to learn how to shoot a bow as well, since sometimes she'd be riding him.

She pushed herself up so she wasn't as stretched out along his back. She did still keep hold of the front strap.

For now.

She'd teach herself to ride him without holding on. She could already see herself doing that.

Yes, she could do this. She'd need to wear her winter jacket when she went flying with him if she was going to be sitting up.

But someday, she'd be fighting from Da's back.

It was going to be awesome.

THE SEMI-CIRCLE OF LIFE

Ulthir is a remote god. He sits on his mountain, high above the world, and he watches the people down below. (His voyeuristic tendencies are not creepy at all. Really.) He rarely interacts with them, and even more rarely still, intervenes.

For all of that, there are a few ideals that Ulthir has passed down that appear to have *stuck*, as it were.

The most important is this: there is no such thing as an afterlife.

Ulthir doesn't want more people on his mountain.

(Sure, he gets lonely every once in a while. When that happens, he seeks out Maloneal or Eowin's company. But after a time, he craves his solitude again. Too many other people around, breathing his air, makes him crazy.)

(Crazier.)

(He is a god after all. Kind of means by definition that he's a little bit off center.)

(Maybe a lot off center.)

So there is no heaven, no pearly gates, no halls full of mead-drinking warriors, no chorus of angels singing Ulthir's praises, no, none of that.

And why would anyone create a hell? Those places just exist to show off the advantages of the *other* place, the place that supposedly isn't hell. And there isn't one of those other places.

There is no reincarnation, no coming back as a peasant having been a princess in a former life. No nirvana or bright light to continue on in.

Nothing.

People have one chance to make it, to live their lives to the fullest.

Then they die. Their bodies return to clay. (Metaphorically speaking, that is. They either get burned or buried or in a few select instances, eaten). The spirit or soul or whatever you want to call it leaves and rejoins the sunlight which gave them life in the first place.

There is the occasional ghost, the poor lost soul who didn't make it and so desperately wants a second chance that they manage to hang around for a while even after their flesh is gone. Most ghost stories are just fantasies. Actual ghosts are as rare as the times Ulthir has stirred himself to do something.

For the vast majority of people, there is the here and now. And that's it.

Despite that, there are creatures called demons. They don't preside over fiery pits or frozen lakes. Usually, demons are merely local gods gone wrong. Some might say turned evil, but good, like evil, depends on how you look at it. They tempt individuals into doing things considered bad by their neighbors, and sometimes, those people succumb.

Why does this forest's goddess inspire those around her to be kind to one another, whereas the people around that one turn into money-grubbing thieves?

Not even Ulthir can answer that question, as that might require some grave philosophical thinking, which is something he's never really been good at. (Seriously. Mud puddles are possibly deeper.) He might have some ideas on the matter. Then again, he might just be full of hot air, even on his perpetually cold mountain.

No matter.

Many dictators, tyrants, merchants, and even priests claim to have the answer and know the One True Way to Live. They manage to get some people to follow them, at least for a while, until the Twins turn against them and their holdings turn to dust.

Fortunately, most everyone else is content to just wing it.

ORLA

During the year of Orla's thirteenth finding day, she discovered that she got to finally (*finally!*) go and spend a night at Da's place, up on his mountain. She'd been asking every time she met with Da for years and years.

Mama didn't approve of her going to visit Da's peak.

Then again, Mama didn't approve of many of the things that Orla did these days.

Orla spent the time she was required to in the house, learning her letters and her numbers, because it made sense to her to be able to read books and to do sums. The latter came in especially handy at the market.

However, Orla had stubbornly stuck to her promise to Da that she would learn how to protect him. She spent part of every afternoon doing physical training.

Right after she'd made that decision, when she'd still been eight years old, she'd gone into one of the taverns looking for a fighter to train her.

She'd ignored the snickers and snide comments, asking everyone in there for help until finally someone pointed her at an older gentleman named Kato who seemed to know how to use every weapon ever invented.

It had taken a lot of finagling on her part—almost a year's worth of pleading and tears—but Da had finally agreed to pay Kato for his services.

So for four years now, whenever Kato was in town, Orla worked with him every afternoon. When he was gone—usually to ride as a guard for a merchant's caravan—she practiced continuously on her own, with the dedication of someone much older than her years.

Orla had her reasons, though. She knew that Da fought brigands. They constantly came into his territory, trying to hurt his people. Da had even missed her tenth finding day as he'd been too hurt to fly to come to see her.

He did come by the next day. Orla would never forget the burn marks striped across Da's back, how stiffly he'd held himself. They hadn't taken a ride that day—Orla had insisted that Da be more gentle with himself.

Those wounds—and the other times she'd seen him after a battle —helped her stay focused on her training.

Mama despaired that Orla would never find a husband, particularly since, at least according to Mama, Orla's features were disturbingly plain. Her eyes were just brown, her hair was unruly, her brow was broad and her nose was overly-wide and kind of melted across her face.

Orla didn't pay much mind to Mama when it came to that. Da looked at her as if she were made of gold. She'd either find someone who looked at her the same way, or she'd be alone. (Besides, she'd always have Da.)

These days, Orla always went out with a short sword attached to her belt. She was still only five feet tall. She had broad shoulders and muscle her sisters didn't, making her seem even more stocky than when she'd been younger.

Though Orla practiced with both a longer sword as well as with staff and bow, she felt most comfortable with her shorter sword. She had no idea if she'd grow taller—no one did, as no one really remembered her actual parents. She hoped she would, so she would have a wider range of weapons available to her.

Papa had given Orla a brand new rucksack for her birthday that year. It was made of leather, with strong yet thin and light pieces of wood that gave it a solid external frame. It was the perfect gift for his adventure-seeking daughter.

Orla had packed it with food and water, as well as her warmest clothes. She didn't know how cold it would be up on Da's mountain, but she would be prepared no matter what. There were clever straps attached to the bottom of the rucksack that she used to attach a roll of blankets. She could use the sack itself for a pillow.

Da had yet to take Orla fighting with him. She didn't pester him too much about it.

Yet.

She figured she could wait until she was fifteen before she really started to push.

Besides, she felt as though she had so much to learn! Not just all the weapons she needed to master, but different fighting forms and techniques.

Da couldn't really help much with that. Sure, he'd once been a great swordsman. However, that had been eons ago. Techniques had changed, and Da wasn't used to fighting with a sword anymore. He barely used his arms at all, if he could help it.

The morning of her finding day for her thirteenth year was overcast, but Orla had faith that the clouds would burn off before too long. Da came to fetch her before noon that day, as it would take a long while to fly all the way back to the center of his territory, where he lived.

Orla had graduated to a single strap over the past year. That was something else Mama didn't approve of, how Orla had built up the muscles in her legs so she could hold onto Da's back without using her hands. Kato had suggested it, that she train to ride Da how she would ride a creature called a horse. She'd never seen one, just oxen.

Da had seemed impressed though. He'd only threatened to do somersaults with her just using the single strap. She was pretty sure she'd be able to handle it, that he wouldn't have to try to catch her as she fell.

Still, the first time they tried such acrobatics might have to be from only a few feet above Rafferty Lake or someplace else where a fall wouldn't hurt her.

She waited in the clear air in the courtyard of the house for Da. All her sisters had long since left to form their own families. Orla had never been that close to them, being five years younger than the youngest, and now all they wanted to talk about were their husbands and children. They didn't want to hear the rumors of a war starting in the west, or even how the attacks against Da's lands had increased over the last few months.

Orla could tell how much Da was fighting. His hands were almost always scarred, and frequently when he saw her, one or more of his talons had been ripped out, due to his clawing something he shouldn't have.

Soon enough, Orla would be there to protect him.

Da came shooting out of the sky. Orla loved watching him hurtle towards her, standing her ground and not giving an inch as he thudded into the courtyard, less than a foot away from her now.

It was a game they played, seeing how close he could get to her without her flinching.

Both of them were too stubborn to ever give way.

Though no one ever said it, Orla still thought it sometimes.

Like father, like daughter.

Da's dry voice rang inside her head. *Happy finding day.*

"Happy finding day, Da," Orla said out loud. She tended to speak out loud with Da when she was at home, so that Mama wouldn't be quite so angry about Orla spending time with Da.

Madam Hayes, Da said in that formal tone of his, looking over Orla's shoulder. *All is well?*

"It is," Mama said with a resigned sigh. "You know how it is with little ones. Sooner or later they grow up and have a mind of their own."

Da snorted out loud. *I would think that this little one has always had her own opinions.*

"True," Mama said. At least she was smiling. "I heard about the MacAffies," she added, growing more serious.

I've been doing everything I could, Da said, sounding defensive. *And those responsible have paid.*

Orla busied herself attaching the one strap to Da's torso, not wanting to get involved in the conversation.

The MacAffies had lived further inside Da's territory, on the outskirts of Millerstown, a major city in the northwest quadrant that was more than two day's ride from the border. Usually, the brigands who came after Da's people stuck to the outer farms. This was the closest to a town that they'd ever gotten to.

And the MacAffies hadn't been able to put up a signal, to tell Da that there was trouble. No, it was only after the tortured and mutilated bodies were discovered that Da had been alerted.

More guards now patrolled the streets and towns. There were also more guards at the openings of Da's hedge, the gates, so everyone who came and went could be questioned.

Not everyone liked these measures. However, Orla understood that Da was doing everything he could to keep his people safe.

If only there weren't so many brigands trying to get at him!

It made Orla growl softly, under her breath, and train even harder.

"You keep her safe," Mama warned.

Orla bristled at that as well. She could keep *herself* safe, thank you very much. Why else had she been training every single day, if not to be able to defend herself, at the very least?

Always, Da said, his tone sounding warm for once.

He glanced down at Orla. *Ready, little one?*

Orla nodded. She looked over at Mama, who raised her arms for a moment, as if considering giving her youngest daughter a hug, then dropping them back down before she did.

It made Orla sad that Mama thought she'd grown too big and that she didn't need hugs. This *was* her first time spending the night away from her house.

So Orla ran over to Mama, gave her a quick, fierce hug, then ran back to Da.

She pretended not to see the tears that streaked Mama's cheeks as she flung herself up on Da's back. Mounting quickly was a trick she'd practiced even when he wasn't there, so that if they were in a fight, she'd be able to mount and dismount quickly.

We'll be back tomorrow, around the same time, Da promised Mama as he sprang into the air.

Orla waved at Mama, then turned away, looking forward to spending more time with Da at his place.

The ride to Da's mountain took most of the afternoon. Da explained that there were headwinds that day. Orla was glad she was wearing her warmest winter leathers to block at least some of the cold from getting through to her. She was going to have to get better gloves, though. And a warmer hat.

Though Orla had heard stories about Da's peak, the sight of it made her gasp.

It stood alone, rising up out of gradual foothills. It wasn't part of a range, just a solitary mountain. (Da explained later that he had knocked down some of the hills that had been closest so that he had a clearer view of all of the surrounding area.)

Show me the base, Orla said.

After a slight pause, she added, *Please.*

Da nodded and flew down, circling the base of the peak.

Orla could see recent rockfall. Probably, Da had bashed his tail against the stone, ensuring that there was no clear path up the mountain, so that no one could reach him easily.

There's a spot over there that you should probably hit again, Orla said, holding the image clearly in her mind. *Someone might be able to scramble over that.*

Thank you, Da said, sounding impressed.

Orla nodded. It had been one of the reasons why she'd wanted to come out to Da's peak in the first place, to make sure that it was safe for him.

While Da didn't like to admit it, her eyesight was better than his. His sense of smell more than made up for that.

Still, it was her job to take care of him.

Scraggly trees clung to the edges of the peak, at least around the base. The boulders changed color as they rose, from reddish brown to a lighter, yellowish white. Bleached by the sun? A different type of stone? Or perhaps a bit of both?

There weren't any trees close to the top, and what vegetation there was had been thinned, probably by constant application of acid from Da's snout. There was no easy cover, no place for an assassin to hide in.

Orla approved, even if it did make Da's peak look kinda naked and un-homey.

The landing pad in front of Da's place was covered in soft, well pounded dirt. Da had told her once that he'd tried sand, but that it had gotten everywhere and irritated his scales.

Da seemed to take pride in how well he landed, so Orla always told him that he'd done a good job. She hopped off and unbuckled her strap, rolling it tightly and tying it off so that she could carry it easily.

She waited while Da took a few moments scenting the area, his red tongue flickering in and out of his mouth rapidly.

No one here besides us, Da said after a few moments.

Good, Orla said. *Wouldn't want anyone crashing my finding day party, now would we?*

Party? We're having a party?

Of course we are. With cake.

With cake?

Orla had to giggle at how panicked Da suddenly sounded.

Silly. Just us celebrating. We don't need cake. Or cookies. Or any such treat. Really.

Are you sure?

She giggled again at how worried Da was.

I might have brought something for me, but I know you don't want anything. She'd learned long ago that Da only ate about once a month, generally something large and fresh. He would frequently take an entire day after that to recover. He'd tried eating smaller meals, but they didn't seem to satisfy him as much.

In the meantime, she patted his torso, then walked into the large gaping hole in the rocks, determined to love whatever Da had done to the place.

Inside was different than what she'd imagined.

First of all, there were many levels to Da's place, all connected with gentle ramps. Da had dug into the yellow-white stone like a worm boring through earth, though the holes were so smooth she had to wonder if he'd used magic to make them.

There were also more windows than she'd expected—though none of them were covered with glass and were more like holes poked through stone. Three-foot-deep holes, which meant that they'd make lovely places to sit on (in) with the right cushion. When it was warmer.

None of the rooms were that big, though the ceilings were all tall. Da just needed room for his upright torso, and was content to let the rest of his tail remain outside the doorway, on the ramp that connected the room to the rest of his place. Frequently, there wasn't enough space for him to turn around in, so he'd just back out.

The walls were the plain, yellowish-white stone. No stitching samplers, framed portraits, or even braids of hay for good luck adorned them, unlike at Mama's house where it felt like every inch had to be overly decorated.

While at first Da's place struck Orla as poor, with its barren walls, she grew used to it quickly. So fast, in fact, that she figured that when she had her own rooms, away from Mama's house, that her walls would also be unadorned.

The top level of Da's place was the nicest, Orla decided. It had really good views, so Da could watch both the sunrise as well as the sunset. There was a fireplace up here, something she hadn't been sure about, making the upper layers seem cozy, even if there was a floor up above the hearth, as well as two below. The fireplace didn't burn wood, but held a magical flame that could warm the place.

Underneath the top level were more rooms and fewer windows. Da lit the place with magical gems imbedded into the walls that flickered on as he approached.

After showing Orla the top level, Da took her down to the bottom-most layer, three stories down, which held the treasure rooms. Orla was appropriately awed by Da's hoard of gold, as well as an entire room dedicated to semi-precious gems. She was happy that she'd never have to worry about making enough money through working or hiring out as a mercenary—Da assured her that he'd always support her, in whatever field she chose.

(She was going to be the fiercest fighter in all the kingdoms. She wasn't quite sure how to make money doing that, as she didn't intend to hire herself out like Kato did. But she would figure something out.)

Da appeared to be hesitant about showing Orla the next floor, but he did when she asked him about it.

There was a single room on this level, that ran at least fifty feet long and about half that wide. No windows, just the magical gems giving it lots of light.

In the room, one entire long wall held a map carved into the rock. Da had done it using a glass nib coated in his acid. The map illustrated most of the lands outside of Da's mountain. His territory sat a little east of center on the wall, the four quarters of it clearly marked.

There weren't written names associated with places, but general features were shown, like meadows, forests, rivers and lakes, as well as the coast, far to the west.

What is this for? Orla asked, surprised. She hadn't thought that Da was that interested in the lands outside of his own territory. *What are you keeping track of?*

Da sighed. He traced a line that ran from the top of the map to the bottom. If she split the map side-to-side, from where Da's territory ended all the way out to the coast, the most prominent line was a little over halfway between them.

This is the current border of the Kingdom of Alfaladon. As was this, and this, he said, indicating additional lines that were closer to the coast.

It looked like a ripple of waves, steadily encroaching across the land.

King Alfa, right? That's the current king? Orla asked.

Da nodded. *The current king always takes that name, so there's been a King Alfa of Alfaladon for about a century now.*

In the upper corner, on the coast, was a strange mark that Orla hadn't seen before, a five-pointed star with an eye in the center of it.

What's that? she said, pointing.

The sign of King Alfa's great wizard. Loalmane.

Loalmane? That was an odd sounding name. There was something about that name that sounded familiar. She'd have to think about it later.

Are you worried about King Alfa? And his wizard? Orla asked.

She was always interested in anything that might threaten Da. It was her job to protect him, after all. And there had been rumors of some sort of war brewing out west, toward the coast. She remembered Papa talking about it at some point.

It will take years before they reach here, Da assured her.

And then what? Orla said.

Da hesitated.

You're worried, aren't you? Why? What is going on with this King Alfa and his wizard?

After a few moments, Da shook his head. *I will not lie to you*, he said. *But I also don't want to burden you. You're still young.*

Orla snorted at him. *I have started my menses*, she said, trying to sound proud of the fact though she wasn't really sure about the whole thing. It was awkward sometimes, and embarrassing others.

I know, Da said, reminding her that his nose was better tuned than most.

That means I'm an adult. I can make my own babies, Orla said, though honestly, thinking about it, it felt more like babies having babies.

I know, Da said again.

You brought me here to show me this, Orla said, walking over to where Da was, reaching out and taking one of his hands in hers.

Da looked her in the eye, his own the color of the gold he loved so much. *Is it wrong of me to hope?*

Orla wasn't sure what he was talking about, but she said as fiercely as she could, *Of course it isn't. You deserve hope more than anyone.*

Da shook his head as if he didn't agree with her assessment, but he didn't argue with her. *I want to show you your room*, Da said. *Where you get to stay whenever you come here to be with me.*

Orla smiled. *I'd like that.*

Then, later tonight, I'll tell you more about the map. And what it means.

Orla nodded. She knew the map and what it represented worried Da. She could see the groove in the floor worn by his long body as he slither/paced in front of it time and again.

No matter what the issue was, she would help Da fix it.

She'd promised.

ALL THAT GLITTERS IS, INDEED, GOLD

Dragons like gold.

They really, *really* like gold.

There have been *unsubstantiated* reports of dragons doing inappropriate things for gold, with gold, while lying on top of gold—you get the point. Just rumors. However, those persistent whispers never quite seem to go away.

There are reasons for this. Most people perceive gold as a shiny, soft metal that has value because of its scarcity and because it looks so good when fashioned into pretty jewelry, pretty crowns, pretty statues, and so on.

For dragons, gold isn't just shiny. It's SHINY. Dragons don't have the best ability to see colors. In fact, most everything appears to have a dull sheen on it, the colors faded and blurry.

Gold is the only color dragons can see clearly. In addition, the metal has a light all its own, as if it's enchanted. For a dragon, gold always glows, even in a dark room.

In addition, for some reason known only to Ulthir, gold feels warm to dragons. It doesn't feel soft, but then again, dragons aren't soft, so that isn't a quality they necessarily value. Their bodies tend to be self-regulating, neither freezing in the snow nor too hot in the sun.

But gold feels warm. Touching it, a dragon's fingers suddenly feel as if they're holding hot chocolate on a cold, wintry day.

Even if gold had no monetary value, dragons would still seek it. The fact that people value it makes it even more precious. The few dragons who live more than a couple of years all talk not just of hoarding gold, but of the great wealth they accumulate, just because.

No one begrudges a dragon his or her gold.

And those who have tried to steal it, well, those are stories for another day.

ORLA

If Orla had to guess, Da had spent a lot of time trying to make her room just so.

He was so clueless. She found it endearing.

There was no bed, as Da couldn't carry one up here by himself. Instead, he'd done the best he could, by buying a bunch of colorful, down-filled pillows that she could lie down on.

She wasn't about to tell him just how uncomfortable that would be. Maybe she could wrap a sheet around them or something, to make them behave more like a solid surface. Otherwise, every time she turned over she'd probably slide off them and her butt would hit the floor.

A tiny hearth had been carved into the side. Looking at it, Orla knew that it would never actually heat the room, no matter how big of a magical fire she had going.

Particularly since beside it was a huge open window—no glass or covering from it, letting the cool mountain air just stream into the room.

Da had gotten some things right. He'd carved some shelves into the wall for her things. There were hooks in the walls for hanging lanterns, so she could have some light that wasn't magical.

And lying in the center of the pillows was the most beautiful bow that Orla had ever seen.

Oh, Da! she said. *The room's perfect, everything's perfect,* she assured him. *And that bow is the best present* ever. *Thank you.*

I'm glad you like it, Da said. *Go on. Pick it up.*

Orla walked into the (really cold) room and picked up the bow. It was a short bow, which was good, as she was short. It had been made from a beautiful lightly-colored wood. She had no idea what tree it came from—that wasn't her forte, being able to instantly identify wood at a glance (unlike Mama who could tell you not only what the wainscoting of the parlor of a neighbor's house might be, but also what it would cost to install).

The middle of it was made out of an off-white material. It looked like old bone. It had finely carved edges and the center itself had ridges across it, to give her a better grip.

It didn't feel warm to the touch, but it felt warm to her senses.

It's magical, isn't it, Da? Orla asked, looking back at him.

It is. How did you know? Da said, curious.

Kato taught me. When Da indicated she should say more, Orla added, *He wanted me to be able to pick up an opponent's weapon in a melee and know if it was just as likely to attack me as anyone I used it on.*

Orla couldn't tell what type of magic a weapon had, or what it would do. Maybe after she had more exposure to different weapons, she might be able to make a more educated guess.

However, she'd never know for certain, as she wasn't a real magic user. She'd have to take any magical weapons she found and have them identified by a wizard using a spell.

Arrows shot from that bow will most likely strike any target they're aimed at, Da said after a few moments.

Really? Wow! Thank you! Orla said.

She couldn't help herself, but flung herself at Da and wrapped her arms firmly around his scaly torso.

She didn't hug Da as often as she used to. Partly that was because it was yet one more thing that Mama disapproved of. She also had her hair up in braids, as it was so much easier to deal with, particularly when she was flying with Da. It did mean that Da's claws would get tangled in it, so he just rested his hands on her head.

The way that Da sighed and relaxed, Orla knew that he'd missed her hugs, probably more than she had. And possibly he'd been a little worried about her reaction.

And the room? Da asked, even though Orla had already told him it was perfect.

It's great, she said, looking at the plain yellow rock walls and feeling the cold winds scouring the corners.

She was determined to make it work. She wanted to come back here, be invited to come back, often.

Da had enough to worry about.

It really was time for someone to worry about him for a change.

***

That night, after Orla had fixed herself dinner from her provisions—glad that she'd brought things that she could eat cold as Da really needed to get some pots and pans—the pair of them talked. (She was just going to have to remember next time to bring a tea kettle (or to buy one for Da) so she could heat up water for tea afterward.)

Da admitted to how worried he was about King Alfa and his wizard Loalmane, how they'd been gobbling up territory like a chicken pecking a line of seed.

Why don't the Twins turn against them? Orla asked. That was what the history books taught, right? Anytime someone tried to take over all the lands, they lost their luck and everything started going wrong for them.

I don't know, Da said. *But that isn't the only worrisome thing.*

Orla nodded, wrapped in blankets in front of Da's fire. Though he hadn't said anything, she knew that by giving her a bow, he was admitting that he needed her help.

It's that wizard of his, Da said. *He thinks he's found the trick to living forever.*

Has he?

Da snorted. *Well, part of his so-called* trick *involves slaying other, older creatures. And doing something with the remaining parts, so as to extend his own life.*

Oh. Oh! Orla said. Suddenly, a whole series of random thoughts she'd had and statements she heard made sense.

He's coming after you, isn't he? That's why you get so many brigands. They aren't after your lands, or your people. They're coming after you. *Specifically. You're one of the oldest creatures they can find. That's it, isn't it?*

Da looked at Orla steadily.

She wished he was more readable. He wasn't shocked, as his whiskers weren't stiff. He wasn't angry, as his yellow eyes had a golden tinge to them. He still seemed...displeased.

I'd appreciate it if you never mentioned that to another soul, Da said dryly. *I've gone to great lengths to hide that from, well, everyone.*

Orla waved her hand negligently in the air. *As if.*

Her casual dismissal of his concern didn't seem to sit well with Da.

I'd never tell a soul your secrets, Orla said earnestly. *I'm here to protect you, remember?*

Da nodded slowly.

He told her everything he'd learned about the wizard Loalmane. According to Da, the wizard had been the court wizard for the last three kings.

Maybe the title is hereditary, like King Alfa, Orla suggested.

Da rocked one of his hands, his equivalent of a shrug. *I've wondered that as well. His believers assert that it's still the same person.*

What's happening to all the little local gods and goddesses in the territory King Alfa acquires? Orla asked. That was another reason why it was so difficult for just one person to take over everything. The local deities didn't take kindly to new people in their realm of influence.

Da hesitated so long Orla shot him a particularly concerned look.

I don't know for certain, he said after a few moments. *I know that in the kingdom of Alfaladon that the gods and goddesses are given a type of hierarchy, ranking some as more important than others.*

How do you even judge that? Orla said, confused. How was it possible that a tree might be more important than a lake? Or a hedge more vital than a rose bush?

There's also rumors, and mind you, these are just rumors, that some of the local gods and goddesses go missing once a territory is acquired by the Kingdom of Alfaladon.

A chill wrapped itself around Orla's shoulders that had nothing to do with the cold night air seeping in through the open window.

You said that the wizard was seeking you, right? Looking for other, older creatures? Possibly to extend his own life? Orla said, her mind racing. *What if he's doing that with the local deities as well? What if he's found a way to, well, harvest them? So as to extend his own life?*

Da looked properly horrified at that.

I never would have thought of that, he said after a few moments.

Now, it was Orla's turn to shrug. Kato had told her more than once that her ability to see disparate pieces and put them together in a new whole was a skill that few had, and encouraged her to use it. He'd frequently stage the end of combat scenes, then only give her a few moments to look at it before she had to tell him about it, put all the pieces together.

So how do we stop them? Orla asked.

Da sighed.

I don't know. I've never known.

Orla nodded. *We'll come up with something. We have a few years before they reach here, right? We have time?*

Yes, we have time, Da said.

Orla couldn't say for certain, but she felt as though Da had just lied to her.

Did he not actually believe that they had time? Or was there something he wasn't telling her?

However, instead of talking more, Da had brought out the checkerboard and they had a few rousing games of checkers, no longer talking about the fate of the kingdoms between them and King Alfa, having such a pleasant evening that Orla put aside all her misgivings.

At least for a while.

WHO WANTS TO LIVE FOREVER?

Turns out, a surprising number of people.

As there is no afterlife, many of those who are living try their darnedest to extend the years that they have, which happens to be between seventy and eighty, on average.

Even the smallest of towns will boast a healer of some renown who supposedly can add years, nay, decades to your life! For just a small down payment of only three coppers/silver/gold/local coinage of your choice. Then continuing small donations for the treatments, which of course are ongoing to the end of your very far-in-the-future demise.

There are more supposed fountains of youth than anyone can keep track of. One enterprising entrepreneur actually wrote a guide to many of them over a five-year period. It featured detailed maps, local accommodations, tavern recommendations, as well as personal accounts of healing.

It didn't sell well at all, as the town nearest each fountain went to great lengths to claim that the guide lied, that theirs was the best of all of them and that the intrepid pilgrim need not visit any other, need not spend their coin elsewhere.

(This didn't deter the young entrepreneur at all, and she went on to write many more books, including several guides to local gods and goddesses, holy shrines to keep you fit, and, a personal favorite, a bestiary of the southern mountains. Unfortunately, the writer died trying to write a second bestiary. Seemed some of the water monsters valued their privacy more than supposed notoriety.)

Unsurprisingly, very few of the treatments, diets, fitness plans, exercise regimes, fasting, or frog-licking schemes actually garnered more years for people. On average, those who are richer and have access to better food will live longer, but not by much, perhaps only two or three additional years.

A few of the less principled local gods and goddesses claim that by worshiping them, a person will live longer. These schemes tend to end in heartbreak, sooner rather than later, as the Twins of Fate turn their face away from such areas and they soon fall into disgrace.

Is there any sure-fire way to live longer?

Of course.

Being turned into a dragon or some other such magical creature works.

However, there is a price to pay.

Always.

ORLA

Orla didn't go and actually fight with Da until long after she was sixteen, almost sixteen and a half.

The problem was always timing. Da wasn't about to stop and fly to pick up Orla when he got word that someone was in trouble. She had to be there, with him, when he got the message.

Orla couldn't spend all her time up at Da's place, though. It was too barren. She needed to carry a lot of food with her. She never slept well there, either, as it was frequently just too cold. (Summers were nicer and almost tolerable.)

They'd come to an arrangement where Orla spent one week a month with him. She'd dedicate herself to training during that time, as there wasn't a lot to do. Though she would go on patrols with Da, when he would fly around one part or another of his border, looking to stop bad people from getting to his territory. (They were sometimes stupid, thinking that if they cut across the land away from the roads that they might have a better chance of slipping in, not realizing that was just a clear sign that they were up to no good.)

Orla believed in being prepared. She'd come up with drills for herself—putting on her heavy flying clothes as well as Da's strap in a hurry—so that they'd be able to leave at a moment's notice.

Da had seemed impressed with how Orla had trained, always refining her actions so that there wasn't a wasted movement. (Kato's influence, as he was the smoothest fighter Orla had ever seen.)

Orla had spent that particular afternoon training with her short sword. She'd never really had a huge growth spurt, so she'd ended up being just under five foot five. She trained diligently with the long sword and the spear, but her primary weapons were always going to be her short sword and her bow. She practiced with an ordinary bow mainly, not wanting to rely on the magic of Da's bow to be able to strike her targets.

She was in the middle of a thrust-block sequence, moving smoothly from one motion to the next, when Da suddenly spoke in her mind.

Someone's in trouble.

Orla was pleased with herself at how fast she was able to make the transition, going from fight to flight preparations.

Be right there.

She ran as fast as she could up the ramps to the landing pad.

Da was already there, with her strap in his hands.

Orla smoothly whipped the strap around Da's torso and attached it, slipped into her chaps and heavy jacket, then hopped up onto Da's back.

Ready, she said as she dug into her bag, grabbing out her hat and gloves.

Hang on, Da warned as he was suddenly airborne.

Though Da would always claim that he found good tailwinds when he flew faster, Orla suspected that he used magic to aid his flight, to get him to the edge of his territory more quickly. She certainly felt the increase in the winds threatening to freeze her into a solid ice chunk, as well as seeing how fast the terrain below them changed.

A pillar of smoke on the horizon beckoned to them.

They tried to burn the hedge, and it fought back, Da said smugly. *Probably why the nearest farm was able to raise an alarm.*

Good, Orla said as Da drew closer. *How many are there?*

Da shook his head. *Two groups, one close to the hedge, one over at the farm.*

Drop me near the hedge, Orla instructed.

Da hesitated. In his ideal world, they'd be together, her staying safely on his back so that no one could get to her, not without going through him first.

Da, you know we need to take care of both groups. So that we don't get too involved with the one and the second is able to sneak up and attack.

Fine, Da huffed. *Just you take care of yourself.*

I'll be fine, Orla assured him. *Besides, I know this big hunky dragon who'll come rescue me if I get into trouble.*

Better you not get into trouble in the first place, Da warned.

Orla couldn't help but roll her eyes. She was ready for this. She'd *trained* for this. For years. Not quite a decade now, but still.

The butterflies in her stomach as she faced her first real combat were just regular nerves. Kato had told her she'd have them. As had Da.

She wasn't afraid.

Honest.

Da flew close enough to the ground for Orla to hop off just north of the spot where the hedge still smoked. She had her bow ready and strung as she raced toward the fire.

Of course, Da hadn't put her down in the middle of things, now, had he? No, he had to put her down *away* from where the bad people were doing bad things, so that they couldn't hurt her.

Orla tried not to grind her teeth as she ran, happy for all the drills and running that both Kato and Da had insisted that she do. Not so that she'd be capable of running away from a fight, no, they'd both assured her. But so that she could join one.

Like now.

She ran forward through empty field, curving along the hedge. Her nose told her when she was getting closer, as the smell of smoke suddenly blocked out everything else.

Only then did she slow down, trying to assess what it was she was running toward, what the people here were doing.

Besides, you know, hedge murder. (Hedgeicide?)

Orla treated it like one of the drills that Kato made her do, to look at a scene for just a few moments and assess what was going on.

Three people formed a semi-circle, facing the still burning opening in the hedge. If she had to guess, they were all spell casters, working to undo the magic in the hedge, so as to open it up more, perhaps. Da hadn't said that there was a third group out there, on the other side of the hedge, but Orla wouldn't be surprised if there was.

Two other people were also there. They were facing outward, toward the field. Guards she first assumed, given their stance. Then she realized that they had matching uniforms and weapons. Hired guards, like Kato, or a town's guard, wore their own clothes, with only matching badges or sashes to indicate their authority.

These were trained soldiers.

King Alfa's soldiers, perhaps?

The three wizards wore long robes that covered them from neck to ankle and flowed down their arms. (Really? Why not plain shirts and trousers? Was there something special about robes that helped one cast spells?) The colors intrigued her: dark red for the center one, deep blue for the one closest to her and bright yellow for the farthest one. Did the colors indicate the types of magic they did? Ranks? Or were they merely fashion choices?

The soldiers wore solid boots, leather pants, a metal chest piece that covered their entire torso, with ringed mail down their arms. They had sturdy helmets protecting their heads, covering their foreheads with a T-shaped flange going down their noses. Bright red plumes stuck out from the top of the helmets. Were those also a color rank, perhaps?

Though Orla could absolutely hit the soldiers with her arrows, she didn't think she would be able to do much damage to them. Their armor would protect them.

She shifted her target to the three spell casters. They would have to go first. Then she could deal with the soldiers.

"He's here," one of the wizards announced.

Somehow, they were connected to the second group, the one that Da had tackled.

That would be a useful trick for an army, Orla knew. In the histories of various wars that she'd studied, more than one battle had been won or lost due to communication or the lack thereof.

Too bad this group wasn't going to have a chance to join their friends.

Orla would see to that.

It hadn't taken her more than a few moments to assess the situation.

Without allowing herself to think about what she was actually doing (taking a life) she raised her bow and cleanly shot the neck of the main wizard between the other two, in the dark red robes, who dropped with a quiet gurgle.

She got off a second shot, into the back of the wizard in the dark blue robe, before anyone noticed something was wrong. His shout alerted them.

She tried to get a third shot into the yellow robed one, but that magic user raised some sort of magical defense, so Orla's arrow bounced off.

Fortunately, Kato had taught her some tricks when it came to getting through a wizard's shield.

Tricks that she didn't have time for at the present.

Then the guards were drawing their swords. Orla knew they'd have reach on her, possibly experience as well.

Good thing she had desperation on her side, but more importantly, she needed to impress Da. That drove her harder than anything else.

She wasn't as well armored as they were. She might have to see about stealing the chest plate from one of them, the smaller one, on the left. She'd always just been focused on her weapons, not armor. Kato didn't wear much beyond leathers, then again, he fought brigands, not soldiers.

Orla dropped her bow and drew her short sword. She let them come to her, away from the injured magic users. She knew that she wasn't far enough away from the magic users to protect her from their spells. However, she wanted a few moments to study her two opponents, to see how they moved.

She'd give them a B-, quite frankly.

Both Kato and her Da would have them running sprints for weeks given their performance.

At the very last moment, Orla roared loudly and charged herself, aiming toward the smaller of the two, as he was definitely the worse one. She wrapped both hands around the handle of her short sword and struck out at the man's well-protected torso, swinging her sword like a staff, striking out with the flat of her blade and not the edge.

The clang of her blow rang through the quiet area.

She might have been a little worked up. She'd hit him harder than she'd intended, the blow reverberating in her arms.

It threw the man to his side. He lost his footing, and went crashing into his fellow.

Orla followed the blow with a kick to the man's groin, causing him to fly through the air and land on his butt a couple of feet away.

Good. It would only take a few moments for him to recover as that area had been covered with armor, but that would give her time to fight the second guard by himself, so she wouldn't be crowded with two opponents at the same time.

She knew better than to get drawn into sword play by either of the soldiers, that semi-polite exchange of thrust and block. She had to get them to fight, though hopefully not as dirty as she was planning on doing.

Instead of engaging with the soldier's blade, she struck at his knees, slicing open the leather there.

First blood was hers.

The soldier narrowed his eyes at her and started to hack at her with his sword.

He had reach on her. And strength, given the way he pounded on her short sword when they connected.

However, someone hadn't trained him much beyond the sword.

Who would only fight with a single weapon, when there were so many at hand?

Orla pretended to stumble as she backed away, turning the movement into an easy roll. She grabbed a handful of dirt on the way up and flung it at the first soldier, who'd recovered enough to start approaching.

Either her aim was good, or the Twins were watching over her, as despite the visor, the second soldier stopped, crying out as he was blinded.

Orla didn't allow the second soldier to deflect her attacks, to give his companion time to recover. She raced in, getting under his guard, shoving his arm *up* with her sword arm while stabbing his throat with the stiffened fingers of her other hand.

He stumbled back, eyes wide with surprise at the move.

Really? Didn't they teach soldiers anything about fighting?

Orla may be on the smaller side. And a girl.

However, she'd been taught how to *fight*.

And win.

Orla struck the blinded soldier again, this time, aiming high with her sword.

He made a half-hearted attempt at a block, but really, it was all over for him.

Her sword skewered his neck nicely.

She saw her mistake immediately.

She'd gotten too close, and now the blood spurted over her, half-blinding her and making her grip on her sword slippery.

She didn't have time to recover.

The other soldier barged in, fighting desperately, finally realizing the danger he was in.

Orla gave ground as she thought, trying to find the next hole in the second soldier's defenses.

He wasn't going to give her the opportunity to get close again.

Orla would just have to force her opening.

So maybe, once again, the Twins smiled at her.

Or Orla had grown a touch more bold than the soldier.

She stumbled, for real this time, but instead of turning it into a roll away, she rolled closer to her opponent, then beyond him.

She reached back with her sword, striking at his legs again, the least protected area of his body.

Her blade struck true, and Orla sliced through the man's calf, above the edge of his boot.

He screamed and faltered, nearly falling on his face when he tried to put weight on the leg.

Orla had a moment of remorse. She didn't want to kill this man. She didn't want to have to kill anyone.

However, these people had come here to hurt Da.

And she needed to protect him.

The soldier still tried to fight, but Orla now got easily through his defenses and rammed her blade through his throat.

That was when the lightning struck her back.

The sole remaining wizard had now joined the fight.

HALLOWED BE THY NAME

If you travel even a short ways through any of Ulthir's world, you're bound to come across yet *another* local god or goddess. They appear to sprout up everywhere, whether there is a population of people around to worship them or not.

What caused so many to come into being?

Supposedly, they were all created by Eomar, as a way for the people in an area to talk more directly to Ulthir. (Again, this is the theory. In fact, it is the rare being who actually makes contact.)

Unlike other worlds, a god or goddess doesn't need belief in order to get along. They do just fine without anyone interacting with them.

In fact, according to the *Guide To Local Gods and Goddesses: Enkala Empire Edition*, there is more than one deity who lives in an inaccessible area, like a particularly rocky beach that you can only reach when the tide's out, and even then, it's a waist-deep slog up the coast for an hour or more. There, a particularly lovely goddess makes her home, watching the tides and communing with the sea turtles swimming by. According to the author of the guide, that goddess had never talked to a person before, and didn't seem all that impressed with the intrepid writer who'd come out to see her.

What caused such a goddess to come into being in the first place, though?

Again, we turn to our expert, the author of those handy guides, who puts forth the following theory.

Leaving aside semi-divine intervention such as Eomar, local gods and goddesses need the perfect intertwining of two elements in order to emerge.

The first is a location where there's plenty of magic. Magic, as we all know, isn't stretched evenly across Ulthir's lands. It eddies and flows, snagging on this tree or that pond, while streaming away from this flat plain or that craggy hill. Ask any magic user and they'll tell you that it's far, far easier to do magic closer to the home of a god or goddess than someplace that's empty of the stuff.

The second is that somehow, one day, a spark of divinity passed through the area. Perhaps the location had garnered Ulthir's attention long enough for some part of him to flow down. Or maybe Eomar or Maloneal passed by, camped there, stuck their fingers in the creek, what have you.

There are only a few highly magical areas that are barren of deities. Such a powerful location is bound to birth more gods and goddesses. And mostly, people don't mind having a local god or goddess handy. Gives the area *character*, personality. Something to talk about when the weather is fine. Plus, when people feel they need an intermediary between themselves and Ulthir, having a nearby deity is convenient. (Priests occasionally try to fill that role. They almost always fail. They just aren't on the right wavelength, regardless of the their claims.)

So what makes a god or goddess different than an extremely powerful wizard, witch, spell caster, or whatever they're calling themselves these days?

Specifically, it's that entire spell casting thing. A god or goddess lives, breathes, and does magic. He or she doesn't need to memorize a spell, and eschews ingredients as well as spell books. They want a thing to happen, so it does—if it's within their realm, and they're capable of it.

For example, taking an injured farmer to a water goddess is just about the stupidest thing you can do. She will assume he's a sacrifice, not someone to be healed, and will be put out when you don't drown him in her lake. Take that same injured farmer to a god living among the trees and he'll heal the farmer up nice and neat. (Most of the times. Sometimes, he also wants something in return. Usually it's produce, like scrumpy or spirits, and not a life.)

A magic user might also be able to heal that same, poor injured farmer, but it would take time to find the right spell, gather up the ingredients, then to do the casting. The farmer might have died in the meanwhile.

Of course, there are always rumors of mighty wizards who don't need spell books, who can just cast magic willy-nilly. Chances are though, that they prepared the spell ahead of time and also cast some sort of preserving spell on it, so they had it at the ready, just to impress the masses.

There's one other difference, though, between a god or goddess and a magic user: their access to Ulthir. Of course, the great god doesn't want to be bothered sometimes. (Okay, most of the time. Truthfully, Ulthir rarely pays attention, even to the minor deities.) But the local deities do have some sort of connection. A shared spark, if you will.

Generally speaking, Ulthir doesn't answer. You have to leave a message.

Which is why sometimes, bad things happen to good people.

Again and again.

ORLA

Orla shook her head and backed away as another zinging bolt of lightning struck her arm. At least she'd slid far enough to the side that it hadn't hit her square in the chest.

Damned wizard hadn't been able to do much while the soldiers had been involved. Probably would have hurt them with the spells she was casting at Orla. But now, as there was only Orla left standing, the wizard had a clear shot.

Orla zig-zagged as she raced back to where she'd dropped her bow, hoping to throw off the aim of the wizard. It seemed to work, as the next lightning bolt sizzled over her left shoulder.

Then Orla turned and started shooting arrows at the wizard. Kato's dry voice was suddenly in her head, drowning out the sound of her own panting, the pounding of her heart in her temples, the pain of the burns and the cuts she'd suffered.

You need to distract a wizard. If they're distracted, they can't shoot spells at you.

The wizard just looked amused as another arrow clattered to the ground after striking the wizard's shield. "Talon must be desperate if he's taken to hiring guards who are so young."

Orla didn't answer. She couldn't afford to talk to this wizard, to give her any sort of hold over Orla.

"Or are you perhaps the infamous daughter? You would be quite a prize," the woman purred as she raised her hands to blast Orla again.

Orla ignored her as she ran forward, never taking two steps in a straight line, while at the same time, peppering the wizard's shield, starting at the top then methodically working her way down, seeking a weak spot.

There didn't appear to be any place that wasn't solid, or if there was, Orla would run out of arrows long before she found it.

That didn't stop her from putting three more arrows into the back of the blue robed wizard, who'd dragged himself into the gap left in the hedge. She wanted to make sure that he didn't move again.

Then Orla dropped her bow and reached for a bag at her waist, one that Kato had always insisted she carry.

A bag full of stones.

Wizard shields were supposed to stop projectile weapons.

Pebbles weren't considered weapons. Neither was dirt.

Using a soft, underhanded throw, Orla lobbed a stone at the wizard.

It went straight through the wizard's shield and pinged against the woman's shin.

The rock didn't strike with any force at all. Wouldn't leave a mark or a bruise.

However, it had gotten through.

The wizard seemed to suddenly realize that she was in danger, as she closed her eyes and started mumbling something in a language that Orla didn't know.

It was a spell. Possibly a big one, able to wipe Orla off the face of the world.

Orla carefully approached the wizard, striking her now with soft pebbles, on the front of her chest, as well as on her face.

The one Orla threw that hit the wizard's temple seemed to do the most damage, as it got her to lose her place and stop chanting.

Again, distraction.

Most shields worked against weapons. Long, skinny arrows, swords, staves, or pikes.

Not bodies.

Why someone hadn't thought to bring that up to this wizard, Orla would never know.

Orla plowed into the wizard, planting her shoulder against the woman's chest and *shoving*.

The wizard toppled back, but her hands were already crackling with more lightning.

Quickly, Orla drew her short sword and plunged it into the woman's belly.

The way that the blood spilled across the yellow robes was a sight that Orla wasn't ever going to be able to forget.

However, that didn't kill the woman. She raised her hands, her eyes glowing menacingly.

Orla chopped at her neck, slicing through the jugular.

Again, she was too close, as the spurting blood blinded her yet another time, coating her in even more gross matter.

Orla was pretty sure she was going to be sick as soon as the adrenaline wore off.

She wiped her eyes clear, then wiped her blade on the woman's robes. She turned, prepared to run over to help Da with his group, when she heard a rustling noise behind her.

Orla whirled and crouched, ready for the next attacker.

Except that no one was there.

The noise came from the hedge.

Whatever spell the wizards had cast on it was only now wearing off, since all the spell casters were dead.

The leaves in the bramble waved back and forth, moving as if being tickled by a wind.

Then the branches started growing, fast enough that Orla could track their progress.

The wizard who'd worn the blue robes had crawled into the opening between the branches. The hedge focused its attack (revenge?) on his body. Thick thorns pierced his robes. Whip-like branches scoured his flesh. The hedge quickly overtook the space he'd been in, absorbing the body into itself.

Orla dragged the bodies of the other two wizards into the rapidly closing opening, hurrying away before those thorns reached for her.

The hedge gratefully accepted the sacrifice, filling the opening quickly with wicked thorns and new leaves.

The slight red tint to the leaves was the only sign of where the wizards had been.

That was one way of getting rid of the bodies.

Hopefully, the hedge would be stronger for it.

Probably meaner as well.

She didn't have time to drag the bodies of the two soldiers into the hedge opening. Besides, she wanted to come back and take some of their armor off them.

For now, Orla had another battle to join.

Her legs felt like lead, as did her arms. Her breath even came heavily, as if all the muscles in her chest had frozen.

I'm coming, Da, Orla called out in her mind.

She figured Da couldn't hear her, not from here. His range of mental speech wasn't much better than the spoken or shouted word.

She still wanted him to know that it was her coming, not some enemy.

Orla forced her tired legs to move, even though all she wanted to do was to lay down and rest.

She could sleep later. After she'd cleaned up. And thrown up.

She still had to go protect Da.

Orla was aware that she made lousy time running from the edge of the hedge into the farm. She felt as though her legs betrayed her. She should be able to do this. She was young. She'd been training to do this for a very long time.

Yes, this had been her first real fight. And she'd killed people. Bad people, who were out to get Da.

It couldn't all be because of the shock she felt? First hot, then shivering, as she forced her legs to pump along?

By the time she made it to the farmhouse, loudly proclaiming that it was she who was coming, Da had already finished off all of his assailants.

There was a large, black scorched area that he carefully slithered around. Orla found out later that it had been a trap, covered magically, set to entangle Da when he strayed over it. He'd spotted it from the air, of course, and had gone ahead and just spat great gouts of acid down on his opponents. Survival was more important than giving a person the honor of a fight, at least these days.

Are you all right? Da asked as soon as he saw her. His tongue rapidly tasted the air between them.

I'm fine, Orla assured him. She gestured to herself. *None of this blood is mine.*

Da nodded at her assessment. He seemed pleased, as well as relieve, that she wasn't hurt.

She told him of the wizards and the soldiers, and how she intended to go back and get some of their armor.

Or we could just buy you some, Da said dryly.

Orla shrugged. *I'll need two sets. One for fighting, stored at your place. One for practicing in, kept at the house in town.*

Da nodded. He also seemed pleased that the hedge had reclaimed the bodies of the wizards.

I'll have to remember to feed it bodies sometimes.

Orla wasn't certain if he was joking or not and honestly wasn't sure if she wanted to know.

Now what? she asked. She was gross and exhausted. Some of the bruises she'd acquired while fighting were starting to make themselves known. Along with a few scratches along her legs. The burns from the stupid wizard also smarted, and needed to be cleaned.

You sit, Da instructed her. *I'll gather up the bodies.*

To toss into the hedge?

Not this time. No, I have a better use for them.

He demonstrated with the first one, by throwing it into the burned area that had held the trap.

Pink vines shot up as soon as the body touched the earth, wrapping thickly around the corpse and holding it tightly, preventing it from getting up again and walking away.

While Da continued his grisly task, Orla started going through the backpacks and rucksacks that she found nearby.

She pocketed the bags of coins she found there, intending to give all of it to Da when they got back to his place. She also found what appeared to be a private journal of one of the soldiers, which she kept. She doubted it would have any interesting military communications; still, it was important to know how her opponents thought.

Or at least one of the dead ones.

She found a pendant of the star and eye that Da had said was the sign of King Alfa's wizard, Loalmane.

Nothing else of value was in the bags. If she knew a local wizard, she might hand over what were obviously spell ingredients. She'd have to ask Da if he wanted to donate them someplace. (While Da didn't necessarily approve of spell casters, he never tried to do something as stupid as forbid them in his territory. There was even a spell-school of sorts, in the northwest quadrant.)

While Da and Orla worked, three men came walking out of a large structure set some distance from the main house—a barn, where they probably wintered their livestock.

All three men were stocky with curly hair, wearing dingy shirts and mud-brown pants. She'd bet they were brothers, based on how they looked.

They came and stood on the far side of the barren circle, watching Talon as he dragged the last of the bodies into it. The magic finally appeared to be wearing off, and only a couple of vines popped up, snagging the corpse's ankles.

"Thank you, Talon. Sir," the man in the middle said. He looked to be the oldest of the three.

You are welcome, came Da's reply, his metal tone at its driest.

Orla stayed where she was to the side. Though the men cast a few curious glances her direction, it appeared that they were determined to not ask about her.

"They slaughtered all our livestock. Used their entrails to make… this," the man continued.

Orla blanched. Those weren't vines? She had just assumed that since they'd come from the ground, though they were that pink color…She fought down the nausea. Again.

I'll bring you recompense tomorrow, Da promised.

The man in the middle shook his head and looked down. "This is the third attack in two years," he said.

I know.

The man looked up. "We're leaving here. Moving inland. Away from the edge." The words came out in a rush, as if he was scared to say them.

I understand, Da said. *I appreciate you staying as long as you did.*

Were the brothers afraid of Da? He wouldn't hurt them. Just those bad men and women. They all seemed relieved when Da had acquiesced so quickly.

Da looked over at Orla, then nodded. *We will leave you now to determine your losses. I'll be back in the morning with recompense.*

Orla wasn't sure if she was invited to come back or not. That wasn't really her business, how Da ran his lands. She was just there to protect him.

After they finished talking, Orla slowly pulled herself up onto Da's back. All she wanted was a quick dip in any nearby river or lake. Then to sleep for a year. Then maybe to figure out how to stop these attacks.

She was afraid of that last problem. There had to be something they could do, besides go and confront this King Alfa and his wizard.

Still, Orla was determined to continue to live up to her promise, to keep her Da safe.

That is, until she met *him*. Then everything changed.

A WIZARD IN TIME

BRENNAN

Brennan MacFarly was only five when he started telling his siblings that the old woods tasted funny.

He couldn't really say more than that. And though his siblings teased him about licking the rough barks of the trees or eating the purple mushrooms, he hadn't. He hadn't even run his fingers across the golden leaves of the big old maple then touched them to his lips, though he had thought about it.

No, there was just something about the trees there, how they grew, that changed the quality of the air. (It wasn't until he was much older that Brennan realized that so much magic pooled between the old roots in the forest that the trees had a vague level of awareness. If the local god Num hadn't already come into being and claimed a different part of the forest for himself, the old woods would have been his home.)

The taste of the woods hadn't been the only indication to Mrs. MacFarley that her current youngest (out of six) was different than the others. He was quiet for a boy, more thoughtful, and capable of a stillness that rendered him adult-like in bearing.

That was, when he wasn't racing around like a crazy thing, playing like a normal boy, scrambling for whatever prize came with winning the current game that his siblings had just invented.

Every once in a while, not very often, he stopped stock still and looked up toward the sky, even when all he could see were leaves and branches. It took a while for the rest of them to realize that Brennan always knew when Talon flew over their woods, patrolling or hunting.

They lived in the northeast quadrant of the dragon's territory, far from the border. They'd heard the stories of those closest to the edge on the western side suffering attacks from bandits and brigands, but they were poor enough, and far enough away, that it seemed as though it happened in a kingdom other than theirs.

So Mrs. MacFarley kept an eye on the boy, watching him mostly when he didn't know it. When Brennan was eight, she found herself pregnant again (with what she knew would be her last boy).

Normally, she took her husband, and possibly the oldest of the children, to seek the blessings of the local god Num. This time, she took Brennan with her.

Of course, Brennan's siblings tried to scare him with stories of how Num was going to eat his heart, or drink all his blood, or even make him carry Mama's baby (the latter put forth by his sister Erin who was always slightly off, at least as far as the rest of the family was concerned).

Brennan held tightly onto Mama's hand as they entered the woods close to Num's domain, starting every time the undergrowth rustled or a loud bird called out. Mama didn't say anything, and Brennan wondered at her amused smile.

The grotto where Num lived was lit with magical lamps casting a golden light across the open space among the trees. Brennan could never say how big the area was. Sometimes it was cozy and intimate, only six feet across and a couple deep. Other times, it was big enough to hold all sixty of the men in the village.

At first, Brennan thought leaves and vines covered the ground, but eventually he realized that it was actually finely woven carpet with a design of golden elm leaves and thick ivy. It felt as soft as moss, as if his feet were sinking into it.

The air here smelled good, of dense trees and baked pine needles, of sweet lakes and casual rain. It also gave Brennan a tingling feeling that he'd come to associate with the old woods that were closer to the family's cabin. (Growing things felt that way. The healthy type of growth, like what you'd get in the fields, not the bad kind Brennan later discovered in the cities.)

A huge tree stood in the middle on one long side of the clearing. If Brennan squinted, he could sort of see a face in the bark, with a big nose, drooping eyes, and a gaping hole for a mouth.

Offerings were laid under that tree: fine bowls full of berries, pretty garlands of woven flowers, or small bottles filled with the best local mead.

Mama set down the large apple pie that she'd carried into the woods, full of crisp goodness and rare spices, the top a fine lattice of dough.

She spoke, now, directly to the tree.

Brennan knew she needed her time with Num, and so stepped back and to the side, trying to be respectful as Mama asked for blessings for her little one.

When Mama was finished, she beckoned Brennan closer. He reluctantly stepped up, under her arm.

Was now when Num would eat his heart?

"This is my current youngest, Brennan. He says the old woods taste funny, and he has a way with the wheat and barley in the field, almost as if he's talking to them."

Brennan looked at Mama, alarmed. He hadn't told anyone that, not his siblings and certainly not Mama. However, she was right. Sometimes it seemed as if the young plants were talking to him, telling them how good the sun felt, when they needed the rain.

A change flooded the clearing, as if a clean wind had just blown away the haze. The tree directly in front of them underwent a transformation. Suddenly, it was *animated* and alive. Eyes the color of pumpkins opened up, staring at the pair of them, with small black dots in the centers for pupils. The gaping mouth closed, then smacked its lips together a couple of times, as if trying them out. A snort went through the big nose, sounding like a startled duck.

The Old Woods taste funny, eh?

Though the lips of the tree-face moved, Brennan knew the words weren't coming from there: they echoed around inside his head, as if it were as empty as his mother sometimes proclaimed.

Terrified, Brennan clung to his mother.

"It's all right," Mama said, running her fingers through his sleek brown hair. "Yes, he didn't seem to be able to explain it much beyond that. He was five at the time he made that pronouncement."

Young. The old tree snorted again. *Come here,* Num ordered. *Let me taste* you.

"No!" wailed Brennan. "He's going to eat me, Mama! Just like Sean said he would!"

Mama sighed. "Can you excuse me a moment?"

Num chuckled. *I think I know how to handle this.*

Brennan couldn't say why it seemed to him that the tree in front of him just shuddered, but it did.

The glowing eyes shut and life faded away from the face in front of him.

A tall man abruptly stepped out from behind the grand tree.

Or maybe—just a more person-shaped version of Num.

His skin was the color of spring moss, rippling over a solid frame. Sightless white eyes stared down at the pair of them. Golden curls, the color of ripe summer wheat, covered his head, and a wreath of dark-green laurel leaves encircled it.

He was obviously a god, but he seemed to be a minor version of one. This was the type of god who would enjoy games with you, chasing after you along the forest trails, playing tag or hide-and-seek. He seemed much more jovial, like Brennan's Uncle Roy, who, according to his parents, liked his mead a bit too much.

The blind god reached out a hand. Mama guided it to her swollen belly.

Brennan's breath caught as he *saw* the blessings pouring off the god's fingertips around the new baby. It was like a miniature purple waterfall, flowing around his new brother.

He also noted that most of the blessings dripped off of Mama's stomach and back onto the carpet. It was as if she couldn't keep them all.

Mama closed her eyes and a look of utter peace and bliss infused her face.

Brennan found himself looking away. It was a private sort of emotion, not one that she'd readily share, not even with her children.

Once Mama was taken care of, the blind god turned his face unerringly toward Brennan. "Come here," he said softly, the words actually spoken. "I won't hurt you."

Though Brennan was still scared, he did walk forward. He could be a good boy. Particularly for Mama.

When the blind god held out his hand, Brennan took it, but he wasn't sure what to do with it. He wasn't about to put it on his belly —though he didn't believe what Erin said about him having to carry the baby, he didn't want to chance that either.

Instead, he lifted up the hand and placed it on his head.

The god chuckled, a warm sound, like a refreshing summer rain.

"Good choice," he said. After a moment, he added, "Yes, you see things. Know things. See the world as it can be, not how it is. That is the heart of all magic."

Though Mama stood as if frozen, the god still turned his face toward her and spoke. "I will send him a teacher, who will be a better judge of his fate."

Though Mama still didn't move, Brennan knew that she accepted the god's gift.

Funny, Brennan didn't see blessings pouring off his head from the fingertips of the god, not like he had with Mama's belly. Had he received anything from the god? Or was the teacher going to be his gift?

He asked Mama about these things, along with a hundred other questions as they made their way out of the woods and back to the old cabin that was their home.

Mama seemed bemused by his questions and not impatient, not until they got home and she needed to talk with Papa.

Seemed that they were going to have a guest for a while, and they needed to make a place for him. Their little cabin in the woods that Papa had made was already bursting at the seams with all the children.

And that was the first time Brennan's entire life shifted and changed.

It wouldn't be the last.

The wizard who showed up—Señor Alberto—smelled funny, and this time, not only Brennan thought so. Even Erin thought he smelled of moldering books and spoiled ink, though she also thought he stank of bread gone bad.

He sounded funny too, rolling his Rs and drawing out his words. His voice was deep and rich, as if it belonged to a completely different man, not one shorter than Papa and skinny. Mama was always trying to fatten him up, getting him to take an extra piece of meat from the roast, or perhaps even an extra hunk of cheese. Señor Alberto politely but firmly declined, saying the extra pounds would just weigh him down, then chuckling at his own (half-) wit.

Brennan, unfortunately, had taken an instant dislike to the man.

Maybe it was his white hair, which hung like tangles of bleached rope off his pink skull and shed copious amounts of dandruff. Maybe it was the way he laughed at his own jokes, though his smile never reached his watery blue eyes.

Or maybe it really was just the way he smelled, of long-dead things that should have remained buried.

Señor Alberto did have a cool robe. The blue was so dark it seemed black when the hearth fire was low. No design broke up the solid color, though there was a border of silver braid around the collar and wide cuffs. He never wore anything else, and it never seemed to get dirty, either, even when Erin accidentally-on-purpose spilled half a bowl of soup down his front. The fabric shed the liquid easily, and Erin never did it again, too afraid that the wizard would turn her into a mouse or something.

Honestly, the robe was about the only thing Brennan liked about Señor Alberto. He didn't like having to sit inside while everyone else was outside, he didn't like memorizing things, and he *really* didn't like when he had to help Señor Alberto do his magic.

There was something unclean about Señor Alberto's magic, something that just set Brennan's teeth the wrong way.

He didn't know why he felt as though the old man was doing it *wrong*. He just did. And he didn't have the experience to be able to tell him, or to figure out what was *right*. Not yet, at any rate.

At first, everything was hard. Learning the correct pronunciation of the magical tongue, memorizing the words, as well as learning the grammar (OMG the grammar: there was a reason why everyone spoke Common and not this other tongue).

Brennan had at one point thought that learning magic would be easy. He could kinda sorta do it already, since he could sense it. When the magic was really big and showy, he could see it as well. That was his biggest advantage and something that Señor Alberto honed like a sharp razor: Brennan learned to detect even the smallest sliver of magic, cast on a single sentence in a book buried amidst thousands of books.

However, in order to cast a spell, there was *so much* to learn.

Ugh.

Still, Brennan tried to study, to learn, to make Mama and Papa (and possibly the god Num) proud.

Whenever Brennan thought he might quit, he went out into the woods on his own, taking a break from the learning (and Señor Alberto always seemed to know when Brennan truly needed the time alone versus when he was just feeling lazy). One of the things that Mama had always said about Brennan was that he had a sense of calm about him that belied his now twelve-year-old self.

Brennan knew that wasn't the truth, or rather, that it was only sometimes the truth.

And whenever it all got to be too much, he took himself off and raced through the woods close to the cabin like a crazy thing, climbing trees and jumping into the creek and swinging from branches and scaling the nearby boulders as well as bravely exploring one of the caves underneath.

Only after he got all that longing for adventure out of his system could he sit and think, generally ensconced in a tree over Ox Creek. The dappled water always helped him find that calm that Mama talked about, that stillness that he appeared to have been born with.

And on those quiet afternoons, the sun glittering on the stream beneath him, as well as gently caressing his sweaty skin, Brennan thought about his future. It wasn't something that all twelve-year-olds did. He knew he was different in that regard.

It always came back to this: no matter how difficult the language lessons were or how onerous acquiring ingredients became or even how *wrong* Señor Alberto's magic felt, there was still nothing else he wanted to do. He didn't want to become a woodsman like Papa, or go into some sort of business like his brothers.

Brennan wanted to do magic. *Real* magic. Magic that suited him and could inspire (and possibly amaze) others.

He would survive his youth and his training. Survive Señor Alberto's mismanagement. Get himself to a real wizards' school one of these days.

And learn, well, how magic really worked.

OF CABBAGES AND KINGS

In the world that Ulthir created, there are as many different types of government as there are groups of people. It isn't all kings, queens, emperors and such.

For example, in the jungles far to the south of where our story takes place, there is the Beloved Dictator. He is a dictator as people define such things, and he has strict rules about how the people must conduct themselves, how each life is supposed to be lived.

His first law is: Be Happy. (It was originally, *Don't worry, be happy* but that was just too long.) He has other laws about loving people, not judging, thinking for yourself, forgiving debts, curbing excess usury, and so on. This is why he is considered a Beloved Dictator. It's a tough job, always striving for happiness and leading a people to joy, but someone has to do it.

More than once a neighboring kingdom, empire, city-state, what have you, has tried to invade the happy dictatorship, particularly as they have no standing army. (Though they do train some of the most deadly monks in the entire world.)

The problem wasn't the resistance that an invading force met.

Instead, those invading usually found their own army turning against them.

The choice was stark: attack people who hadn't done anything to you, either depriving them of their lives and quite possibly losing your own, or turning against your masters and having a chance at being happy.

So most of the surrounding countries left the Beloved Dictator and his strange people to live their contented lives all on their own.

The government of the archipelago of islands to the east of the main continent is a little harder to pin down, as at least half the population live on boats that travel between the islands, and some of the islands appear to…wander, let's just say. Something like a series of city-states, as each island is law unto itself, with its own rules, customs, and frequently, currencies.

One of the smaller islands has less than fifty inhabitants. They insist on eating all their food (and fish) raw, as if fire had never been invented. They worship a local turtle god named Jar-Jar who speaks to them in gibberish. No one understands him, but no one really minds him either. They just go about their days as they always would, certain that they're living the True Way though no one really knows what that way is for sure.

As for the kings, queens, emperors, consorts, republics, and such, one of the most important things to remember is that Ulthir is a remote god. Though he's always watching, he so very rarely acts, so there is no divine right of rulers. Sure, a little local god or goddess may have a go at it, but no one pays them much mind, as eventually, the Twins turn against them and all that they've accumulated falls apart.

Kingdoms, democracies, empires, timocracies—they all rise, join together, fall apart, regroup, implode, burn down, fall into the swamp, develop a new twist on ancient ideas, and so on.

The thought of a single king, emperor, or other royal type

uniting and then leading the world that Ulthir created is ridiculous. None of the local gods or goddesses would accept such behavior. And the Twins of Fate would firmly set their faces against it as well.

But sometimes, someone decides that they know better than everyone else, and they just have to try.

BRENNAN

The god Num never apologized for sending Señor Alberto. He was a god, after all. How was he to know that there were different types of magic? It was all the same to him.

However, once it finally became clear that Señor Alberto's type of magic worked with the dead (with bones, skin, and plants long since dried) and that Brennan's magic worked with living things (like still-chirping crickets, fresh flowers, and even that field mouse who'd wandered too close that one time) Señor Alberto was sent on his way.

Brennan was sent away as well.

Only this time, the god Num arranged for Brennan to go to the city of Millerstown, to the wizards' school there. He was to travel with Trader Fionuala, as she made her way to the markets there. Brennan never learned the details of their bargain, though Mama seemed happy enough that he had someone to see him safely along the road.

The wizards' school wasn't the best in all the countries. No, that would be the school out on the west coast, in the kingdom of Alfaladon. However, Millerstown was still part of Talon's territory, in the northwest quadrant, and only about a week's journey from the woods where Brennan had grown up.

So at the age of fourteen he said goodbye to Mama, Papa, all his siblings and their respective families, as well as the familiar woods. He hitched his smaller backpack higher on his back (his larger rucksack with all his belongings stowed away in the trader's cart), and walked away next to the cart, his head held high, his eyes on the horizon.

He was going to learn how to be a proper wizard. That thought propelled him forward, even when he possibly, *maybe* wanted to run screaming back to his mama and never ever leave.

There may have been some tears in the dark of the night, when Brennan thought no one could see or hear him. Along with an aching in his chest that he believed nothing would ever fill.

During the day, Brennan walked beside Trader Fionuala's ox cart as they made their way along the market road. She dealt with exotic herbs and magical ingredients (like the purple mushrooms only found in the old woods) and had a touch of magic herself. She was self-taught, though, from an old book left to her by her mum. Her accent was atrocious, and Brennan couldn't understand her when she cast a spell, though he could see the effects.

Trader Fionuala didn't look like a wizard, or any type of spell caster for that matter. She was a happily plump woman with rosy cheeks and a grand smile who always found joy in everything. She wore a plain shirt, plain trousers, and good stout boots. She also wore a bright hat woven out of dried straw that Brennan knew had a trace of magic braided into it. He assumed the magic was to keep the hat's wearer cooler in the sunlight, dry in the rain, and warmer in the snow.

The trader constantly puffed at her pipe, and the smoke that surrounded her was only sometimes mundane. Brennan didn't know if it would protect her against arrows. At the very least, it kept the bugs away, unfortunately, leaving them with no target other than his own delicate flesh. (The oxen also seemed to be immune.)

Brennan found himself shivering when they reached the first town and he had to spend his night out under clear skies without the comfort of tree branches overhead.

There were places in the forest he'd grown up in where the trees lost their leaves at the start of winter, where the sky could be seen through the bare branches. Seeing the clear blue above him, even in the middle of summer, made him feel cooler despite the sun beating down on him. It always reminded him of a winter sky.

Trader Fionuala at least appeared to understand how hard it was for him to leave the trees, and so they walked slowly along the market road, letting Brennan find his feet (and possibly learn to pick up his jaw) as they meandered from smaller villages and towns until they finally reached the city.

Millerstown wasn't the grandest of cities in all of Ulthir's lands. Several other cities lay claim to that, particularly those with magnificent structures, or where most of the buildings were blindingly white and perched over brilliant blue seas, or even filled with natural beauty and boasted many parks complete with waterfalls.

The one thing Millerstown did have going for it was that it was built up on cliffs above a river (the Wadun) which provided all the power for the mills at the base of the city. From across the river, it certainly looked impressive, the tiers all shades of brown and green as they stacked up against the yellow-white of the cliff.

Brennan got dizzy thinking about all the souls who lived there. It was going to be more people than he'd ever seen before, more than all the inhabitants of the towns and villages they'd seen on their way there.

Trader Fionuala had spent at least half of an hour bargaining with the ferryman to take her oxen cart across the river, rather than spend the two days it would take to travel up to a fordable location and back down again.

"Not as many traders come this way," she told Brennan when she finished, puffing angrily on her pipe, her teeth biting away at the stem. "There are some who come by boat, from up river, but they don't carry the goods I do." She took a deep breath, trying to settle herself. "My hope is that as a rarity, we'll make a better profit once we set up, down here at the base of the city, on the lower tiers."

Brennan nodded. Trader Fionuala had tried to educate him in the ways of trade while they were traveling to their destination. He had learned some of what she had to teach him, though it would be a while before he figured out the value of her lessons, that knowing more about how the whole world worked would be useful.

He was still focused on the single aspect of magic. Nothing else mattered, at least not then.

The passage across the broad river was smooth, the city rising up, and up (*and up*) above them as they approached.

Brennan found the air was getting thin as they got closer, all those other people breathing it in.

Yet, at the same time, there were all these exotic smells: The mouthwatering scent of dough being fried in oil; the stench of the garbage that was dumped every day into the river, expecting it to carry the load away and do all the work; as well as the cloying odor of ground grain that underlay everything.

And there was the smell of magic. Sometimes it reminded Brennan of Señor Alberto, sometimes it smelled dark and dank like rotting mushrooms under a log, but still other times it had that fresh, complicated odor of the old woods, alive and powerful.

Brennan helped Trader Fionuala set up her stall in the market place, selling herbs and concoctions off the back of her cart.

It didn't take long before word appeared to get out that she was there, with high quality ingredients to sell. A small line formed, always two or three deep, but constantly replenishing.

All of her customers wore robes. Maybe it was a uniform of some sort, that all magic users had to wear. Brennan didn't have any robes, and he wasn't sure he wanted to wear one either.

Would be hard to climb a tree in one of those, that was for certain. Or possibly to run away fast.

Come nightfall, Trader Fionuala seemed pleased with her profit, and splashed out on rooms in one of the nicer inns on that level of the city. "Oh, they'll get even fancier up the hill. Mark my words. Tomorrow, I'll take you to the wizards' school."

"Don't you have more herbs to sell?" Brennan couldn't help but ask.

Sure, he wanted to go and learn more about magic. But it was all going to be so foreign and different than what he was used to. And that was a little intimidating. Even to a fourteen-year-old boy who tried hard not to be afraid of anything.

Trader Fionuala gave him an understanding look. "I do. I plan on taking tomorrow and seeing my errand fulfilled. Then I'll remain here, in Millerstown, for at least three more days. Possibly five. So you can get your feet under you, knowing that there's someone you know here."

Brennan didn't really blush. His skin, though white, had dark undertones to it. He still felt his cheeks grow a little warm as he thanked the trader for her kindness.

Not that he would turn tail and run at the first sign of trouble. He wasn't one to do that. He'd stuck out the years of Señor Alberto not teaching him the right magic.

He could survive the wizards' school as well.

He'd just have to remember to find his calm when everything threatened to overwhelm him. He'd done it instinctively as a younger boy. As a teen, it had been more difficult to remember to breathe.

Hopefully, as he grew older, it would get easier again.

Despite Brennan's expectation that they'd be up and gone as soon as it was light, Trader Fionuala took her time breaking her fast, and had just settled in for a second cup of tea when Brennan finally realized the cause for the delay.

Two wizards approached the cart. They seemed older than Señor Alberto, though they were both skinny and tall, wearing long red robes. One had a shaved head but made up for that with a gray beard that nearly reached his waist, while the other 's white hair stood out all around his head like a mane. His skin was almost black, the darkest that Brennan had ever seen.

The bearded one was Mr. Pembrooke, while the other was Mr. Okura. Once they'd finished their business with Trader Fionuala, they turned to Brennan expectantly.

"Can I help you?" he asked, concerned about their stares.

"You sure he's the one with magic?" Mr. Pembrooke asked, throwing a glance at the trader.

"Aye. Brought him here special. Sponsored by the local god of their region," she added.

"So what can you do?" Mr. Okura said to Brennan. At least he sounded curious and not challenging.

"I—I—I don't know, sir," Brennan stuttered.

"Are you self-taught?" Mr. Pembrooke said, looking concerned.

"No, I had Señor Alberto as my instructor for a while," Brennan said.

"What happened?" Mr. Okura said, frowning at Brennan.

"He—I—Our magic isn't compatible. Sir," Brennan said.

"Nonsense," Mr. Pembrooke said. "Magic is magic. You weren't trying hard enough."

"I was," Brennan said, instantly protesting. "All I've ever wanted to do was magic. But his ingredients were all wrong. Skin and bone and dried things." Brennan couldn't contain his shudder. "I work with living things." Both of the wizards still looked skeptical, though Mr. Okura did at least give Brennan an encouraging nod.

Trader Fionuala primarily carried dried goods. But she did have a single pot with something living: an exquisite orchid, with yellow petals as bright as sunlight on a field. The scent was light and sweet, unlike any other flower Brennan knew. She used the petals in very expensive skin ointments, as orchids weren't native to this part of the world. She always had to maintain the pot using spells, and had taught those to Brennan, making it part of his duties to make sure the flower grew well.

Brennan reached for the smooth clay pot holding the orchid and raised his eyebrows at Trader Fionuala, asking permission silently.

She nodded, giving him a bemused smile as she pulled out her pipe, sitting back as if about to watch a show.

Brennan started the spell, pronouncing the words clearly. Out of the corner of his eye he thought he saw the two wizards glance at each other, possibly impressed. But he couldn't really pay any attention to them, focusing instead on his magic.

The growth spell had to be delicately administered. Too much, and the plant would burn out. Too little, and it wouldn't have any effect. Keeping his touch light, Brennan stroked the stalk of flowers, from the base up to the three existing blossoms.

A second stalk branched off from the main one. Brennan coaxed it along, all the while still chanting. Two buds appeared, then blossomed. The smell of the orchid flooded the air, sweet and uplifting.

Brennan tried to hide his shaking hands as he passed the plant along to Mr. Pembrooke.

The old wizard looked at the stem and the junction of the new stalk critically before handing it to Mr. Okura, who took a deep breath of the scent, smiling as he handed it back to Brennan.

"You say you worked with Señor Alberto?" Mr. Okura said.

Brennan nodded, fear striking through his heart. How badly had Señor Alberto messed him up?

"Well, your pronunciation is so deliberate and clean I think that a non-magic user could possibly understand you. But there are a few words, like *egy* and *költözik.* where you're starting to slack some. Need to keep up your exercises," Mr. Pembrooke said.

"Thank you? I think?" Brennan said, still unsure about his performance.

Mr. Okura stepped forward, patting Brennan on his shoulder. "You did well. Yes, you belong in our school. If you're ready to join us?"

As Brennan had already packed up his rucksack, all that was left was for him to say goodbye to Trader Fionuala.

"Thank you," he told the woman as she gave him a hug goodbye. He wasn't sure how she'd arranged the audience with the two wizards who later turned out to be two of the seven elders who sat on the school council.

"Eh. Num felt responsible for ye," Trader Fionuala said. "Wanted to see that ye had a better chance."

Brennan nodded. He hadn't planned on writing his parents—neither of them could read. But maybe he should send a letter or two back with Trader Fionuala anyway, so that when she passed through Millerstown again, she could read out loud to them.

Brennan shouldered his rucksack and walked away with the wizards, up the numerous steep roads of Millerstown. The lower levels had so many people! Brennan was forever feeling hemmed in on all sides. At least people didn't walk boldly into the wizards, but kept clear of them, which meant that for the most part, he wasn't jostled from side to side, like some of the others walking around him.

And there was so much to see! Shops and professions he'd never considered. Like bathers. And buckle makers. Watercarriers. Old clothes shops. On and on.

At least the main road was fairly predictable. He'd get lost on the side streets almost immediately, he was certain. But on the main road, he'd always be able to find his way.

Finally, they left the lower levels and the street improved. Cobblestone instead of dirt. Street cleaners rapidly scooped up any remains from a passing ox. The shops were bigger. Jewelry shops. Candle makers. Purse makers. Inns that smelled of sour beer.

The road climbed, twisted back on itself, then climbed some more.

Instead of wood, the houses were now almost all made of stone. Larger. More important. The air cleared as the mass of people dropped away. Below them, the Wadun river started to look less brown and muddy and almost shone in the sunlight.

Finally, they reached the edge where the wizards' school perched, hanging slightly off the hill on one side. It was all stone and grand arches, carvings of dragons and brilliantly painted gates.

Brennan had never felt so out of place. Not a single tree to be seen.

Of course, the mayor and several important merchants lived above the school. He glanced up at the cold blue sky and told himself that he was lucky to be there, that it wasn't a bad place to spend the next few years, learning, growing, and finally becoming the person he was always meant to be: a wizard.

Or so he desperately hoped.

STIRRING THE MAGICAL POT

Maloneal didn't mean to always be stirring the pot, as it were, causing trouble both for Ulthir as well as whatever poor people were involved.

It just happened. Really. Honest.

Okay, so maybe there was that one time when he felt compelled to stick his hand in it, to change the fate of everyone as much (if not more so) than the Twins ever managed.

And that was when Maloneal decided that magic shouldn't just be bound up with the gods, whether that be Ulthir or the little local ones.

No, people should be able to use magic as well.

Maloneal adamantly denies that he was feeling jealous of Eomar, who'd taken it upon himself to go create all the little local gods and goddesses, setting up little caches of magic for those with a divine spark to use. All the people loved Eomar for that, as it at least made them *feel* as though they had a way to contact Ulthir (not that the big snot ever listened to anyone).

Maloneal wasn't envious at all of how many people regularly included Eomar in their prayers. Not at all. Nope. Nothing like that.

The people had survived both the floods as well as the fires and volcanoes and such that Ulthir had thrown around like a spoiled child, only eventually relenting after Eowin had talked some sense into him. (It was too much to hope that she'd actually smacked him, for which Maloneal would have paid good money to see.)

Now, though, it was time to better the lives of those poor wretches.

Maloneal had carefully watched Eomar a time or two when he'd created the little local gods and goddesses. May have even tried to create a few himself, only to discover that he was missing an essential *something*. His creations were generally misshapen and rarely lived longer than a few days, often terrorizing those they were meant to look after. They were also completely non-magical. (Which, given their crazed temperament and destructive tendencies, was a good thing.)

There had to be a trick when it came to directing the divine spirit. It wasn't because Maloneal was selfish and not good at sharing, well, anything.

Honest.

Since Maloneal couldn't create his own cadre of gods and goddesses, he decided that maybe he could gather his own followers among the people by gifting them with magic.

Bringing magic to everyone, well, that would surely make him more popular than Ulthir. Right?

However, his reputation as a trickster made it difficult to get people to regularly interact with him, let alone pray to him.

It was a tricky problem. Fortunately, Maloneal was good at solving those sorts of puzzles.

People tended to believe what they saw. The world is as it is.

As stated before, magic involves not just a firm belief in what is, but in what could be.

All people could already touch magic. It was inherent in them, placed there by Ulthir when he brought the sunlight under their skin.

The people just needed an extra push to get them all the way there.

Maloneal first tried sharing mushrooms that had psychedelic effects, as a way of expanding people's minds.

While that led a few of his followers to see the possibilities, they no longer had a firm enough grasp on the here and now to make effective changes.

Plus, they kept stripping naked and rolling around on the grass, wanting to feel all the possibilities with their skin. While this led to some truly inventive spells and lawncare products, it wasn't what Maloneal had in mind.

Next, he tried asceticism, denying oneself not only pleasure, but more importantly, food. Starving people were much more likely to do anything to bring themselves relief.

However, too many of those who followed this path tended to stick with it, and not try to end their suffering. Maloneal hadn't believed it would be possible, but there were people who thrived eating only a few grains of rice a day.

Ugh.

Though the ascetics had the most potential magical power (and when they did let loose with a magical curse or blessing, it could be earth-shattering), they also wouldn't leave their craggy mountaintops or caves. And they certainly made lousy followers, always judging Maloneal for his own indulgences. (What? Just because he was asking them to give up all earthly pleasures didn't mean he had to as well.)

Maloneal eventually realized that he needed a middle ground, something between the hedonistic tendencies the mushrooms brought and the grinding discipline of the ascetics.

It was only after listening to two people who both supposedly spoke the Common tongue misunderstand each other both due to local idioms and pronunciation, that he realized the potential that existed in language.

Could he create a magical tongue? People were gullible enough to believe that they needed aids to cast magic, something to channel their power, instead of just dipping into the magical well that existed in each and every one of them.

Maloneal spent some time visiting islands and mountainous regions, isolated places where Common existed but so did a thriving second, native language. Places where every single movement word was conjugated (from behind was different than to behind, which was different from standing still behind something), where they had ten different forms for every verb (I, you, he, she, it, we, y'all, he plural, she plural, and it plural), where different shapes had different numbers used to count them (flat long things used one numbering system, round oval things use another, counting backwards used different numbers than counting forwards, and so on).

He concocted a language from all of those. It was mostly regular and pronounced exactly as it was written, or nobody would have bothered learning it at all.

He may have spiked the water for some of the more extreme ascetics, encouraging them to write down this divinely spoken language, capturing the word of the gods and creating the first grammar books, as well as the first spell books.

And it worked.

Sort of.

The language of the gods is what people always thank Maloneal for, for enabling them to harness magic. Some even went as far as to say that Maloneal actually brought magic to the people.

It may have even brought him a few more followers.

Most, though, continued to contentedly along their existing paths, not flocking to Maloneal side. Ulthir, Eomar, Eowin, the local gods and goddesses, even the Twins remained much more popular.

So Maloneal continued to seethe in jealousy, trying this ploy and that until he finally was able to turn the tide.

At least for a while.

BRENNAN

Two weeks after Brennan started at the wizard school, the attack on the MacAffies occurred.

Brennan felt as though he was still trying to find his feet, to figure out where his classes were, which students were like his weird sister Erin and best either placated or ideally, avoided, and which students could become friends.

Brennan was lucky that the boy who shared his room—Holgi—was also from out of town as well as relatively new. Holgi was happy to bring Brennan along on his explorations of Millerstown. Holgi was a year older, but he'd grown up in a very small mountain village, so the city was as new and different to him as it was to Brennan.

Everyone was shocked at the attack. As Brennan had grown up in one of the western quadrants of Talon's territory, as well as far from the border, he hadn't ever heard of one this close before.

That didn't mean that the house he'd grown up in didn't have a flag in a bottle like everyone else that they could uncork and place outside in case something happened. Talon took care of his people, or at least, did the best that he could.

Holgi burst into their room later that afternoon, after the bodies of the poor MacAffies had been found.

"Come on!" he said just sticking his head in but not actually stepping into the room.

Brennan was already rising out of his chair. "Where to?" he asked as he followed Holgi out of the room.

"To the MacAffie house," Holgi said.

"Wait. What?" Brennan said, slowing down, not wanting to go anywhere near such a tragedy.

"Come on, already!" Holgi said. "It'll be our best chance to get a good look at Talon!"

Nodding, Brennan followed along.

He'd always been aware of the dragon whenever he passed over their woods. Mama told him that he'd been able to do that even when he'd been a very little boy. Brennan wasn't sure if it was because Talon was magical or if it was something else.

He'd never seen the dragon before, as there had always been trees in the way.

A few others from the school appeared to have the same idea, as a steady stream of boys and girls made their way through the front gate and down the steep street.

Neither Holgi nor Brennan had any idea where the MacAffies had lived. Others appeared to have a clue though, so they just followed along.

The house was stuck in the lower part of the mid-city, back from the edge and buried in a cramped neighborhood with other similar houses. They were all made of wood, a single story, with thatched roofs. A few of the bigger houses with two floors had plaster with boards floating in it to make them stronger.

On every corner stood a magical barrel, an unending supply of water to be used in case of a fire. The wizards' school kept those filled as part of their agreement with Talon, who, Brennan was shocked to learn, didn't really like wizards, witches, or any sort of spell caster.

(Seemed he still held a grudge against the wizard who'd originally turned him into a dragon, something everyone knew and no one blamed him for.)

The wizards constantly needed to prove themselves useful to Talon or they wouldn't be allowed to stay in any of his cities. This meant more than one magical improvement to the city—like the water barrels, lights at night, and free healing clinics. While the wizards oversaw the activities, the students frequently did the actual work. Brennan wouldn't get assigned one of those duties until after he'd been in the school for a few months.

Brennan was still looking at the magical water barrel and nearly walked into Holgi's back.

"Whoa," Holgi said.

Brennan gasped, and so didn't repeat the word.

There was Talon, the dragon in charge of their lands. He took up much of the street before them, not because he was that wide but he was really long, perhaps thirty or more feet of tail slithered out behind him.

Brennan kept looking up and down, from Talon's head to the tip of his tail. It took him a few moments to realize that he was looking for, well, *more.*

Talon just wasn't that impressive as a dragon. Not majestic at all.

First, he was a muddy brown-green color. His scales were matte, not glossy or glittery. Yellow-green scales covered his segmented belly. It wasn't a natural color, not unless you considered baby-puke natural. Tiny arms jutted out more from his front than the sides. They didn't look very strong at all. However, the black claws that tipped every finger appeared razor sharp.

His face was something between a snake's and a hunting dog's, one of those with a huge muzzle. Long, gray whiskers drooped from the sides of it. Golden eyes with a vertical slit dominated his expression as he stared with obvious disapproval at the MacAffie house. He raised his nose to the air, like a dog, as if scenting for the killers.

(Brennan knew that was exactly what he was doing, as Talon would go and find those responsible and make them pay. He always did. That was one of his promises to his people, that he always kept.)

Brennan had expected magic to be dripping from Talon, like it had from the god Num when he'd given a blessing.

Honestly, though, he didn't feel that much magic from the dragon. Maybe it was because he was merely talking with the mayor and not doing something, well, magical.

Large wings lay folded up on Talon's back. They stirred every now and again, as if being folded that way wasn't comfortable. Brennan had heard them described as bat wings, and was looking forward to seeing them in action.

While the mayor spoke out loud of what a tragedy it was, Talon was silent. At least, until the very end.

I will find those responsible for this massacre, Talon promised.

Everyone who was nearby heard those words.

Brennan took a step back, as did many of the others. It was shocking to suddenly have words that weren't yours echoing in your head.

Talon raised his head and looked out on all the young wizards who, quite frankly, took up most of the street now.

I will find them and they will pay, Talon added.

Brennan found himself nodding along with everyone else.

How had they gotten so far inside Talon's boarder? Why had they targeted the MacAffies? And how was Talon going to stop the next attack?

Brennan suspected that nobody knew.

Talon flung himself upward, toward the sky, his great wings unfolding as he grew airborne.

Magic streamed from him as he gained height.

Huh.

Did he even need his wings to fly? Were they just to steer him? Was his flight actually magical?

Brennan had so many questions!

However, he quickly learned that asking questions about Talon, or trying to study the dragon, was strictly forbidden. Talon didn't trust magic users one bit. They were tolerated at best, because they had proven themselves useful.

Still, Brennan decided that it would be in everyone's best interest if he continued to study Talon, at least from afar.

What harm could there be in doing that?

ON CORRUPTION

When all you have are spoken words, it's pretty easy to set up a whisper campaign against some fall guy to take the blame for whatever shenanigans you might have thought up.

Usually, at that point, the Twins catch onto what you're doing, and that whisper campaign turns against you.

There is a chance that maybe, *perhaps*, King Alfa had sent some spies into Talon's territory, there to stir the pot and not much else.

(He would deny it, you can't prove it, and besides, such things are obviously beneath him.)

(He is a very good, believable liar, as we'll see in a while. Particularly when it comes to lying to himself.)

However, things are a bit different in the territory of said dragon.

Namely, he doesn't speak. Not out loud.

And though few comment on it, for the most part, it's *really easy* to tell when Talon is lying, even if it's just a lie of omission, or if he says he's certain about something when he has some doubts.

Those sorts of things are almost impossible to hide given the way he communicates.

So, perhaps someone tries to stir things up by claiming that

Talon is being greedy, that he actually demands more than just a cow and two sheep from every quadrant each year. (His people don't pay taxes. What would Talon do with the money? He doesn't need a nicer place to live, or better food, or a court of fools surrounding him. Cities can raise their own taxes, but if Talon ever gets wind of any massive corruption or misuse of funds, whoever is found to blame had better learn how to fly sooner rather than later, because Talon will take the person high up into the air and then just drop them into an uninhabited part of a forest somewhere. Or onto the hedge, depending on how angry he is.)

In addition, there are too many people who travel to the biggest city in their quadrant for the Feeding Day celebration, when the quadrant gives their gifts of food to Talon. There are huge markets and lots of festivities around that day every year. It's treated as a holiday.

In addition, as many people as can be crammed into a square show up, and all of them (yes, *all of them*) listen to Talon make his demands as well as express his appreciation of what is given.

So hinting that Talon might be getting greedy just doesn't work. There are too many people who've listened to him, who *know* on an instinctual level that the dragon is telling the truth. What the quadrant provides is enough, and he doesn't want any more.

There might have been a time when people tried to spread rumors about the *unnatural* relationship that Talon has with that girl, Orla.

Not as many people had heard about her. That rumor takes hold a bit better, but again, when more attacks start happening, more people get affected, and they all get to see Orla in action.

Besides, Orla calls Talon, "Da," which is just heartwarming, and Talon (and others) have talked freely about her being his adopted daughter.

In the end, this whisper campaign fizzles out because people just don't think Talon would do such things, and besides, Orla is too nice of a girl, for all her fierceness.

Then there's the most insidious campaign of them all—that since it's Talon's territory, and he's the one in charge of it, he's the *only one* responsible for its protection. No one else should stir themselves to help him. People live in his territory voluntarily. They'll move (and they have moved away) if they no longer feel safe, if Talon can no longer take care of his lands properly.

This is the only whisper campaign that actually takes root and produces fruitful results. No one offers to help Talon (only Orla, but she's a different matter). No one thinks twice about demanding that Talon do more (though no one has a good suggestion of what he *can* do about random attacks). No one volunteers to build their own defenses, or send more people to work as guards (though Talon does pay well, if grudgingly, from his hoard).

It's Talon's fault these brigands are coming in the first place. He's the one who needs to take care of them.

When the wizards stepped in to help, that was quite a blow to this campaign. People started waking up to the fact that King Alfa's lands were swelling, and that perhaps Talon's territory was next on the chopping block.

Holding a people inactive is actually quite easy. You merely have to appeal to their selfish, lazy side, which is readily accessible.

But sometimes, that can also work against you, as we shall see.

BRENNAN

One of the tasks that Talon assigned to the wizards was to help on the upkeep of the magical hedge that grew all the way around his territory.

Over the three years that Brennan had been at the wizards' school, he'd heard much about the hedge and its properties. Some of it couldn't be true—such as it would attack any enemies who tried to sneak through. If that were the case, then none of them would make it, would they?

Brennan had kept track of all the attacks he'd heard of, brigands crossing the border and assaulting farms.

The attacks were increasing.

It used to be three or four a year.

Now, they appeared to be happening once a month.

Brennan traveled five days from Millerstown to the eastern most part of the hedge. Three other wizards from the school were sent out at the same time. All of them did the same sort of magic Brennan focused on, working with living plants and ingredients. Those three wore robes. Brennan still thought they were stupid and stubbornly stuck to wearing trousers and shirts. There was no advantage to wearing a robe, except to be immediately identified as a wizard.

Twice a year, wizards traveled from the school down to the border. They always sent four wizards, each one working a single quadrant of the hedge. They'd start at one of the gates and make their way clockwise, to the next gate.

On average, it took a person about a month to circumnavigate all of Talon's territory, walking along the edge of the hedge. Each wizard was given a week's time to walk their quarter of it, starting at one gate and making their way to the next. Once a wizard reached their initial assigned gate, they'd turn right and walk every day until they finally reached the next gate before going back to Millerstown.

The more experienced wizards went to the western edges, while the less knowledgeable ones went to the eastern sides.

Everyone knew that it was primarily people from the Kingdom of Alfaladon who were attacking Talon's territory. No one knew why, though. Of course, there were rumors about Talon having insulted King Alfa, questions about whether Talon, before he'd been cursed, had come from that kingdom (he hadn't), and mad speculation about the treasure that must be buried at the base of Talon's peak, in the center of his territory (while there was some, it was a modest hoard at best).

The hedge rose up above Brennan's six-foot-tall head. Even with his arm stretched out all the way up, he couldn't reach the top of it. It grew at least three feet wide close to the gate, though he'd heard that it was thicker in some places.

Brennan had also heard that the hedge might be sentient. He never got involved with such arguments, as he remembered the magic curling around the roots of the old woods and had often wondered about the level of awareness of the trees in that region.

The hedge was made of blackberry bramble, long vines intertwined with vicious thorns prominently displayed. As it was midsummer, a few green berries poked out of the mass of leaves.

Brennan had the impression that reaching for even one of those would end in tears and blood. He'd bet that the berries were a trap. The hedge would pull them back as a person reached for them, until they found their arm completely entrapped in thorns.

Standing next to the hedge, Brennan sensed a malevolence emanating from it. It wasn't pleased with its current circumstances. Not at all.

Before he'd come down here, his instructors had explained that the hedge wanted to grow unchecked, not be kept bound tightly to the perimeter of the territory.

Still, the hedge had a purpose. It didn't like strangers. It couldn't tell good strangers from bad, though. It had only ever slowed down some of the attacks. It couldn't prevent them.

Brennan had heard about some wizards who'd tried to burn down a portion of the hedge the previous year. Rumor was that it had absorbed all the corpses once Talon had killed them. That the dragon purposefully dropped brigands onto the top of the hedge, feeding it.

That was certainly one way to get rid of the bodies.

Brennan spent the next two days walking along a portion of the hedge, chanting a growth spell, feeding the hedge magically (though honestly, he wasn't sure how much good it would do, because the hedge was already so strong). His fellow wizards did the same on their portion of the hedge.

Brennan enjoyed his time traveling between the small villages close to the border. They reminded him of his home, so far away. (He'd tried angling for getting a different portion of the hedge to walk along, but it was traditional that the first time was always the southeastern portion.) He had dutifully gone to see his parents once a year, in the old woods. The trees there were both familiar as well as slightly claustrophobic, at least until he adapted again. He'd gotten used to more open spaces, being able to see the sky anytime he looked up.

The area he was working in that day was so very different than where he'd grown up. It was primarily flat, full of fields interspersed with small, well-trimmed, lines of trees marking the borders between the farms.

Strange.

Brennan tried to work with the hedge and not to force his magic on it. It appeared more or less indifferent to him—again, he figured whatever he fed the hedge was merely a trickle, barely noticeable to its thirst for *more* of everything.

Midmorning, while Brennan was taking a break and snacking on some of the good bread that he'd brought with him, he felt the hedge tremble.

Either a really strong wind had just sprung up on the other side of the hedge or someone was trying to hack their way through.

Brennan swallowed around a dry mouthful.

What should he do?

All his teachers had been very clear that the brigands were *Talon's* problem, not theirs.

Brennan was no fighter. He hadn't learned any offensive spells. Those were reserved for fifth year students.

Still, he had to do *something*. He couldn't just run away, though he suspected that was exactly what his teachers would advise him to do.

Brennan made himself run forward instead.

He heard the sound of the battle before he saw it. A thin line of birch trees marked the edges of two farmers' fields. Brennan stopped just past the edge of the trunks, trying to take in what he was seeing.

There were three—no, four—wizards there. They were focused primarily on the hedge, trying to dismantle it. They'd managed a huge hole, at least ten feet across. However, the opening didn't reach the top as the hedge still arched over their heads. A few vines dangled down it, bristling with thorns. Based on the torn robe Brennan saw one of the wizards wearing, they may have gotten too close.

Brennan wasn't too worried about the hedge, though that was supposed to be his primary focus. It would take care of itself. Those wizards had no idea what they were up against.

In the meanwhile, a short, mighty warrior in a breastplate and helmet fought to free Talon, who'd been caught in a net. The dragon was also working to free himself, those long claws of his tearing at the rope.

The warrior kept having to stop hacking at the net as four soldiers tried to pepper him with arrows, or race up and engage him and his sword.

Brennan couldn't throw missiles or bolts of lightning at the fighters. He hadn't learned any of those sorts of spells yet.

He could, however, encourage the grass beneath the feet of the soldiers to entangle them.

Brennan started chanting quietly, figuring that no one was paying any attention to him, at least for a while.

He couldn't help his elation when he saw one of the opposing fighters stumble.

Uhmmm.

The grass quickly wrapped itself firmly around all the limbs of the fighter, hiding him from sight.

Maybe Brennan had given the grass a little too much magic in his excitement.

He saw strands of it reaching for the feet of the other soldiers. One had stopped attacking Talon's protector to slash at his feet, trying to free himself.

Then Talon broke free. A long stream of acid struck the nearest soldier. The man's screams broke Brennan's concentration. The grass lay flat again, and the soldier who'd fallen was able to rise, green staining his silver breastplate and arms. His helmet was gone, and dirt streaked his face.

Quickly, Brennan started chanting again, calling the grass and nearby vines to aid him.

He kept his concentration up this time as the next soldier died, skewered by Talon's warrior.

However, now the wizards turned from their attack on the hedge.

There was nothing the poor warrior could do against lightning strikes.

Brennan turned his own attention toward the wizards. They were sure to have shields up, so no arrows could get through. The hedge, for all its malice, couldn't move from beyond its set location—as much as he might like to ask a vine to reach out and snag the wizards who'd now turned their back to it, that would take magic far beyond his training. (If it was possible at all. Very powerful magic restrained the hedge. Undoing that would take much more training and power than he had.)

So Brennan did the next most logical thing.

Blow the wizards toward the hedge.

It wasn't a very powerful spell. Then again, he didn't need much. Just a strong enough gust of wind to make the wizards take a step back.

Toward the hedge.

Again, they had no idea what they were dealing with.

Two of them stumbled backwards, into the opening that they'd created.

The hedge attacked. Long vines of thorns whipped around them, immediately ensnaring them.

Their screams threw off at least one of the remaining wizards, long enough for her to drop her shield so Talon could send a blast of acid into her face.

Fortunately, at least for her, that also made her step back.

The hedge took care of the rest, quickly putting her out of her misery.

That left a single wizard, as well as three, no, two, soldiers left.

Talon withstood a lightning strike easily. Huh. Good to know those didn't really affect him.

Brennan had heard a theory about that. As Talon dealt with acid, lightning wouldn't hurt him, nor fire. However, ice probably would. Of course, no one knew for certain and those were just rumors, idle speculation by students well away from any instructors.

Brennan tried a new spell. He glanced back at the woods he stood in, found an appropriate fallen branch and cast magic on it.

It worked!

The tree branch rose up like a club, then hurled itself into the back of one of fighters, distracting him from Talon's warrior long enough that he got another good strike in.

Moving more quickly than Brennan could track, the warrior sliced, pivoted, then sliced again, downing both of his foes.

The wizard was no longer standing by the time Brennan turned back to aid Talon. He wasn't sure what the dragon had done, but the wizard was nowhere to be seen.

The battle was over.

Brennan stayed where he was, just past the tree line, panting, unsure what to do next. His ears had a weird ringing in them, and he wanted to shout out in victory as well as go puke.

Talon turned toward him, those golden eyes tinged with red. (Was he still angry at those who'd attacked?)

And you are?

Brennan heard the words echoing between his ears. He shook his head to clear them as he slowly started walking toward the pair of them.

"I'm Brennan. Sir." He stopped briefly, and managed a stiff bow. "From the wizards' school. Sent here to, uhm, strengthen the hedge."

The hole the evil wizards had opened was already rapidly closing. As he'd thought, the hedge could take care of itself, given a chance.

Thank you for your help, Talon said.

Was it just Brennan's imagination, or did the dragon sound strangely stiff himself?

"I thank you, too," said the warrior as he—she!—removed her helmet.

Brennan couldn't help but stare at her. Her copper colored hair was bound tightly back in a long braid. Clear green eyes coolly appraised him. Though her skin was pale, it was dotted with orangish freckles.

"You are both welcome," Brennan said. At least this time his bow was a bit more genuine. "I am Brennan," he said, addressing them both.

"I'm Orla," she said. She turned to Talon. "I didn't know you had the wizards' school doing maintenance on the hedge."

I want them to be useful, Talon said.

"Does the hedge actually need help?" Orla asked.

Talon gave a soft sound that might have been a snorting laugh. *It doesn't hurt.*

That was exactly what Brennan thought. The hedge didn't need their magic. Why was Talon having the wizards come down and work on it twice a year?

Because it showed them who was in charge, he realized.

"I'd like to help more. Sir. If I could," Brennan found himself saying.

How? Talon asked, his voice sounding dry enough that Brennan found himself starting to be thirsty.

"Now, Da, don't be that way," Orla said.

Da? Was Talon her father? How in all of Uthir's lands did *that* work?!?

(It wasn't until later that Brennan remembered that Orla was Talon's adopted daughter.)

"I was useful in this most recent battle," Brennan said. He wasn't sure where all this courage was coming from.

Possibly from the smile that Orla was giving him.

"He entangled a couple of the soldiers, so they couldn't get to me," Orla pointed out. "He rammed that one in the back with a tree branch."

"And I sent a wind, to make at least some of the opposing wizards step back, into the hedge," Brennan added.

Hmmm, Talon grumped.

"There are other wizards who could help, too," Brennan said. "Ones who have a lot more magic than I do. Who could be useful."

What, am I supposed to stop by the school in Millerstown and just pick someone up whenever there's trouble? No, Talon said. *That would take too much time.*

He did have a point.

"You could talk to the wizards about setting some of us to patrol the perimeter more regularly," Brennan said. "So that if trouble occurred here, we could be close enough to help."

Talon grunted.

Brennan knew his idea had some merit. "The wizards would help you," he said. "If you'd let them."

He actually wasn't positive that would be the case. Most of his instructors were pretty clear that the brigands were Talon's responsibility, if not downright fault. But surely some would decide to help.

I did ask for help before, Talon said.

"But that was before the attacks started coming once a month, right?"

The golden eyes staring at him tried to bore a hole through him, but Brennan stood his ground. *Who told you the attacks were coming once a month?*

"No one, sir," Brennan said. "But it's pretty obvious to anyone who's paying attention."

Talon nodded and looked away, back toward the hedge, which was now almost completely recovered.

"I think he's right, Da," Orla said softly. "We could use the help."

And what happens when they get killed, ambushed by wizards stronger than them?

"Then they die," Orla said, her cool tone overshadowed by the sadness Brennan saw in her eyes. "As your people have been for long enough."

"Do you know who's behind these attacks? Why King Alfa and his wizard hate you so much?" Brennan asked.

He regretted his question instantly. If Talon could shoot acid from his eyes, he would have, based on the stare Brennan received.

"We think we know why," Orla said. "And nothing less than killing my Da would satisfy them. Oh, as well as swallowing all of his territory. And probably killing most of the local gods and goddesses."

"What?" Brennan said, surprised. He hadn't heard about that at all.

"Ask your teachers about King Alfa and his wizard," Orla said. "What happens to those gods and goddesses in the territories he acquires."

"I will," Brennan said.

What would happen to the people if all the little local gods and goddesses were destroyed? Who would they make sacrifices to? Who would rain blessings down on them? Or stand in for them, if they had to gather Ulthir's attention?

No, if this was real, it had to be stopped.

Nothing was resolved that day. Orla and Talon said their goodbyes. (And yes, Talon did, indeed, drop all the corpses onto the hedge. As soon as they touched the top of the greenery, the rustling started, and the bodies were pulled down. The only remaining sign of them was that the leaves nearby gained a red tint.)

However, Brennan was resolved to help.

It couldn't just be Talon's work to defend the territory and their homes. It had to be the work of them all.

BRIBING THE FATES

It's easy to get someone to do nothing. Particularly when there are all these tales and myths about the Twins of Fate showing up and turning the tables when someone is getting too big for their britches, as it were.

The Twins aren't accessible—whether they live at the top of a tree in a grand forest, or up on the mountain with Ulthir—they aren't easy to reach. The little local gods and goddesses have no access to the Twins. Fate just happens to whoever the Twins turn their attention to, for both good and ill.

So if the Twins are divine and have no wants or needs, and Maloneal has no way to get to them, how does he go about bribing them to turn their eyes away from what he's doing?

No one knows for certain. But there are speculations, rumors, nay, merely whispers, of a method that will work for the short run. Never for the long run. However, Maloneal might not need a long period of time, at least not how the gods count time. Just for long enough to get his foot in the door, as it were.

The Twins still love the game, "Make the Frog Jump," even though they've been told that it's impolite to call people that, to treat individuals that way, that they need to have more respect for those whose fates they twist, and that they need to be more careful with Ulthir's people. (They've only made Ulthir angry once. It isn't something that they ever, *ever*, want to do again.)

So they can't just randomly change people's fates like they used to. They have a few (not many) rules that they're supposed to follow.

However, what about a people who Ulthir doesn't claim as his?

Maybe there's a group of islands that's far away from the continent that Talon and the rest live on, where the people have declared themselves descended from something silly like apes, that they have no god and they need no god. Or perhaps Maloneal finds a link to a mirror world: something that's very similar to Ulthir's world, but just different enough that they aren't his people. Or maybe Maloneal creates a shadow people for the Twins to play with.

The Twins aren't breaking the rules. They aren't adjusting the fates of *Ulthir's* people willy-nilly, causing them to twist and turn randomly.

However, the Twins can mess with these *other* people to their hearts' content.

Which distracts them away from what is actually happening with Ulthir's people. So that maybe between their distraction and Maloneal's concealing magic, they don't necessarily see what's going on in Ulthir's world.

Again, their attention won't be turned away for a long time, not as the gods measure time. Eventually, they'll look back again at Ulthir's people.

When, though, remains the question.

BRENNAN

Brennan wasn't there when the discussions between Talon and the seven elder wizards at the school were held. It wasn't up to him. He didn't have a say in the matter.

However, he was determined that the wizards should start helping out. He couldn't believe that they'd gone for this long without volunteering.

Then again, the attacks hadn't been that bad before now.

Why had they increased and were now so frequent?

It was only then that Brennan learned how the border of King Alfa's lands kept creeping closer, heading directly toward them, like a diseased wave.

Of course, everyone expected someone else to do something about it. Where were the Twins? Why hadn't they turned the king's fate against him?

What Orla had said about the little local gods and goddesses turned out to be true. They were frequently *absorbed* by the approaching army, disappearing from their groves, lakes, rivers, and other places of enchantment.

All Brennan could think about was the way the hedge had *absorbed* the corpses dropped onto it, until nothing remained.

Most of the students were eager to help. Only a few felt it was *below* their position to do such menial work as patrolling the border of their lands.

Brennan snickered when he saw the first posting. Those who had complained the loudest had been sent to the western portions of the hedge, the places where they were most likely to see combat.

The first group sent out saw one of those students die.

Perhaps unsurprisingly after that, no one complained about the task. It was, after all, turning out to be necessary.

In addition, the elders changed the curriculum, so that offensive spells started being offered to students after just three years of study. (And OMG the complaints about that! Brennan sometimes thought his fellow students were more like old grandmothers always complaining about how different everything was instead of enjoying the prospect of learning something new.)

Finally, after two more years, just after Brennan turned nineteen, he was sent back to the border.

As the border was constantly being patrolled, a few of the farmers had built extra rooms on their farms for the wizards to stay at.

The attacks came less frequently with the constant border patrols. However, when a group of attackers did arrive, they were generally bigger now, better prepared to deal with a wizard. In response, the wizards' school had started sending out pairs of wizards, at least for the western border.

Every wizard was given a small vial. It contained a small piece of cloth that held a strong odor. Once uncorked (or broken) Talon would know there was an attack and come flying to the rescue, if he could, or to avenge who'd ever been attacked, if he couldn't.

Brennan (and a few of the others) worried about a coordinated attack, with more than one group striking at the same time. It hadn't happened yet, but it was a fear.

Talon had taken to patrolling his border more often as well. Brennan heard stories about him frequently being sighted flying above the hedge, on the lookout for anyone crossing the territory on foot instead of following along on the road.

The guards at the gates had foiled a few attempts as well.

Still, the brigands came. Now that the school was participating, it was very obvious what the attackers wanted: Talon.

They *wanted* the vials broken, the signal called, so that they could set up their nets and bring the dragon down. It was also obvious that they wanted him alive. They weren't trying to kill him outright.

How much were these brigands being paid? None of them survived for long. Didn't they realize it was a suicide mission?

Or had some survived? Had they purposefully left some of their party outside the gate, who returned to King Alfa to report their failure?

Brennan thought about all these things and more as he walked his portion of the hedge that morning. It was clear and sunny out, the end of summer approaching. The hedge grew tall and broad, a solid wall of greenery and thorns, to his left. Fields lay to his right, equally full, though with tall stalks of wheat, almost ready for harvest. Bees buzzed between the flowers that edged the fields. Birds who made their homes in the hedge sang cheerfully. Brennan was thankful for the straw hat that kept the sun out of his eyes. He stubbornly still wore a shirt and trousers, with good heavy boots, though he was teased about it sometimes by the other students.

Every now and again, Brennan would stop and send a trickle of magic through the hedge. Part of that was to help support and feed it. Part of that was just to keep his awareness centered there, hoping to notice anyone else doing magic before he stumbled across it.

He'd just finished his spell when he felt the hedge tremble.

It wasn't quite a shudder. Just a quick passing of an ill wind, rustling the leaves.

Brennan started his chant up again quickly, trying to sense what was going on.

Yes. The hedge noticed his magic for the first time, drawing on it, sucking into itself as much as it could.

Mouth suddenly dry, Brennan fumbled for the vial he kept carefully wrapped in a pouch he wore hanging from his belt.

Someone was attacking the hedge. The spot wasn't in front of him, no, it was a behind him, far enough away that he couldn't see it.

Had the brigands finally figured out the routes that the wizards took? And were trying to time things better?

Brennan opened the vial and ran with it, heading back the way he'd come.

Hopefully he could do something about the group coming through.

And hopefully, Talon would arrive sooner rather than later.

Brennan got to the area under attack just about the same time as the wizards finally burned their way through the hedge. He wasn't sure how long it had taken. Quarter of an hour? Half of one, perhaps? Given how winded he was, he'd bet it was the latter. (It was.)

There were no handy trees for him to hide behind. No spell he could cast that would turn him invisible. He could cast a quick shield around himself for protection (which he did).

And he could try to slow his opponents down.

Fortunately, he'd been practicing this.

Taking his cue from the hedge, Brennan called up a wide field of blackberry vines.

Okay, so maybe he was a little enthusiastic about it, and possibly he kinda sorta entangled himself as well.

And those thorns *hurt*.

But he wasn't the only one taking damage. His opponents were all stuck where they were. The soldiers were too busy hacking at the vines trying to pull them down to take any pot shots at him.

As were the wizards.

Brennan slowly started stepping back, out of the patch of hungry thorns.

He'd nearly broken free when one of the wizards finally noticed him.

Uh oh.

She looked him square in the eye and raised her hands above the bramble.

Crap.

At least his little shield took most of the damage caused by the shooting gouts of flame. And he continued to concentrate, keeping the field of blackberry bramble alive and angry, trying to engulf all of those in its grasp.

Brennan took one last stumbling step backwards, finally free of the vines which still smoked from the attack by the other wizard.

The second attack occurred before he could do much of anything else.

His shield took less of the damage. Brennan felt himself knocked back, but damn it! He wasn't about to lose control of those vines.

Those were his best protection.

Particularly if he ended up having to fight all of this group on his own.

Another gout of fire came his direction. Brennan was more prepared this time, and used a strong wind to push it to the side.

Unfortunately, that singed more of the bramble.

He gasped when he realized that the wizards were going to burn the bramble he'd called up, freeing themselves.

As well as their soldiers.

This was *not* how Brennan wanted to die.

He readied himself as a second wizard stopped fighting the bramble and faced his direction, starting a new spell, attention focused inward and not on the vines encasing him.

When he finished his spell, this was going to suck for Brennan.

At the last possible moment, the wizard raised his hands.

A steaming gout of acid splashed down out of the air.

What the—

The wizards didn't appear to notice. It fell harmlessly around them, as if shielded by an invisible umbrella.

The soldiers, on the other hand, all started screaming.

The wizard with his hands raised sent a huge fireball—the biggest that Brennan had ever seen, at least six feet tall and wide.

But it wasn't directed toward Brennan. No, it flew through the air, directly at Talon's wings, as if an invisible spirit or wind guided it.

Talon screeched—a horrible sound that made Brennan want to puke. Possibly that was because not all of the noise was made out loud: some of the dragon's painful scream had occurred inside his head.

The dragon wobbled and just managed to turn before hitting the edge of the hedge.

Brennan knew, *knew* that Talon didn't necessarily need his wings to keep him airborne.

Steering, however, was another matter.

Brennan took a moment to perform a different spell, one he could do while still maintaining the bramble. It set off a loud clap of thunder in the area just before him, causing all of his opponents to flinch and stop whatever it was they were doing. It disrupted the wizards' spells, which was his primary goal.

The soldiers—well, he didn't think they had much of a chance. Particularly not when Talon took another swooping run over them, coating them in acid.

Talon landed with a heavy thump just beyond the patch of blackberry bramble that Brennan had managed to still maintain.

That turned out to be a mistake, as a second fireball struck the side of his body and dancing flames encased his wings.

Howling, Talon turned and charged into the area, Orla at his side. Brennan dropped the entangle spell immediately, not wanting to hurt his companions.

The shield of the wizards couldn't withstand the force of a dragon getting a running start, then barreling over them.

When Brennan saw his chance, he cast another burst of wind and pushed one of the wizards back through the opening they'd made in the hedge, letting the angry wall of thorns take care of her.

He had no wooden tree branch handy, so he couldn't strike an opponent that way. He did, however, have the ability to shape and throw ice daggers. It took some concentration to form each dagger, so they were a slow way to battle.

However, they could get through the shields of the wizards. While their damage was minimal, each successful hit broke the concentration of a spell caster, which would interrupt the spell they were trying to cast.

Talon also joined in the battle, spitting long streams of acid when Orla was out of the way. (It wasn't until later that Brennan realized just how careful Talon was of Orla, how he focused on protecting her above his own safety.)

It started out as four against three. Then the odds were even. Shortly, though, the last wizard standing fell, and the fight was over.

The groan that Talon gave wasn't just in Brennan's head.

Orla raced to Talon's side.

Brennan couldn't hear their conversation, though he had no doubt they were having one.

Interesting. Everyone else who ever talked with Talon had to do so out loud. Orla obviously didn't.

Orla wrapped her arms around Talon and lay her cheek against his chest. The dragon had very gently laid one arm over her shoulders.

From where Brennan was standing, Talon's posture looked painful. There were burn marks all along Talon's side, starting from his elbow, up along his torso, and then over his wings.

"Sir?" Brennan said, taking a small step forward. "I have some ability at healing. If that would help you."

Heal her, Talon said immediately, using his hands to gently turn Orla around so Brennan could see the scorch marks that ran across the metal of her armor. The leather covering her arms had been blasted away, and she was bleeding fairly heavily from one elbow.

"No, Da," Orla said. She raised her chin stubbornly. "I'm fine."

No, you're not, Talon said firmly.

"I'm better than you are," Orla replied coolly. "You can't even fly home right now. Can you?"

Brennan wasn't sure what the following conversation entailed, but he could guess that it was something along the lines of *Don't say such things in front of* him!

"Da, he isn't about to just leave while you're hurt like this. Right?" Orla said, turning and piercing him with a fierce gaze.

Talon looked away, toward the hedge that had already started repairing itself.

Heal her first. I want to make sure that you know what you're doing before I let you tend to me, Talon finally said.

Brennan bit back his flippant reply, something along the lines of he'd try not to add a second head to Orla, but no promise.

Now wasn't the time.

While Talon tossed the bodies of their opponents into the opening of the hedge, Brennan cast a healing spell to take care of Orla's wounds. It worried him that she was still carrying wounds and bruises from her last battle as well. He did what he could to patch her up, while at the same time, not use up all his magic.

She seemed to understand, and after taking a deep breath, thanked him. She appeared to be moving better, her breath rising and falling easier. They both knew, though, that she wasn't all the way healed.

"Here, Da, let me get the last of them," Orla said gently as she pushed Talon in Brennan's direction.

Brennan couldn't help but gulp as the dragon drew nearer. He was *huge*. His head alone was probably as long as Brennan's torso. The smell of acid, sour and biting, emanated from him. He had a presence to him that seemed to take up all the space surrounding Brennan, and then some.

And he'd thought that living in Millerstown was claustrophobic! Talon easily took up all the air in the room And more.

You sure you're up for this? Talon asked as Brennan took another deep breath.

"I am, Sir. I just need to concentrate for a few moments." Brennan made himself close his eyes, though he could still *feel* the dragon beside him.

Fortunately, it didn't take long for the spell to form.

Brennan understood that not all wizards could see magic as it was being performed; in that, he was particularly gifted. The magic of the gods was always a deep, rich purple color. The color of wizards tended to be a pale blue, though frequently it would be tinged with some other color. Señor Alberto's magic had a red outline to it, while Brennan's was green.

All of the magic Talon did, particularly when he flew, was the same yellowish-green of his torso scales. Brennan had never met a wizard whose magic was that color. (He won't learn until much later that it's the color of all transformations.)

When Brennan raised his hands, he saw that he'd been focusing so hard that the usual light green of his magic had shifted, and was now a rich green-blue.

Most of it stuck to the dragon as well, landing solidly on his wings and sinking into the dragon's body. More than usual, in fact.

Seemed that Talon was particularly susceptible to magic. Was that just healing magic, or all magic?

Brennan could also tell that what he'd done wasn't enough to completely heal Talon. The dragon bore some deep injuries.

That's it? Talon asked after a bit.

"I'm afraid it is," Brennan said. "After I rest, I can heal you more."

Talon looked away again. He shifted his wings, trying to determine the amount of damage they still had.

What are you doing? Talon asked.

Brennan looked around, guiltily. He hadn't been doing anything!

Then he realized that the question hadn't been directed at him.

"We're spending the night here. In the morning, Brennan will be able to heal you up enough that we can fly home," Orla said.

She'd been pulling things out of her backpack, which she'd dropped at some point, and appeared to be setting up camp.

No, we're not, Talon said. He sounded angry.

"Well, you can go and fly off, then," Orla responded. She actually sounded amused. "I'm spending the night right here, so that *I* can get healed more after Brennan rests a bit."

Oh, Talon said. *I'm sorry, little one.*

"It's okay, Da." She turned to Brennan and gave him a smile. "Unless you have to be someplace else?"

"No, no, I'd love to spend the night with you," Brennan said.

The anger that radiated off Talon made Brennan take a step back and consider what he'd just said.

"No, no, not like that," he said, holding his hands up, trying to appease a very large, very terrifying, angry father.

Humph was the only response he got.

Brennan quickly hurried over to retrieve his own rucksack, the one that his father had given him when he'd left for Millerstown, so many years ago.

Between Orla and Brennan, they quickly set up a rough camp,

sharing their stores of food and water while Talon spent the time communing with the hedge, one clawed hand holding onto the bramble.

Every once in a while Brennan thought he saw a trickle of magic flow between the dragon and the hedge, though he was never certain which way it was going. Sometimes it appeared that the dragon was giving the hedge magic, other times it was the hedge's magic flowing toward the dragon. (For all that it was a green and growing thing, the hedge's magic was more black and red than the color of its leaves. Brennan wasn't sure what that said about the living wall of thorns: if that was just its anger that tainted its magic or something else.)

After they'd eaten dried meat, part of a travel roll, and some dried berries that Brennan happily shared, Brennan and Orla started chatting. He learned about how Talon had found her, how she'd adopted him as much as he'd adopted her, how they'd started fighting together against the brigands.

Talon had crept around them, encircling them with his body and tail, a living border, intent on keeping them both safe for the night.

Finally, Orla gave a soft sigh and said, "Good."

Brennan shot a quizzical look at her.

"He's asleep," she said, her voice not much above a whisper. "He needs to rest. That will help his healing as well."

Brennan nodded and silently mimed going to sleep.

Orla laughed softly at his antics. "Naw, nothing more than a loud scream will wake him at this point."

"And what about you?" Brennan asked, though he still kept his voice quiet. "Do you need to sleep? Or do you want to talk some more?"

He was dying to ask her questions about the dragon, particularly now that Talon was asleep. He trusted Orla's judgment in such things, as they were mentally connected somehow.

He'd told her about his own upbringing, coming into magic, leaving his home and going to the wizards' school in Millerstown.

After a moment, Orla firmly replied. "Talk. Then sleep."

So they talked more about their different paths, about all the memorization that Brennan had to do for learning spells and the magical language, as well as all the physical drills Orla did for fighting.

Finally, Brennan saw his opening.

"We know that it's King Alfa who's attacking us, right?" he said softly. "Do you or Talon know why?"

Orla bit her lip and looked to the side.

Brennan knew that she'd given him a hint before, that the other kingdom wanted to capture Talon for some reason. Keep him alive. Presumably to do something to him.

"You've heard about the king's wizard, Loalmane, right?" Orla asked softly.

"There are some at the school who swear that he's figured out the secret to longevity," Brennan told her.

"You know that?" she said, sounding alarmed.

Brennan shrugged. "No one knows for certain. But there haven't been any ceremonies in Alfaladon welcoming a new court magician for decades, perhaps centuries now. Either they happen in private, which is unlikely, or it's the same person."

Orla nodded. "And what does the wizards' school know about the missing little gods and goddesses?"

"As you once said to me, they're disappearing. They get absorbed," Brennan said with a shudder. "Kind of like how the hedge absorbs bodies."

Orla gave a heavy sigh. "We have to stop him. Both the wizard and this latest king."

"I agree," Brennan said. "But until there's a formal declaration of war between Talon and the king, no one will support an army." He lowered his voice. "Sometimes I think that King Alfa has sent spies into Talon's territory, to live and work among us, and to continue to claim that all of this is Talon's responsibility, that the people have nothing to do with any of it. That others are keeping us, well, passive. Instead of stepping up and acting in our own best interest."

Orla nodded slowly. "I hadn't thought of that. But Da's people have never known war or strife. Or even bad taxes. Not for a couple centuries, now. He's coddled and protected everyone. Now, no one wants to step forward. He's never let anyone help him."

"You help him. You fight with him, protect him," Brennan said.

Orla gave him a lopsided grin. "He might not have had any choice about that." Then she sobered and sighed. "But how many others are going to be as stubborn and insistent about it, as I was?"

Brennan sighed in return and nodded. He remembered how much resistance there had been at the wizards' school about forming a patrol. And they knew more about the attacks and what had been going on than most.

What would the farmers say? Or the men who worked in the mills? The captains on the boats that plied the rivers? The regular traders and merchants? Or even those who dealt with magical ingredients and concoctions?

"We have to do something," Brennan insisted. "Has Talon ever sent an ambassador to King Alfa, to talk about the attacks?"

Orla gave him a wry smile. "He has, in fact. King Alfa refused to meet with the man. Said that there was nothing to talk about. Though he was very sorry that our little territory was under attack, we couldn't *prove* that it was him ordering them. And did we want his protection? Of course, that would mean Da giving up his claim to the land."

"Is he just after Talon? Or is there something here that he wants as well?" Brennan said, musing.

"We've always assumed it was just Talon, that they somehow think they can use him to further their plans. However, he's recently found some spies scouting the base of his peak. No matter how much they try to smell like the local wildlife, Da can still sniff them out," Orla said with some pride in her tone. Then she sighed again. "But we don't know if they were just there to see if Da was vulnerable, or if they really think there's some treasure buried there. I mean, beyond Da's hoard."

Brennan nodded as if he already knew about that.

Talon was a dragon. Of course, he had a hoard. As Orla didn't appear to think that was what anyone was after, he would believe her.

"Can we make a formal declaration of war against King Alfa?" Brennan said after a few moments.

"No one in the territory would support that," Orla said. "No, King Alfa has to officially declare war on us." She paused then said, "I have a different question to ask you about."

"All right," Brennan said. He was just happy to talk with her longer. She was intelligent, articulate, had a wicked sense of dry humor (something he suspected she'd acquired from Talon) and was fierce in a way that warmed his heart.

He didn't know what Talon would have done without her. Probably been killed or captured already.

Orla dug into her bag and pulled out a pendant. It had a star with five points, and an open eye in the center of it.

"Do you know what this is?" she said.

Brennan nodded. "Yes."

"You do?" Orla asked, obviously surprised.

"It's one of the old symbols for Ulthir," Brennan said. "Though there's some argument that it's actually a sign for Maloneal. It hasn't been used for ages, though."

"That's funny," Orla said. "Because we find these pendants around the necks of almost every wizard, as well as quite a few of the soldiers. We think it's the sign of Loalmane."

"That's really strange," Brennan said. "Wait. Loalmane. Maloneal. Loalmane. Maloneal." Something was familiar about those names. Something he felt that he should see.

"What is it?" Orla asked after Brennan ran the two names together a few more times.

"Is Loalmane the same as Maloneal? Composed of the same letters?" Brennan said after a few moments. His breath caught. "I think it is."

"If that's the case, no wonder the Twins haven't turned against King Alfa," Orla breathed out.

"But what are we going to be able to do about it?" Brennan said. "If the trickster, himself, is out to get Talon?"

Orla took a deep breath. "It isn't just to be able to extend his own life, if that's the case, if we are right about this." She looked over her shoulder at Talon, who still appeared to be sleeping. "Something else is going on. What is he doing? Why is he doing this?"

"Maloneal, in all of the stories we know about him, has never done something like this before. Something this big," Brennan said firmly. He wasn't certain why the wizards' school had so many classes on myths, and insisted that the students learn such stories. Not just local variants, but those collected from the islands off the coast as well as some handed down from the Benevolent Dictator.

"But the trickster has always been second, right?" Orla asked. "He's either getting into trouble, or getting someone else out of trouble. He isn't Ulthir, sitting up on his great mountain, looking out over everything and brooding."

"You think this might be Maloneal's big play for power? To usurp Ulthir?" Brennan said, the horror of it drawing over him.

He did *not* want to live during times when the gods were at war. Nothing good ever happened during those times. No, he wanted to live a long and peaceful existence, do his part as a wizard and protect other people, and maybe, perhaps, work up the courage to ask Orla out on a date or something.

"I don't know," Orla said, shaking her head. "This is all a lot of supposition with no facts to back it up. Maybe Loalmane and Maloneal aren't the same person. Maybe their names are just a coincidence."

Brennan sighed and nodded. "I know. I just...I want to figure out what's going on. And I'm afraid that the only way to do that is to leave Talon's territory, and go find out."

"I can't leave Da. Won't leave him all alone," she said, looking fondly at the soundly sleeping mound of dragon wrapped around them.

"Maybe the wizards' school can send a contingent out to King Alfa," Brennan said. "After all, the wizards on the coast are supposed to be the best there is."

Orla snorted at that. "They must send their rejects here, then," she said. "Because they don't survive. And why do they keep attacking the hedge?"

"There isn't an army poised out there, ready to come rushing in once it's down?" Brennan said.

He'd spoken his words lightly. However, Orla frowned and looked worried.

"Da—Da's very particular about not really patrolling past the edge of his territory," she said. "He does deal with some of the closer, smaller towns. They've learned to never give sanctuary to anyone who's attacked farms here. But he also doesn't get involved in their affairs."

They weren't able to resolve anything that night. They did linger, though, talking about it, coming up with alternative plans, speculating wildly about all the attacks and what they could do about them.

They might have stayed up a little later, just because they both needed someone to talk with, who was in their world and yet not too close, so they could both teach and learn.

Eventually, they both went to sleep, well apart from each other, so that an angry dragon wouldn't have anything to complain about in the morning.

Even though secretly, they might have both needed some additional comfort.

ON WINNING WARS

It is only the rarest of instances that someone starts a war that they don't believe they can win. The vast majority of the time, whoever starts such a conflict is confident that they will be victorious at the end.

Even Maloneal must believe that his chances are better than fifty percent. Perhaps not much better, maybe merely fifty-two percent. Still. Better than even odds.

In addition, Ulthir's people don't believe in an afterlife. If they're going to be throwing their lives away (because people will die in war) they had better have a pretty good reason why.

King Alfa Edwardo actually has three very good reasons why either he, or one of his descendants, will win his family's war.

The Prophesy. (And yes, it is always referred to as The Prophesy, with that level of emphasis). It was first revealed to his great, great grandmother, King Alfa Regina. (All the rulers are called King Alfa, regardless of gender identity or pronoun preferences.) The Prophet (yeah, he also rarely gets a name, though he'd have you know that he prefers Sir Seguin III) may have been speaking about the Kingdom of Alfaladon when he predicted the rising wave of power engulfing the land. Or he could have been talking about the next sunrise. We'll get into this more, later.

In addition, Loalmane and his mages have, so far, been successful. Not just in subduing the little local gods, but in the sacrifices they've made to keep the hands of the Twins of Fate tied. It didn't hurt that as far as the current King Alfa knew, Loalmane was the original mage who'd developed the plan with King Alfa Regina. The mage was onto something, and had promised that once they'd captured Talon, the current King Alfa would become the permanent King Alfa.

(Although Loalmane and his wizards had yet to capture Talon, despite trying for more than a decade, now. There was an entire wizards' school dedicated to bringing the dragon in. Each month, the graduation ceremony culminated in going to Talon's territory and capturing him. The joint reward was spectacularly high at this point: both gold from King Alfa as well as promises of longevity from Loalmane. It needed to be, as practically no one ever made it back alive.)

The third reason King Alfa felt assured of his success, that *he* would become the permanent King Alfa, was in part because success breeds success. As no one, not the Twins, not the little gods or goddesses, nor even Ulthir himself had stepped down to stop any of the King Alfas, the current one was starting to believe his own press, namely, that maybe, perhaps, his quest *was* holy. He *was* doing the will of Ulthir and the Twins. He was *destined* to become king of all the lands, as spoken of in The Prophesy (see point above).

Usually, such a belief is a good setup for the Twins to come in, giggling like the teenaged girls they still are, just to swat the person down like a negligent fly.

As it hadn't happened yet, maybe it wouldn't.

Time will tell.

BRENNAN

Brennan healed both Talon and Orla a bit more in the morning. The sleep had done wonders for the dragon—he was practically back to new, and only needed a little aid. Orla took more, which Brennan was happy to give.

They'd all packed up and were saying their goodbyes when Talon suddenly froze, his snout lifted to the air.

Trouble, he pronounced loudly.

"That's my cue," Orla said grimly.

"Let me come with you," Brennan said, speaking before he could consider the consequences of his words.

"What?" Orla said.

No, Talon said immediately.

"I can help, sir, if there's a fight. Particularly if someone is attacking again so soon. They must be getting desperate," Brennan said.

He wasn't sure what Orla added to that, though he was certain that she'd just said something private to her Da.

Fine, Talon said after another moment. *But I'm dropping you if you cause any trouble.*

"No trouble! No trouble at all!" Brennan assured Talon.

Orla gave him a bemused smile and jumped up onto the back of the dragon with practiced ease.

Brennan didn't have any experience with riding an animal. He gamely put his foot where Orla told him, swinging his leg awkwardly over Talon's back. He rode behind Orla, his arms clenched tightly around her waist, his hands wrapped around his own arms so that he wouldn't accidentally touch her and make her adopted father angry —well, *more* angry.

Talon threw himself up to the sky.

Brennan's stomach objected as it dropped to the bottom of his torso. At the same time, breakfast threatened to make a re-appearance, shooting up the other direction. Fortunately, the cold cut down on his nausea, as the chill wind of Talon's rapid flight whipped at him.

"You all right back there?" Orla said. She still sounded amused.

"Y—y—yes," Brennan stammered. He made the mistake of looking down at the ground that was far, *far* too far away, all the way down there, then shut his eyes tightly.

"It won't take us long to get there," Orla told him. "Seems some idiots are at the western gate."

"Good," Brennan breathed out, because nodding his head sounded like a really bad idea.

After a timeless time, when Brennan finally felt as though he could take a deep breath and not puke, Orla said, "We're here."

Oh God.

Descending was worse than taking off.

Cold winds threatened to dislodge him from his seat. He opened his eyes then closed them again, the speed of the ground rushing toward them making him want to scream. His stomach wasn't sure which way was up anymore.

They landed with a solid thunk. Brennan bit his tongue as his head came down, his jaw connecting with Orla's solid shoulder.

After a few moments, Orla patted the arms still tightly clenched around her. "We're here. You can let go now."

"Oh. Sorry, sorry," Brennan said.

He opened his eyes and was instantly even more sorry, as the world still appeared to be spinning.

However, he had to pull it together. Now. Particularly if Orla needed him.

Except, he didn't hear any sounds of fighting.

Forcing his eyes back open, Brennan looked around.

They were just inside the western gate, which was thrown open. It was wide enough for two carts to go through side by side.

On the other side of the hedge stood a large collection of wizards in many colored robes, as well as a few people who were dressed up. Brennan had seen silks and brocades a few times before. They were the sorts of fabrics woven into clothing for the Mayor of Millerstown and his family.

These people made the mayor and his ilk look like paupers.

There was silk. And lace. And feathers. And brocade. And more than one fancy ring on every finger. Necklaces that hung on shining silver or sparkling gold. Scarves that fluttered in pockets or across shoulders. Hats that looked too fine to be real.

And...by Ulthir's balls...were they riding *horses*?

Orla and Talon looked at each other, some sort of exchange taking place, before Talon went barreling through the gate, racing at the party gathered there, stopping just a few feet before them.

The horses didn't even twitch.

Brennan had never seen anyone have such control over those creatures.

There were three noblemen, with three times as many wizards. Once Brennan got to the other side of the gate, he saw that there were two dozen soldiers, all standing, not riding, fanned out behind the group.

To what do I owe the pleasure of this party's call? Talon asked.

Brennan, along with everyone else, could feel the grumbling underneath the words. (Seemed that when the party arrived, they demanded to see Talon, though they refused to set one foot in his territory. The gate guards had finally uncorked one of the vials meant to bring Talon in case of trouble.)

"We are here by order of King Alfa," one of the noblemen snootily replied. "He is displeased with the number of attackers you have sent against the kingdom and—"

I have sent no one to attack your kingdom, Talon said clearly.

Brennan knew that Talon spoke the truth. Anyone who heard Talon did as well.

The foot soldiers behind the group suddenly looked a little less grim and a little more unsure of themselves.

The wizards...did not. They knew that it was a trumped-up charge. As did the three nobles.

Brennan tuned out the dragon and the others, keeping his focus on the wizards. He wanted as much warning as possible if they started casting an attack.

Fortunately, this was Brennan's forte. Three years at the wizards' school had honed his natural abilities even further.

The group had some low-level spells running—probably shields and other types of protection. Plus—ah, there it was.

Horses reacted badly to any and all magic. Everyone knew this. He detected a spell that he'd never seen before, that felt different than any of the spells he'd learned. It was like a constant drip of cool water running along the reins of every horse.

Quite possibly, that was what was keeping the animals under control.

He'd bet that if he cast a very targeted dispel magic spell, the horses might freak out, if not immediately, then the next time any sort of spell was cast.

Based on what he could sense, he doubted that this mob was here for a fight. They weren't prepared enough. And there weren't nearly enough soldiers. Particularly not with Talon here.

"Be that as it may," the noble said, speaking over Talon's objections, "King Alfa has decided to declare war on your territory."

Really.

Talon's response was so dry Brennan found himself swallowing reflexively.

And how do we stop this war? Before you needlessly kill more of my people?

The noble seemed surprised by this question.

One of the wizards spoke up instead.

"Why, give yourself up, of course," she said, her tone dripping with haughty condescension. "Allow us free access to all of your territory. Tear down your damned wall."

What was it that these wizards hated so much about Talon's hedge? Why did they always come and try to tear it down? Was it just because of what it represented? Or did it do something else that Brennen wasn't aware of?

I will need to think on this, Talon said. *Meet with the mayors of the quadrants. I will give you an answer in a week's time.*

"No," the nobleman said. "We need your answer today."

Talon's rumbling laughter filled the area. *Why the rush? This is an important decision, one that needs care and deliberation.*

The nobleman sniffed in disgust. "All you'll do is spend the time raising an army."

Talon didn't deny it.

"King Alfa has shown you enough leniency," the noble declared.

Talon just snorted at that.

"What is your reply?" the noble demanded.

You said I had today, Talon said. *You will at least give me the appearance of grace.*

The nobleman opened his mouth, then shut it again abruptly and glared churlishly.

Looked as though no one had told him *no* in far too long of a time.

Talon added, *Or should I show you the same* leniency *that King Alfa has been showing me?*

The threat was obvious. Everyone in the party bristled.

"You could try," the noble said haughtily.

You're not worth the effort, Talon said as he turned his back on the party. *I'll be back before sundown. Make yourself comfortable* outside *my walls.* He paused, looking over his shoulder at the wizards. *If I feel even one of you trying to touch my hedge, you are all going to die. And it won't be pleasant.*

The wizards stiffened as one, as if a cold wind had just encased them. Slowly, they nodded.

Go to your families and loved ones, Talon told the gate guards. *For you will be leaving them again soon enough.*

The four guards looked at each other. Two nodded and turned away abruptly. The other two stayed.

Well? Talon said to them.

"Our duty is here, sir," one of the guards—a woman—replied. "Our family as well. We have done little enough since the attacks began. The least we can do now is to stand by you."

Brennan couldn't help but gasp, just a little.

What the guard said was true. People *had* stood by and done nothing for far too long.

Maybe the guilt would prod them into stronger action, now.

Thank you, Talon said. *I am truly grateful.*

He glanced over at Brennan. *I leave it to you to tell the wizards. I'm going to visit the mayors of the quadrants. See what sort of response we can give those assholes over there.*

"Yes, sir," Brennan said.

He knew he'd have to suffer through another flight on Talon's back, back to Millerstown.

And though the prospect of war chilled him to the marrow, his traitorous heart leapt at the thought of getting to spend more time with Orla.

Fortunately, the mayors all agreed that if King Alfa was declaring war on Talon and his territory, that they must go to war themselves, to defend themselves if nothing else.

Brennan thought Talon was very smart, telling the mayors that King Alfa had accused him of sending his own brigands, which Talon had not done.

No one doubted Talon's word. They knew him too well, knew that he wouldn't lie about such a thing, that he kind of couldn't.

Not all the mayors knew that it had been King Alfa sending his own brigands into Talon's territory, but that just goaded their anger.

Though Talon did report back that day to those gathered at his Western gate that his territory was rousing, it still took a couple of weeks before everyone was ready to leave.

During that time, scouts reported back about the large army just a few weeks' march away. King Alfa had been preparing for this for a long while. (The scouts hadn't necessarily gone to see the army themselves. Seemed that the little local gods and goddesses were keeping track of the force, because they knew what was coming.)

Talon had at one point been a leader of men. Though it had been a couple of centuries ago, he still knew the basics, and was able to help his own people organize, as they'd never had need of an army before, let alone warriors and soldiers.

So those who streamed out of the western gate two weeks later weren't necessarily well equipped in terms of weapons or armor.

What they had was grit, determination, and a sudden revulsion at their own laziness, that they'd let it come to this.

Brennan had thought that he'd be marching with the wizards, or assigned a group to protect as the other wizards had been.

Instead, at the last moment, he was told he'd be riding a large cart, at the back of the army.

He chaffed at the assignment, though he didn't object to it. Or say anything out loud about how unfair it was to anyone except his friends.

It wasn't until he saw that the driver was Orla that he understood the honor he was being paid.

The cart was for Talon, to ride in the back of the war effort, at least at the beginning. Slowly, they'd make their way up to the front, to lead the army.

"I wasn't sure you'd agree," Orla said as Brennan hopped onto the cart beside her. Two solid oxen pulled it, more placid and unimaginative than most. (Even the most calm of beasts still has issues when pulling a *dragon*. These animals, however, had been specially trained.)

"Why wouldn't I want to spend more time with you?" Brennan asked, perplexed.

The warning rumble of a dragon perched behind him gave him pause.

Orla merely rolled her eyes. "Because of *that*," she said, throwing a look over her shoulder at her Da.

"You know I respect your daughter and mean her no harm," Brennan said hastily.

Depends on how you define harm, Talon replied.

Before Brennan could defend herself further, Orla broke in. "Da, you're going to need to address everyone before we start off."

Fine, fine, Talon said. *After this, I'll need to spend a month alone in my cave. All by myself.*

"I know, Da," Orla said.

Brennan couldn't help but feel how his heart rose at the sight of Talon flying over their amassed troops.

They were outnumbered, at least two to one. They didn't have the training, the weapons, the discipline, or much of anything that the other army had.

What they did have was a dragon leading them.

All their struggles were sure to be turned into legend and song.

Wouldn't they?

A RECIPE FOR WAR

PROPHETS, FORTUNE TELLERS, AND OTHER LIARS

In a world where there's magic, *real* magic that people can see, touch, taste, as well as perform, you'd think the number of those faking it would be minuscule.

Never underestimate the power of people wanting that which they don't have.

Plus, actual magic takes discipline. Sure, you can cast some spells just by taking enough psychedelics or other mind-altering substances. However, frequently, those leave your mind, uhm, *altered*. Occasionally, there is no coming back from one of those trips.

And not everyone has the discipline to learn the magical language necessary to cast magic. Of course, there are always those instances when someone is faced with an impossible situation, like a raging river sweeping away their baby, when they find their magic because they couldn't live in the world that *was*. Through sheer force of will, they alter circumstances until the world they want comes into being.

The actual number of times that happens is relatively rare.

In addition, maybe because there are wizards, hedge witches, spell casters, what have you, people think that magic can do everything from keeping you alive forever to telling the future.

The latter is actually tricky.

Partly, that's because of the Twins.

Say you have someone who predicts the future. The Twins might step in to twist things so that what has been predicted occurs exactly as stated.

Or they might change events so that it only kind of happens.

For example, there was an oracle who predicted a flood washing over one of the pretty little coastal towns, a huge wave of destruction. The oracle was very convincing, had times and dates and everything, not just, "I see something hot. No, warm. Maybe it starts as a cool day, then grows heated. There's a sun out. Mostly. Then this thing occurs. It's a bad thing. Trust me. I know this."

This one oracle convinced the townspeople to build row upon row of houses up at the top of the cliff behind the village. (The existing houses were built out of white stone, with red tiled roofs, or carved out of the nearby hills, with large windows and doors facing the water. Very picturesque.) All the new houses were built on stilts so the rising waters wouldn't get to them. (Not so pretty.)

Did I mention that the oracle's brother-in-law worked in construction and possibly grew tremendously rich during this building frenzy?

A wave did come at the predicted time. And it did great damage. Many lives were lost.

However, it was a wave of *locusts*, not water. They swarmed the town and ate everything that was organic.

Which meant the stilts of all the houses up on top of the cliffs. Those houses tumbled down. Some of them even fell all the way down to the ocean below. Many of the people up there were killed, including the oracle, his family, and the brother-in-law who'd made so much money.

The poor people, below, still in their houses made of stone with the tile roofs, were mostly safe, as long as they stayed indoors until the wave of locusts passed, and kept all children and pets indoors as well. They had very few deaths.

So prophesy is a tricky business. Certainly not for the faint of heart. Most true prophets keep their predictions to themselves. Even if what they end up predicting turns out to be true, it might only partially be true. Or be a twisted truth.

Then we come to those who could be called charlatans. Those who make grand predictions because they *want* them to be true, not because some divine spirit or magical seeing actually foretold the event.

Even these people have a better than average hit rate. Frequently, that's because of the Twins, making everything a particular prophet say come true, lie after lie, until the big day comes for whatever big event, and everything…fizzles.

Was The Prophet, i.e., Sir Seguin III, one such being?

Yes.

And no.

Sir Seguin III did have the capacity for small magics. His mind was flexible enough to manage such things. There's also a good chance that when he was a young man, he did have an affinity for predicting the future. For example, one year he instructed his father's servants to cover the rose bushes with straw early, on a clear fall day that was sunny and warm, only to have a huge storm blow up that evening and snow covering the grounds come dawn.

This story may, perhaps, have been exaggerated a *tiny* smidgen, such that the story that reached King Alfa Regina's ears was that he'd warned his dear departed grandmother not to leave the manor grounds that afternoon because of the change of weather coming. She hadn't listened, and so had died in the storm. (She'd actually died cozy and warm in her bed, not bestirring herself when the snow arrived. She *also* may have had a touch of foreseeing, and had chosen where she'd wanted her end to find her.)

So King Alfa Regina invited Sir Seguin III to visit the court and regale her with some of his tales.

Sir Seguin III came prepared. He had charts. Dates. Times, even, when he dared, of certain events occurring.

As the third of four heirs, with hearty and hale siblings, he knew that chances of him inheriting were slim. He was going to have to make a place for himself elsewhere.

The king's invitation suited him to a tee.

How many of the numerous predictions were real? How many of them were fortuitous? Did the fickle Twins help his position along? Or was it the court magician who gave those extra twists when needed?

No one can really say. He was right often enough, though, to inspire King Alfa Regina to commit to The Plan of taking over the world. To believe They were responsible for this wave of power emanating from the west, flowing over the land and uniting it under a single rule.

So the kings committed, and followed The Prophecy and The Plan and everything fell into line neatly.

Except for that annoying dragon Talon.

TALON

To be honest, Talon had given the idea of the eventual war with King Alfa a lot of thought. How he would organize his people, how they would get slaughtered. How he'd lose his daughter, his home, his life.

All right, so maybe he'd given it a lot more *worry* than strategic planning.

He'd also hoped that the war was many, *many* more years in the future, after Orla had found a husband. In his best-case scenario, she'd be so heavily pregnant that she wouldn't be able to insist on coming with him.

However, Talon's dreams weren't known for coming true.

So now, he rode ignobly on the flat back of an over-sized cart. It had been specially built for him over the past week. Though he didn't physically use his wings to fly, flying for hours and days at a time still would have left him tired.

Besides, he needed to stick close. Meet with his "generals," though most of them didn't have any actual military experience. They were mainly composed of mercenaries (like Kato, one of the few whom he had a good opinion of), a couple of merchants with large houses who were actually excellent at logistics, as well as a few armchair warriors who'd never held a sword before, let alone led people into battle.

Talon was well aware that chances were, he and his army were marching directly into a trap set by King Alfa and his very well-trained people.

Not only that, he suspected that at least some of the people traveling closest to him were spies, set on double-crossing him at the least opportune moment. Or the most opportune, depending on how you looked at it.

Talon intended on double-crossing them first.

Which was why he'd actually been the one to suggest that Brennan, that *boy wizard* as Talon tended to call him, accompany them on the cart.

Orla, needless to say, had been shocked.

What, do you actually like *him, Da?* she'd asked, glaring at him suspiciously.

It was a week before their company would depart Talon's territory. They were resting in a field outside of the southernmost large town there. While Talon had suggested to Orla that she find a nice inn in the nearby town to stay in, and that he'd pick her up in the morning, she'd scoffed and had insisted on finding them a nice farmhouse instead.

Due to the increase of wizards patrolling the hedge, many had built extra guestrooms, and Orla had decided to take advantage of one of those.

The farmhouse in question sat in the distance—a large building, painted white, with a cute little stone cottage standing beside it. Some wizard had reinforced the walls, so the cottage was warm and cozy and no cool drafts snuck through any cracks. It came with a large stone hearth, a huge bed topped with a down-filled mattress, as well as indoor facilities. It was sheer heaven as far as Orla was concerned, as she'd figured she'd be sleeping on the ground almost every night after this.

I don't mind the boy, Talon groused. *I'd prefer a wizard who had more offensive spells. But he's a good healer. I want someone able to take care of you if you get hurt.*

Da, Orla said, rolling her eyes. *I don't need my own personal healer.*

Talon didn't reply, though it was obvious that he thought she was wrong, that she did, indeed, need not only her own healer but her own personal bodyguard.

However, Talon didn't trust any of the other wizards. He only had to look at his elongated snout to remember what wizards could do.

Orla hadn't objected too strenuously to Brennan traveling with them. That part of Talon's plan had gone well.

And Talon had tried to keep his growls and grumbles to himself as the pair of young people chatted easily, amiably even, throughout the first day.

It wasn't until later that evening, after Orla had fallen asleep, that he'd talked to the boy.

Brennan, Talon said, his thoughts directly only at the wizard.

As Talon had suspected, the boy hadn't fallen asleep yet. He was too keyed up from the travel, the talk, the upcoming battles, everything.

Orla, of course, was much more practical. She'd fallen asleep immediately.

"Sir?" Brennan had replied quietly as he'd sat up on his bed roll.

Direct your thoughts at me, Talon directed the wizard. Not everyone could communicate silently with Talon. People who used magic regularly tended to be able to—he suspected it was the discipline required for their practice. Kato and some of the other mercenaries could as well. Again, discipline.

Can you hear me? Brennan said tentatively, as if afraid that he might end up shouting inside of Talon's head.

I can, Talon said. *You know I have a use for you, right?*

Beyond healing Orla?

Boy was quick. Talon would have to give him that.

Aye.

Talon looked around. The army was camped all around them, quiet campfires banked. Not only had more people joined him than he'd expected, more kept marching up. It was as if every free hand from his territory had decided to join them.

Odd.

What are the chances that we are walking directly into a trap? Talon asked.

Brennan paused. Talon could tell he was considering lying. Before he could warn against it, Brennan responded.

Better than fifty-fifty.

And what are the chances that some of the stalwarts surrounding us are actually spies? Planted by good King Alfa to capture me when I least expect it?

Brennan snorted. *Also better than fifty-fifty.*

Talon kept his sigh to himself. There had been a part of him that had hoped he was wrong, was just being a cynical old curmudgeon.

That Brennan had agreed with him so quickly meant that Talon was potentially seeing the situation as it actually stood, and not just his fears talking.

I propose that we circumnavigate those assholes.

How? Brennan asked, instantly suspicious.

You're going to betray me, trick me, then take me to King Alfa yourself, Talon said.

Why would I do that? Brennan asked, alarmed.

Talon didn't bother hiding his amused snort. *Money. Power. Potential immortality. That's what they're promising anyone who brings me in. Alive.*

What happens after we reach King Alfa's court? Brennan said.

We double-cross them, Talon assured him. *You will free me, once I've been brought before the king. And I will do the rest.*

That doesn't sound like much of a plan, Brennan said, shaking his head.

We'll develop more of it on the road. But trust me. It's better—so much better—if you turn against me, rather than someone I can't trust.

You trust me? Brennan asked surprised.

Talon rolled his eyes, glad of the darkness so the kid couldn't see. *I know you have nothing but good intentions toward Orla.*

"Oh, I do, Sir, I do!" Brennan said, forgetting himself and speaking out loud , then flinching at the noise.

They both looked over to where Orla was stretched out. Still asleep. Good.

But you can't tell her about it, Talon warned. *Not one word.*

But—

The double-cross has to look real. Not just to the casual bystanders, but to her, especially to her. Otherwise, the goons in King Alfa's employ won't believe it's real.

Oh. Brennan sighed, looking down at his feet. He shivered and slumped further.

Talon held his tongue, letting Brennan come to his own conclusions. This decision couldn't be forced. He had the rest of the night to convince the youngster that this was in everyone's best interest. Maybe one or two nights after that as well, but not as many as three.

And he doubted it was his paranoia that was telling him that.

You'll be saving so many lives by doing this. So much bloodshed, Talon said softly. *Their main objective is to capture me. Once they have that, the rest of the war won't matter. The people can go home.*

Brennan nodded absently. *There will still be a fight. They won't just give you up lightly.*

Talon sighed. He'd been used to his people not doing anything. That they were all suddenly *involved* was a new thing.

Then you'll just have to spirit me away, keep me away from the troops.

And how am I supposed to do that? Brennan asked, sounding perplexed.

I don't know. You're the one who's supposed to turn me in to the opposing army for a grand reward.

Wait. So you want me to approach the other side?

Of course! I don't expect you to do this all on your own. They'll never fully trust you, he warned. *They just need to trust you enough.*

"I see," Brennan said softly.

He was quiet for so long that Talon felt the stars shift above them.

Will you do it? Talon finally asked.

Aye, I will.

Though Brennan didn't sigh, Talon still felt the weight those words bore.

He supposed he had just placed a rather large burden on the boy's shoulders.

Hopefully the boy would prove man enough to be able to bear it.

I need one promise from you, Brennan said suddenly. *That when this is all over, if Orla survives, that you will tell her the truth. Everything. Particularly if I don't make it.*

I promise I will tell her everything, Talon said, knowing that Brennan would hear the truth of his words, despite the fact that he had many, *many* doubts about making it out alive.

Particularly if stopping this war was somehow being twisted by the Twins to be *Talon's* fate.

All other dragons had come into being with a purpose.

Was this his?

It didn't feel like it. Didn't feel personal enough.

Time would tell.

I'M NOT AS THINK AS YOU DRUNK I AM

Though Eomar is generally credited with bringing alcohol and other spirited beverages to the world, it was actually Eowin who did it. (She was always the practical one, who would see a need then do the necessary work to fix whatever was wrong. Often while shaking her head and perhaps muttering about the uselessness of men.)

It started easily enough with fruit left too long on the vines, and observing the odd behavior of the birds who pecked at such fruit.

It took a bit of experimentation. (Not too many deaths. No, really.) Finally people figured out how to "rot" the fruit without really rotting it, to turn it into a beverage that at first tasted like fruit that had gone off to becoming a drink that was actually palatable.

When grain came into the picture, that was a whole additional step forward on the inebriation scale. Instead of using fruit, which was harder to grow and therefore much more expensive, you could make booze from grains, which grew in abundance.

There are many types of alcohol in the world, though all of it has the same purpose, namely, to elevate one's spirit and possibly alter one's mind. (Mushrooms are still much better for that, particularly when it comes to casting magic. However, while they're relatively easy to find or grow, processing them is so very complicated. Get just one step wrong, like drying them with too cool a temperature, so they form even the slightest bit of hidden mold, and your customers end up dead. Experienced practitioners learn to never trust a new grower.)

Magic can't really create food or beverages out of nothing. You need a base, something to start with, that your local wizard can then transform into something else.

However, those spells are tricky, both to cast as well as to maintain. You do *not* want to give a haunch of lamb that's gone off to your local spell caster to fix, so that the meat is tender and good again, just to have the spell die mid-meal and your stomach is now full of rotten food.

So people primarily eat and drink the old fashioned way, using local ingredients.

Scrumpy is a favorite in certain parts, as it's relatively easy and uses whatever fruit is left on the tree. It's left rough and only tastes of apples because the brewer back-sweetens the batch. Just a cup can also knock a grown man on his ass.

Talon, unfortunately, didn't really get inebriated, no matter if he drank an entire barrel of scrumpy, which he only tried once. It didn't taste that good, and all he got was a slight tingling in his fingers.

While grapes can be used for wine, so can pretty much any fruit that's currently in abundance: berries, figs, plums, pears, and so on. It gets the appellation "fruit wine" and it's best not to make any further inquiries after that.

While some insist on "pure" beverages, made with a single fruit like "peary," most just aren't that fussy.

Someone as rich as King Alfa may have a specialty beverage, designed just for the King and their court.

They will have their magic user take a rather bland wine that's just composed of grapes, then modify it to be utterly delicious and delightful.

The local winemakers then have the rest of the season to match the creation, or at least come as close to it as they can.

It's as good of an excuse as any to get drunk and have wild orgies.

Because why do people drink?

To forget. To lose their inhibitions.

And to find their courage, as many in Talon's army were currently imbibing.

Including one wizardling in particular.

BRENNAN

Brennan didn't like the solution that Talon had come up with. Not just the whole "betraying" Talon, even just in pretend.

But that it was *Brennan* who needed to pretend to turn Talon in.

He also didn't have a better plan.

Like Talon, he was suspicious of some of the people who walked near the cart. They either wouldn't meet Brennan's eye, which he put down to not everyone being comfortable around wizards. Many of the people in Talon's territory didn't like spell casters, particularly since Talon didn't.

Though how would they know he was a wizard, since he didn't bother with the robes?

Then there were the other people who were *too* interested, too friendly. They wanted to know all about Brennan, what his capacity was, how long was his range, what type of magic he did, and so on.

Jude had been one of the latter. Brennan didn't trust the man, didn't trust his shifty eyes, the way he carried his staff (as if always looking for an opportunity to trip someone), how he hunched in on himself, as if the war had already started.

He also claimed to be a poor farmhand, but his clothes were

nearly as good as some of the merchants and shopkeepers who traveled with them. In particular, his boots were solid leather and well-cared for, something that seemed beyond the inept Jude.

Brennan would assume that Jude was a spy.

Now, if Brennan had some time, he'd make the effort to befriend Jude. Bring him into his confidence. Learn what he could about the man before making his case that the dragon needed to be turned in so this whole war could be ended *now*, before everyone died.

Time was the one thing Brennan didn't have. Like Talon, he believed that it was only a matter of days before King Alfa turned up the heat and attacked without warning.

There would be no grand meeting in the field of battle. No chance for victory. They'd all be slaughtered, and then Talon would be led away in chains anyway.

Better that they take the matter into their own hands.

Plus, if Brennan was a free agent, he could claim a spot in the room when Talon was brought in. He'd have to make himself useful, not just in the capturing of Talon, but in the continued subdual of the beast.

And yes, he'd have to use that language. To call Talon horrible things, so that King Alfa and his minions would trust Brennan.

He was smart enough to know that they'd never completely trust him. Only a stupid person trusted a traitor. Or a desperate one. However, he had to get them to trust him at least some.

So Brennan took the fastest route he knew to opening men's mouths and revealing their true hearts: booze.

In particular, a bottle of scrumpy that his father had gifted him with the last time Brennan had visited his family.

This was no ordinary scrumpy. Sure, it actually tasted like apples due to the back-sweetening. And it was vaguely carbonated from the fermentation.

No matter how tasty it might be when it first hit your tongue, it felt like a fireball rolling down your throat, then igniting somewhere in the vicinity of your navel, taking your brain out with the resulting explosion. You might remember your next drink. Or your next memory may be of waking up with your pants on backwards while sleeping tucked in all the way under your bed with chalk drawings covering your entire body. Not that Brennan had ever had that happen to him. At least not more than once.

This particular scrumpy was a favorite of the god Num. Papa had told Brennan that the god had blessed this bottle before he'd insisted that Brennan take it.

Brennan believed Papa that the god Num had been involved somewhere along the line. There was the slightest hint of magic running along the sides of the glass. In the right light, it practically shone.

First, though, Brennan cast a spell on himself so that he wouldn't get as drunk as those he was drinking with. That spell had been handy when he'd been at school, because it meant he could go out with his friends and have a good time, but still be able to get to classes the next day.

Then he took the bottle, apologizing to Num as he splashed some of the contents on himself, as if he'd spilled the contents of a glass all over his clothes.

Jude was in his tent already by that time of night.

Again, how did a lowly farmhand afford his own well-oiled tent? It was low to the ground, just room enough for a man to crawl in and sleep. Still, most of the people traveling with them slept rough, on the ground.

Brennan crawled right into the tent with a magelight glowing over his head.

Jude woke with a start, his eyes wide and scared.

"What are you doing in my tent?" Brennan asked as he sat up, aiming to keep his tone somewhere between confused and belligerent.

"Sir! This—this is my tent. Sir," Jude said. He gestured to the side. "That's my bag, my staff, and those are my boots."

"Eh. Really?" Brennan said. He blinked at the man as he rolled to the side, landing heavily on his elbow in order to look at the man's boots.

"They look too good for the likes of you," Brennan said. "Oops. Sorry. Didn't mean that."

Jude gave him a tight smile.

"My employer gave me those. And everything else, when he sent me off to war. If I make it back, I'll have my own cottage," the man said defensively.

Brennan merely nodded. "But what if you're killed?"

Jude just shrugged. "Better me than the farmer's son."

"Wait, so the farmer's son is supposed to be here?" Brennan said. "Are these his boots?"

Jude's mouth formed a hard line. "No, *I'm* supposed to be here. Not him. That was the whole point."

"Does the farmer know your agreement?" Brennan asked. He was afraid he was sounding too shrewd for as inebriated as he supposedly was, so he followed up with a swig of his scrumpy, managing to spill more than what went in his mouth, before thrusting the bottle toward Jude.

"Here's to you and your fine tent. This isn't my tent, is it?" Brennan added, looking around owlishly.

"No, it isn't," Jude said. He took a cautious sip from the bottle, his eyes practically crossing. "Wow. That's, ah," he cleared his throat before he continued, "that's really something."

Brennan grinned at him as if Jude was now his best buddy *evah*. "Blessed by the god Num," he said solemnly. Then he leaned forward, lowering his voice. "Them gods sure know how to party."

Jude nodded. "Harvest festival out on the farm is something else, let me tell you. No one questions who your father is when you're Harvest born."

Brennan nodded as if he understood. He just barely grasped the concept, as his family had been loggers and woodsmiths, not farmers.

"Are you? Harvest born?" Brennan said. Though he knew the question was inappropriate, he also knew it was in character for a drunk to ask such a question.

That got him a sly look. "Aye. Which is why it's right for me to be here. Instead of someone who may or may not be my half-brother."

"Ah. I see," Brennan said. And he did.

Jude wasn't what he appeared, that was, a rich farmer's son.

Nope. He was a farmhand dressed like one.

And chances were, he knew nothing about the enemy and was completely loyal to Talon.

Brennan sighed, letting the disappointment of his soul shine through. He'd been so certain that Jude would be the one he could approach.

Now, he had to go find someone else. And make a fool of himself again. More of a fool.

"Well, keep up the good work, soldier," Brennan said, giving the man a clumsy salute.

"I know it's not my place, but why are you drinking so heavily?" Jude asked as he handed back the bottle after taking a second, very small sip.

"We're all going to die," Brennan said solemnly. "Unless I do something to fix it."

"Don't you think that the Twins or Ulthir or someone will step in soon?" Jude said plaintively.

Brennan had already turned around and was about to crawl back out of the tent. He turned his head and looked over his shoulder at the other man.

"Not soon enough."

SPY VERSUS SPY

Being a spy in a land of magic isn't necessarily the easiest job in the world.

Sure, you might be a magic user as well as a spy, and able to deflect attention away from youself, get people to not notice you, perhaps even turn yourself invisible. Perhaps you craft a spell that allows you to listen to a meeting from three rooms away. Or maybe you can influence others, get them to bend to your will.

(You're not flying around with a jetpack on your back dropping bombs on your enemies. And you do *not* have an enemy who wears the opposite colors to yours doing the same.)

However, there are all those pesky *other* wizards and such. Who have come up with good defenses for your spells, such as encasing important meetings behind a shield so that no one can spy on them. Or who regularly look for invisible people (or assassins), as well as magical influence on others.

This means spying is generally done the old-fashioned way, by embedding a double-agent deep in your opponent's organization.

There are always problems with that as well. Your agent may

decide that they like the new gig so much they don't want to go back. They may double-cross you.

So of course you put in spies to watch your spies. And then more spies to watch them.

It's a difficult, expensive, thankless task.

The various King Alfas have had various spy masters over the years. Some were more successful than others. Lady Abernathy, for example, who was the one who'd originally came up with the whisper campaign blaming Talon for everything. (Though that might be in the process of backfiring. Time will tell.)

Then there's Lord Flemming, who convinced one of the neighboring kingdoms to surrender without King Alfa having to commit any troops. That was a masterpiece of misdirection, fake spy reports sent to the other kingdom, falsifying battle accounts, men injuring themselves to give realistic battle wounds, and so on.

Loalmane was the one who finally pointed out to King Alfa that Talon had never sent any spies. He'd also never tried to subvert anyone in their court, at least as far as anyone could tell. The royals regularly passed any and all loyalty tests.

It wasn't because Talon was stupid. Far from it. He just didn't see the point.

He knew what was coming. War was inevitable. Any "inside knowledge" from the court wouldn't help him in the least.

He may, perhaps, have considered sending a wizard or two to the coast to see what they could pick up.

However, Talon could never bring himself to trust a wizard enough with that sort of mission. And he had no way of verifying if any report was the truth. While Talon's method of communication guaranteed no lies, that wasn't necessarily the case the other way around.

But Loalmane (and the various King Alfas) were certain that the dragon *must* be spying on them.

The only explanation they could come up with was that he was reading their minds from far away.

That wasn't how it worked. Not in the least. Talon could only read thoughts that were clear, as well as distinctly directed *at* him. Plus, his range was limited, about what you could hear from someone shouting across a meadow.

However, Loalmane never figured that out. So he spent *years* perfecting devices sure to protect against any mindreading.

The hats were made out of a thin, shiny material derived from tin and made into sheets. They were distinctly uncomfortable, capturing all body heat, and likely to leave the wearer sweating profusely.

Did they work?

They appeared to. And Loalmane gave everyone reassurances that they did.

He may, *perhaps*, have found it amusing to watch the royals wearing their tinfoil hats and sweating whenever they had an important meeting.

If Talon *had* had any spies, he would have known to watch those closest to him who were sweating the most.

Brennan didn't know that either.

However, he did have one advantage over most people.

As he staggered from Jude's tent, unsure where to go next, he turned abruptly from his own tent outward, toward one of the larger ones on the side.

Why did he turn that way? Were the Twins finally getting involved? Was it luck? Or was it part of a dragon's fate?

Whatever.

Brennan knew that no wizards had been allowed close to Talon or the wagon, not while they walked, and certainly not when they set up camp.

Yet, someone was casting magic. Powerful magic. In that large tent. Right over there.

Brennan decided that was his next best bet, so he staggered over that way.

BRENNAN

Brennan could never say what attracted him to the tent doing magic, how he'd managed to see it.

His head was a muddle from the scrumpy. Sure, he'd bespelled himself so the effects wouldn't be *as* bad. That didn't mean he wasn't feeling anything.

Plus, his first sure-fire bet hadn't turned out. At all.

Yet, there was that tent. It practically *glowed* with magic.

Not with the purple lights that came from the gods and their blessings, but a cool blue light. Brennan's own magic was more green colored, though a lot of the defensive spells he'd learned were more red in nature.

Blue was for water. For making things smooth.

Could it also be used for communication?

Brennan didn't know, but that was the definite feeling he got.

Fortunately, the tent wasn't warded in any way. That would have been calling too much attention to it, he suspected.

It was a larger tent, made for four people, with poles so that you could actually *stand up* instead of always having to crawl in and out.

The oiled canvas was thick enough that though there were lights inside, Brennan couldn't even make out shadows.

His skin buzzed with magic as he drew closer. Was the magic really powerful? He had to stop and think for a moment.

Huh.

The scrumpy appeared to be enhancing his own natural magical abilities.

Strange. That had never happened to him before.

He'd have to remember to think about it later. (Fair warning: he forgot all about it.)

Could he just go stumbling into that tent? That didn't seem like a good idea, as he was likely to get blasted with a face full of magic if he did.

No, he had to draw them out. Get them to invite him in.

Though he knew better, he took another sip from the scrumpy, then staggered over to the door flap of the tent. (The staggering may or may not have been real, given the amount of alcohol now replacing his blood stream.)

"Yoo hoo!" Brennan called. He tried to keep his voice somewhat low, though he was also aware that he wasn't necessarily succeeding.

Just like someone kinda drunk. Which he might have been. Just a little.

That last hit had really sent him over the edge.

"Anyone there?" Brennan called again. "I know you're in there." He lowered his voice. "And you're doing *magic*. I can tell these things. I'm a wizard."

The physical lights in the tent suddenly went out. The magical ones greatly increased.

"Oooooh, pretty!" Brennan said. "It's all blue and swirling. What is it?" He may, perhaps, have let his voice get a lot louder just then.

The tent flap opened. An older man glared out at him. He glanced around, making sure that Brennan was alone, and that no one was actually paying any attention to them.

"Get in here," he ordered.

Brennan happily obliged. "Want some?" he said, offering the man his half-empty bottle of scrumpy.

The man sniffed suspiciously at the bottle while Brennan looked around the tent, not hiding his curiosity.

Strange. He would have sworn there were other people in here, but only the one grumpy mage stood near the door. There was only a single cot and a small bag sitting next to it. Something shiny lay on the top of the cot—was that a hat? Brennan hadn't seen anything like that before, but he didn't go further into the tent.

"Where are your robes?" Brennan asked as he turned to study the man.

He was probably in his fifties, though he hadn't had the easiest life, not based on the number of wrinkles and craigs spread across his white face. The top of his head was bald, though short black and gray hairs hung on along the edges, as if threatening to make a comeback. Dark eyes sucked at Brennan, as if trying to discern all his secrets. His nose was large and hooked, giving him even more of a dubious character. He was cleanshaven, or had been a couple of days ago, as now black and gray stubble covered his jaw. He was dressed like Brennan and many of the merchants accompanying Talon, wearing strong boots, thick wool trousers, a linen shirt and a fancy, brocade vest.

However, he was no merchant. Brennan was betting his life on that. The man had scars on his gnarled hands, across the knuckles. Brennan now saw some of the scars on the man's face, tucked in among the wrinkles.

A fighting mage? It was possible. Orla had mentioned that a few of the wizards who'd come recently had been able to fight with a sword as well.

"Where are your robes?" the man asked.

Ah. So he could tell Brennan was a mage.

Brennan just smiled at him and shrugged. "Don't like 'em."

The man gazed curiously at Brennan, before he nodded and took a cautious sip of the scrumpy.

"Whoa," he said. "Strong spirits."

"We need them, tonight," Brennan said seriously. "Drink up."

The man nodded to himself, sighed, then took a larger swallow of the alcohol.

He ended up coughing as the fire went down his throat, his eyes watering.

"My name's Brennan," he said guilelessly, introducing himself as he pulled the bottle away from the other man's hands, before he dropped it, taking the smallest of sips himself.

"Concha," he said in return, shaking his head.

Brennan tried not to make too much of the man's name, though it was *such* a west coast name. "What were you doing before?" Brennan asked, still trying to sound more innocent than he felt.

"You know. Praying to the gods. Trying to get more protection. The sort of thing you do before you march into a hopeless battle," Concha replied.

Brennan let his eyes grow wide. "I know!" He took the smallest sip of the scrumpy and handed the bottle back to Concha. "It's all useless, though. We're all doomed to die."

"You don't think Talon's army can win the war?" Concha said.

"Army. Yeah. Right. Those farmers and merchants and such? Not a chance. If only Talon wasn't being so selfish!" Brennan said.

He realized his voice had grown louder of its own volition.

"Shhh," Concha said. He glanced around, but then he gestured for Brennan to continue.

"I mean, we all know that all that King Alfa wants is Talon, right?" Brennan said. "I go to the wizards' school in Millerstown. I've lost friends to those brigands."

That much was true. Brennan paused for a moment, letting the sadness take him.

"If Talon turned himself in, this war would stop in an instant. All those people out there would be safe. They wouldn't all have to die," Brennan insisted.

"Don't you ride on Talon's cart?" Concha said, suspicion flaring in his dark eyes.

"I ride on the cart with *Orla*. Who Talon is selfishly keeping to himself," Brennan said darkly.

It was the best excuse that he could come up with. If Talon was gone, then he'd have a chance with Orla. Pretty much anyone could see that as a motivation.

Like any lie, simplicity was a major component.

"I see," Concha said. There may have been a hint of a condoning smile lurking on his face, making the wrinkles multiply. "But how would you convince the dragon to go?"

"You can't," Brennan said bleakly. "Not without a lot of people dying." He sighed loudly, then made a show of looking around the tent, as if checking to see that no one else was listening. "There is a way, though, to trick the beast." He nodded, contentedly, to himself.

"Really?" Concha said. "You know that those disgusting brigands have been trying to trick or trap him for close to two decades now."

"*They* don't know his daughter," Brennan said smugly. "Or her worries."

"I see," Concha said. "So how would you do it?"

And Brennan told him the plan he'd come up with.

Concha had a few quibbles, but on the whole, agreed that it might be the best and easiest way to trap a dragon.

Because what did Talon love? Besides Orla?

Gold.

THE DIVINE IN ME GREETS THE DIVINE IN YOU (NAMESTE?)

All the people in Ulthir's world have a fleck, a spark, that tiniest bit of *light* placed there by Ulthir. Or so the majority of the people believe. (There's still that one group out on those distant islands who believe we should be genuflecting to monkeys instead. Weirdos.)

In any case, since most of the people in Ulthir's world believe that everyone, everywhere, has a touch of the divine in them, they tend to be slightly, *vaguely* less horrible to one another than people generally are.

Sure, it can be argued that *we* (whatever group that individual is involved with) have more of a spark than *them* (whatever group that individual is opposed to). Chances are, the opposition feels the same way in return.

But the divine is *everywhere*. It can be sensed in the trees and brooks. Flowing across fields, snagged up against mountains. Blown by desert winds or pooled in ocean inlets. It can be found in more abundance in the areas surrounding the little local gods and goddesses. Remember, they aren't just magical beings with a smidge more magical juice. They also have that spark of the divine, placed there directly by Eomar.

So what about Maloneal? Is he divine?

When Eowin woke him from his icy casket, and the light fully shone on him, did that imbue him with the tiniest spark of the divine?

Or is Maloneal a true child of the stars, his life maintained by a different force?

Of course, the tales vary, depending on the teller as well as the audience.

In terms of the hierarchy of the divine world, Ulthir sits on top. Just beneath him are Eowin and Eomar. The Twins are either up on their level, or one half step below. Then the local gods and goddesses of the world, followed by the people.

Where does Maloneal fit in that structure?

He puts himself up on Ulthir's level. He considers himself just as capable as the brooding idiot to sit on his great throne and look down on the world, entertained by the little people below.

Seriously. What else does that fool do? Even one of those monkeys could do *that* job.

Ulthir, in reply, would say that he'd done his great works, creating the world and all the people below. (Though he hadn't done most of that—Eowin should get most of the credit, though she rarely insists on taking it.)

Ulthir *also* looks out for people. Kinda. Sort of. If he ever bothers to pay attention to the little local gods and goddesses who sometimes plead a person's case with him. He isn't some sort of *help desk*, though, answering prayers and requests. People find their own way. He's provided them with everything they need.

Besides, they all lead such short lives. It isn't as if they have time to really screw anything up.

Where does Ulthir think Maloneal fits?

He doesn't agree that Maloneal is his equal in any way, shape, or form.

But he does think of Maloneal as family. A distant cousin, perhaps, who is always getting into trouble.

Does Ulthir's belief in Maloneal give him that spark of divinity? Make him a god, though with a little "g"?

Time will tell.

ORLA

Orla didn't understand why Brennan was so stupidly moody that morning. Or why he'd spent a *second* night not in his tent, but out doing "wizardly things," or so he said.

At least that morning he didn't smell like a distillery. Unlike the first.

And when she tried to talk with Da about it, all he said was that different people climb into different cabinets, whatever *that* meant.

Everyone around her handled the stress of walking into battle differently, that much she'd agree. Kato had grown cold and distant. It wasn't as if he was that warm to start with, but he calculated angles and odds all the time now. Fights had broken out among the merchants, something stupid about proving their worth both in terms of money as well as fighting.

No one thought that this war was a good idea. That was the biggest problem. It was all so *unfair*.

And unnecessary. If only King Alfa wasn't being so selfish!

Midmorning, the front of the long column of people walking across the land slowed. No one knew what was happening up front.

Talon stirred himself from the cart. *I'll just pop up and see what the issue is.*

No, Orla told him sternly. *That's what they want you to do. To isolate you.*

I'll be fine, Talon assured her.

He paused for a moment.

Wait, was he talking with Brennan directly?

Cool!

Talon had been using Brennan as his liaison with the wizards' school, sending him off with messages to the elders there so that Talon didn't have to talk with them himself.

But he'd always used his words before that morning.

It was awesome that he was talking with Brennan directly, particularly as he continued to not use his name but to refer to him either as, "the boy" or "that wizardling."

Brennan nodded and glanced at Orla, then jerked his head forward, the direction where the rest of the wizards were traveling. "I need to go talk with them. Again." He rolled his eyes at the uselessness of the communication.

Orla merely nodded. "I'll be here," she said. Still at the back of the army.

She was suspicious that Da had placed her there on purpose, as if trying to keep her safe.

It didn't matter. When the fighting came, she'd be on his back. For better or for worse.

Da took off, throwing himself at the sky.

She got a huge sense of relief from him. She couldn't help but nod sympathetically. Da was *tired* of riding in a cart, and really wanted to fly some more.

Brennan also quickly disappeared, and Orla was left with her thoughts.

The upcoming battle didn't fill her with as much dread as her traveling companions. Then again, she'd been fighting by Da's side for years now.

Would they all die? She honestly didn't think so. Surely before the battle began, the Twins would turn their way.

Wouldn't they?

Orla passed a few moments of conversation with Jude, a poor farmhand who'd come in place of the farmer's son. He'd described Brennan as a "great drinking companion" and had hinted more than once that he wouldn't mind sharing more of that fine scrumpy of his.

Time passed, but the great stretch of people in front of Orla didn't move.

She tried to reach Da, but he was out of range.

Wait.

Da had just taken off again. He'd landed for a while, probably talking with whoever was up there.

Why was he going away from her, instead of *sensibly* flying back her direction, toward the cart?

He should *not* be heading straight toward the opposing army.

Particularly without her.

"Clear out! Clear the way!" Orla called out to those people in front of her.

A few moved. But most still stayed where they were, chatting with their neighbors.

Orla ground her teeth in frustration. The ox cart was huge, and she'd never get through that crowd with it.

At least, not quickly.

With a sigh, she slipped off the cart, grabbing her weapons as they were right there. (And she may have, perhaps, practiced that move more than once after the cart had been built. Getting on and off the cart quickly in one smooth easy motion. Just as she'd practiced getting on and off Da's back.)

Fortunately, she lived in the larger pieces of her armor—a breastplate made especially for her, leather pants, and heavy boots—

at least during the day. She had gauntlets and her helmet in her bag, which she slipped on quickly.

Suddenly, one of the oxen dropped to its knees.

Orla didn't see any blood, but she suspected that magic had been involved. Particularly given the way the cart now sparked with electricity.

Crap.

Someone *was* attacking. And they'd targeted her.

Where was Brennan? Where was Da?

Orla ducked her head and raced sideways, not going in the direction expected of her. That would be the surest way to run into someone's blade, she was certain.

She heard screams behind her as others were struck down. The mass and chaos would play to her favor, at least for now.

There were traitors in their midst.

Da was in trouble.

Only Orla could save him. She was the only one he could trust.

She darted around folks, some of whom had sat down and started eating a picnic lunch. She didn't spread any kind of warning to them, or shout at them that they were in danger.

Either they'd see her and figure it out, or they'd find out soon enough.

After running a while, she risked slowing down enough to look back.

No one appeared to be following her, at least as far as she could tell with the masses of people around her.

She'd never had that final growth spurt, so she couldn't see over pretty much anyone's head.

All she had was a growing sense of terror in her gut that something was *wrong*.

Where was Da?

Even with all the running drills that Kato made Orla do, it still took her longer than she wanted to get to the front of the large army.

And she was more winded than she'd like to admit. Though she frequently ran in full armor, the terror she felt sapped at her strength.

She could finally see Da in the distance, circling some ways away.

Then he dove in for a strafing run.

Go Da! I'm on my way! Orla called, though she doubted that he could hear her.

There was someone riding away from the front line of their army, toward the enemy army which was just visible on the horizon. No, two people.

Were they on a *horse*?

Orla blanched when she saw the figure glance back.

That was Brennan.

She was certain of it.

How had he gotten to the front of the line ahead of her? He *had* had a good head start, but still.

As the horse raced away, Orla saw another group running toward them.

The warriors of King Alfa, who they'd all feared.

Crap.

Da was off in the distance, fighting someone.

Surely it was a trap.

Brennan had betrayed them all.

Now, Orla was here, having to guide the troops, all on her own.

Maybe Da was right to never trust a wizard.

ON FIGHTING DRAGONS

The proper defense for fighting any dragon has always depended on the type of dragon that you're facing.

For example, take the wizard Soliki's dragon, who was born in the ice caves where she'd buried the frozen dreams of her people. That dragon (who'd taken the name Akiki) could not only breathe out terrible cones of icy breath that froze people, she could also send great gouts of lightning at enemies.

Mirrors work incredibly well for those sorts of attacks, deflecting the icy breath as well as sending the bolts directly back at the caster. (It doesn't work with all lightning, otherwise Orla would have learned to carry a mirror with her.) Plus, having an entrenched stronghold makes it more difficult for a dragon to get at you.

Soliki was able to defeat her enemy (and it wasn't just some dude, but an entire kingdom's army, pretty much single-handedly, as the rest of her people were dead) not just by having a dragon at her side, but by being clever.

The strafing run of a dragon is a horrible, destructive thing, even if you are well prepared for it. And even fireballs and acid won't do much against an ice dragon.

However, if all your defenses are directed *up*, you're not watching the base of your stronghold.

Nor are you prepared for a dragon to act as a battering ram on some of her strafing runs.

It was luck that Soliki was able to get to the idiot king on the first try. (Or perhaps the Twins helped.)

Chopping off the head of the enemy did a lot to get them to back down. Especially given that his son was much more interested in Soliki than in pursuing a stupid war, and they ruled peacefully for many years. (Yes, it's something of a classic love story, true sworn enemies to lovers, but that's neither here nor there.)

Little Irvine's dragon, Norbert, spewed fire that was terrible to behold. Particularly since toward the end, Norbert not only spouted fire, but fire that had liquid iron ore blended in, that splattered and cause a *lot* more damage.

Ice weapons were effective against Norbert. But like Soliki, he continued to draw the enemy's attention *upward*, causing them to forget that he was an iron dragon, and perfectly capable of fighting in the skies during the day, then taking a couple of hours at night to tunnel closer and closer under their stronghold.

This meant that when Little Irvine wasn't so little, and had raised an army of his own, he was able to storm his enemy's castle *from below* with a great force.

Talon's breath weapon, while nothing to sneeze at, wasn't as, uhm, *robust* as some of the other dragons from history. (Or perhaps their abilities grew as the tales about them spread.)

It's still terrifying to have death falling on you from the sky. Shields only work so well for this sort of thing. A wide range shield won't give enough protection: every individual has to have their own. Otherwise the acid either gets through (something about mass and weight and force) or it hits the ground and because it's *magic*, splashes up against the person's boots and legs.

However, the acid only dribbles out. There aren't great gouts of it, like there are with fire or ice. Talon has never figured out how to send it out in a great spray, with less damage but a wider area.

Fire works best against Talon—he shrugs off lightning and ice. And he's learned to better protect his wings.

His second greatest advantage is flight.

As long as he's in the air, he's relatively safe, and your shields will wear down eventually.

Everyone who's ever fought with a dragon eventually learns that the best way to engage them is to get them onto the ground, then keep them there.

Talon had been fighting brigands and wizards sent from the coast for a long time. He knows better than to land, or even to come close to the ground.

Honest.

TALON

Talon wasn't exactly certain what Brennan had planned with enemy. Brennan told Talon everything he could, but there were things that the enemy had withheld from the wizardling.

How could they trust him? This foolish young wizard who was betraying an old dragon, just so he could have the dragon's daughter?

Quite a lot, it seemed, as Talon glanced back and scented that Brennan was on a horse, drawing near.

That had been part of the bargain that Brennan had struck, that he be able to accompany them to the coast to collect his reward for having turned in the dragon.

Seemed the other side was honoring it.

At least for now.

Then something shiny caught Talon's eye.

He'd been called to the air, challenged by some of the wizards from the coast. They'd managed to somehow augment their minds such that he could hear them in the distance.

They lied to him, of course.

He still took the challenge, roaring as if he were merely some dumb beast.

Had to make whatever it was that Brennan had planned look good.

Still, instead of flying directly toward the encroaching wizards, he found himself circling back.

What was down there?

Was that gold?

He snorted to himself.

Were they really that stupid, to believe that a large pile of gold that was *obviously* boobytrapped in the middle of a clearing would tempt him to land?

It did look awfully shiny, though.

Talon found himself flying closer even though he knew, *knew* it was a trap.

It wasn't that he couldn't stop himself. He could fly away at any time. He didn't *need* more gold.

No, really.

Though Talon couldn't see the magic surrounding the pile, he could smell it. A sickly sweet scent that made him want to collect up all those lovely coins and trinkets and give them a good soak in a nearby lake.

He suddenly swooped back up toward the sky, realizing just how close he'd been getting to the ground.

Damn. That trap was *good*. It was going to distract him. Even if he didn't fall for it and continued on his quest forward. The temptation alone would put him off his game.

Had Brennan come up with this? (He had.)

Surely that wasn't it. (It wasn't.)

Just then, a voice spoke in his head.

Da?

The voice wasn't quite right. It didn't feel exactly Orla. And Talon had spent enough years talking with his adopted daughter to know.

However, it came awfully close.

Go away, you imposter, Talon said as he continued to circle the area with the gold, knowing he shouldn't, knowing he needed to get away.

What do you mean? It's me. Orla, the voice insisted.

Talon had to admit whoever was on the other end was good. Very good.

Like the gold, though, the voice was a trap.

Da, they tricked me. Just like they're tricking you. Don't fall for it. Fly away! Now!

That sounded a touch more like Orla, who only ever wanted to protect him.

Surely that wasn't what his opponents really wanted, was it? For him to fly away?

Maybe he should heed the voice's warning. Fly far from here. Go back and protect his people.

We're already fighting here, the fake Orla said. *The soldiers have started attacking.*

Damn it! Talon had to leave. To go help his people.

However, if the attackers were there, focused on his army, maybe there wouldn't be as many here, to protect the gold?

A young woman came out from the surrounding trees. She'd been hidden from his senses.

She wore Orla's clothing—or rather, something that smelled like her. He'd never be able to see the person's features, as his eyes weren't good for that sort of detail.

There was magic wrapped around her. She walked jerkily, as if being compelled.

Maybe that was why her voice sounded funny. Because she was being forced to talk with him.

Help me, Da! the false Orla in his head cried out.

She went and draped herself over the top of the pile of gold.

Talon sighed and shook his head, trying to wipe the image from his mind.

He couldn't.

Nor could he help himself.

Though that wasn't his daughter, and he knew the gold was false, he still swooped lower.

Maybe he could catch whoever that was up in his amazingly puny arms without stopping.

He never had the chance to find out.

Archers appeared out of nowhere. They'd actually managed to hide their scent as well. He should have realized they would.

Brennan's doing, he was certain.

Arrows pierced his wings, tearing the leather flaps between the bones to shreds.

Then came the fire arrows, an entire barrage of them, blinding Talon as well as making him scream.

He tried to pull up. Fought with the air currents to rise back up to the sky.

The net landed on him before he gained too much height.

This net had weights in it, in addition to all the magic that drained him.

Talon struggled, knowing he didn't have much time before he'd be helpless.

His claws tore at the ropes, only to discover that this time, they weren't plain rope.

Seemed that metal had been woven into the strands. Metal he could have melted, if his snout had been free and he could have dribbled some acid on it.

Talon screamed again. While a part of him was playing for the audience, making sure that his capture looked real, in too many ways, it *was* real.

He was being taken prisoner for the first time. Even if he'd arranged it. Even if he had a spy in the court who could set him free later.

The net hurt a lot. It aggravated the burns on his back, the tatters of his wings, where his tail had been bashed.

With the last of his consciousness fading, the false Orla said, *There. Isn't that better?*

The laughter in his daughter's voice hurt the worst of all.

SHAPING THE FUTURE

One of the overarching characteristics of Maloneal, that everyone can agree on, is that he is malleable. He changes shape and form as best suits the situation.

There aren't any silly requirements on needing to see or touch whoever he changes into before his shift.

No, his greatest strength is that all he needs is an idea of the right person, then he can bend the *viewer's* mind to behold that which they think is true.

For example, if you were told that you were going to meet a tall, dark, handsome male stranger, your mind would provide all the details when you saw Maloneal. You would fill in the hair and eye color, how light or dark his skin was, how tall he seemed. Whereas someone else in the same room—who had a fear of tall, dark, handsome strangers—might see a slim blond instead.

This way, Maloneal stays innocuous, only revealing himself when absolutely necessary. Very few ever witness his silver eyes or white hair.

It had been a serious challenge to imitate Orla, Talon's foster daughter. It was a brilliant scheme, though. He'd have to thank the wizardling traitor who'd come up with it.

Projecting his thoughts at the dragon hadn't been difficult.

However, eyes could be fooled more easily than minds.

Getting the pitch right, the voice and tone, *that* had been a challenge.

The dragon had almost not fallen for it. Not until Maloneal—sorry, Loalmane—had walked out himself.

He didn't even have to look that much like the girl. Having her clothes so that the dragon smelled her was the key.

If only his own stupid wizards who he'd sent time and again to attack the dragon's territory had figured that out! That the beast relied on his nose more than his eyes!

Then they wouldn't have needed such measures, like hauling the entire army halfway across the continent. Loalmane wouldn't have had to accompany them, though he had done what he could to at least make *his* passage more comfortable.

Nothing too much. Nothing that couldn't be explained by being a competent wizard.

Though he knew that some suspected the truth of his being, most had no idea.

Loalmane lay there sunning himself on the pile of false gold while his wizards dealt with the beast, carefully holding onto the ends of the net so that they didn't loosen as another group levitated the creature onto their own flat-bed cart.

The dragon would slumber for most of the trip back to the coast, given the magic embedded in the net. A good deal of his power would be drained off, but that couldn't be helped.

Once the beast had made it to the court and been shown off to the king, Loalmane could get down to the serious business of dismantling the dragon.

He would have to allow the dragon to return to its full strength before he started. However, he would have the beast tamed and cowed by then, so it wouldn't be a danger to him.

And once Loalmane had removed all that luscious, divine power from the dragon, well, then he could start the serious business of challenging Ulthir, once and for all.

BRENNAN

Brennan bit his tongue and looked away.

Reminded himself once again that *he* was the one who'd turned Talon in, after all.

It wouldn't look good for him to cry out, "Stop! Don't hurt him!"

That was all that Brennan wanted to do, though, as he rode along (on a horse!) with the rest of King Alfa's wizards, back to the castle on the coast. They covered the ground quickly, much faster than Brennan would have expected. Partly that was magic. Partly, though, that was because they'd left much of the army behind. They'd still be a few weeks trailing along.

Brennan had no idea if Orla lived or died, though his *captors* (let's call a spade a spade—Brennan was as trapped as Talon at this point) assured him that the takeover of Talon's lands had been peaceful.

Seemed they'd had more spies mixed in with the mayors, many of whom had sent representatives with the army. They quickly came to terms with the invaders.

Brennan knew that Orla wouldn't agree. She was either dead, or hopefully, trying to arrange something resembling a rescue.

Because they might need to be rescued after they reached the court.

Talon appeared to be in a daze most of the time. He didn't speak to Brennan, or to anyone else, as far as Brennan could tell.

At least Brennan and the others no longer had to wear those stupid, uncomfortable hats made out of some sort of thin, tin sheets. Brennan had been able to convince Loalmane and the others that Talon couldn't randomly read their thoughts. They had to be *directed* at him.

Though maybe he shouldn't have said anything, because if the dragon was no longer a threat, it meant people could be *brave*. Or something.

Soldiers, wizards, or sometimes even Loalmane, approached Talon and poked him with a handy, nearby spear, making him twitch, moan, and try to get away, just to be caught more firmly in the net weighing him down. The really brave would occasionally rip off one of his long black talons, looking for a souvenir, until all the easily accessible ones were gone.

Talon's wings were still in tatters from where he'd been struck. Burns streaked across his back. He must be in agony, but Brennan didn't dare heal him.

He knew the original plan was for Brennan to free Talon once they reached the court, figuring that once he was free, he could wreak his vengeance. Maybe even take out the most recent King Alfa.

Just freeing Talon wasn't going to be enough, though. Not now. He was in too bad a shape to take matters into his own hands. He was going to need a lot of healing before he would even be able to gather up his magic and fly away.

What had Brennan done?

He tried to stay focused on the plan, though. He was here to learn as much as he could about King Alfa, Loalmane, and the wizards from the coast.

As well as what had happened to all the little gods and goddesses in the conquered lands.

Fortunately, Brennan was the one who was probably best suited for the latter task.

He'd always been able to see magic. Señor Alberto had trained that ability, and his three years at school had honed it further.

It only took a little unfocusing of his eyes to detect the magic in the lands they passed through.

As mentioned before, magic didn't flow evenly across everything. It pooled in places, while disdaining others.

No one, not even the intrepid author of the various guides to local gods and goddesses, was able to come up with an overarching theory as to why that happened. (There was a reason, of course. However, it was far beyond the people's ability to figure it out, as it had to do with how Eomar crossed the lands so many centuries ago.)

However, once Brennan started paying attention, he realized that the magic spread across the land was now surprisingly *even*. It felt like a thin blanket stretched across too much bed.

It took him a while to think through the consequences of that. Fortunately, (or perhaps unfortunately) while people kept an eye on him, no one wanted to ride with him, chat, or be friends.

Such even magic meant that instead of unpredictable results, everyone's magic was going to be the same, everywhere. You weren't going to get wild crazy bursts when people came upon a new pocket of power.

It was all to be ordered, now.

The realization chilled Brennan to the bone.

While magic needed discipline, it also needed, nay *demanded*, a certain flexibility of the mind, the ability to imagine not just what was, but what the magic user thought should be.

While such flatness of magic might even out the playing field, in the coming years, all hedge-witches, wizards, and spell casters of various ilks were going to have a smaller creative spark than previous generations. They would have so much less to draw on.

Was this why the brigands had continued to attack the hedge surrounding Talon's territory? They'd lost some of the ability to think creatively? Think differently? Move their thoughts outside of the usual ruts?

Brennan found signs of where the little local gods and goddesses had once resided. They were actually easy to spot. While the rest of the carpet of magic spreading across the land was a mixture of blues, reds, greens, and whites, the sacred groves, foothills, rivers and lakes still held a brilliant flare of purple.

Like the purple of the blessings the god Num had at one time poured over his mother's pregnant belly.

Brennan didn't know what exactly had happened to the little gods and goddesses. Had they been sucked up with the smoothing out of the magic? Dispersed? Perhaps subsumed?

He tried to cautiously ask Concha about them, but either the man didn't know, or the act was considered a great secret that he wasn't about to tell a traitor.

Brennan rode along noodling on all these things when out of the corner of his eye a bright white light approached.

He squeezed his eyes shut tightly, rubbed them, then opened them again.

Loalmane was there, riding beside him.

Brennan had talked with the wizard once, the second night after he'd met Concha. King Alfa's people had infiltrated Talon's camp. (And hadn't Brennan yearned to tell Orla and everyone else how *easy* it was for their defenses to be penetrated!)

(It was just as well that he hadn't, though. Loalmane wasn't a normal wizard, and no one else could travel as he did, or transport people around.)

Brennan nodded his head in hello, though he didn't expect the great wizard to come and talk with him.

He was wrong.

"Hello, Brennan, isn't it?" Loalmane said as he rode up.

He wore robes, of course. That appeared to be the fashion of all the wizards from the coast. (It made Brennan secretly glad that he'd stubbornly stuck to his own fashion sense and still wore shirts and pants, even if he also felt as though he looked dowdy sometimes.) The rest of the wizards were all color-coded, wearing blue, yellows, reds, greens, purples, and so on. Only Loalmane wore dazzling white with sparkling silver trim around the cuffs, collar, and bottom edge. He presented as a tall man, thin, with pale skin that somehow looked good in white, long black hair, and disturbing gray eyes so pale they didn't seem colored at all sometimes.

"Yes, I'm Brennan," he said. "How can I help you, sir?"

"Tell me what you see," Loalmane directed, gesturing around them.

Brennan inwardly shrugged, figuring it was some sort of test. "I see a grove of trees, in the distance, that way. Undulating plane all around us with summer grass starting to poke out between the rocks. Blue sky and—"

"No, not with your physical eye. With your magical senses," the wizard said, peering closely at Brennan.

Brennan sneaked a look at Loalmane, but he appeared to be merely curious and not threatening.

Brennan allowed his eyes to unfocus and he talked about the magical eddies he saw, the evenness of the former pools, even the one or two places where he assumed there had once been a local god or goddess.

When he returned his attention to Loalmane, he stiffened in fear.

The wizard stared at him with malevolence.

"Who taught you to see such things?" Loalmane asked, his voice cold.

"I've always had the ability," Brennan said. "Even when I was a small child and had no idea what I was seeing." He figured it was better to be honest with the wizard than to lie.

Besides, he'd always considered himself a lousy liar. He appeared to have acquired the ability in the last few days, though.

"Hmm," Loalmane said, sounding even more displeased. "What do you see when you look at me?"

Brennan sighed. He really wasn't certain if the truth was better at this point or not.

"Don't lie," Loalmane added. "I will know if you lie."

Brennan bowed his head, took a deep breath, then looked up, allowing his eyes to skim over Loalmane's frame. "I see white light," Brennan admitted. "Blindingly white. It flows strongly from you, flavors all your magic."

This actually seemed to please the wizard. "That's right," Loalmane said after a few moments. "Like starlight." He paused and gave Brennan a meaningful look. "I suppose you already know what that means."

Brennan shrugged. "I have guesses. As do a lot of people." Wasn't Maloneal also called the Star Child?

Loalmane nodded and they rode in silence for a short while.

Abruptly, the wizard leaned over toward Brennan, causing him to jump. "It's true," the wizard whispered, the words so soft Brennan had to lean over to catch them. "I am the Star Child."

With a nod, Loalmane urged his horse ahead, riding up toward the front of the group.

Brennan shivered. Though he'd speculated that Loalmane and Maloneal were the same person, it was an entirely different prospect to know the truth.

He knew that Loalmane wasn't lying. There was something very different about the man. Whenever Brennan looked at him, that brilliant white light shone through. He'd never seen any other person with that sort of intense light.

None of it was ever tinged with purple, though.

And the shadows that wrapped around him were the purest black, like on the cape of an evil wizard.

MAINTAINING AN EMPIRE

While conquering a people may be fun—between planning for the battles, the actual competition, then all the celebrations and victory dances afterward—ruling an empire can be *exhausting*.

Not that all those people you conquered are going to feel sorry for you. Not one little bit.

But if you want to keep your empire, you're going to have to constantly remind those people over there, who are new to your kingdom, that they are, in fact, *part* of your kingdom. They need to obey your laws, follow your rule, and send in all that wonderful tax money.

Having a dragon over there, with a large territory where there are *no taxes,* is just a bad example for everyone in all empires, everywhere. (That wasn't completely accurate. While *Talon* didn't have taxes, some of the bigger cities did. But they were always fair, and there was a certain degree of transparency as to what the money was spent on, because no one wanted a pissed off dragon flying in to take over their treasury. It only happened a couple of times. No one ever did it again after that, or if they did, they managed to hide their extortion better.)

So how to maintain all these disparate glops of land now held together under the title of the Kingdom of Alfaladon?

Statues are a start. Let everyone know your face, so you aren't some force over yonder issuing orders. No, they can *see* you. All taxes are paid directly to your likeness. This was part of The Plan, as put forth by The Prophesy.

Building roads takes more time and resources. However, they convey a lovely message: we might have marched through swamps and over mountains to get to you, now, we've got easy access to you.

It does work both ways. It means that a lot more people find their way to the capital, for better or for worse.

While oxen have been used for millennia, you start curbing some travel by cart as well. And yes, this is according to The Plan.

Your people, of course, use horses. They are controllable with enough of the right kind of magic. (Those spells might all fall apart when a certain court wizard leaves, but that's neither here nor there, at least at this time.)

Everyone else walks. Or at least that's the direction you're headed in. A walking population is a controlled population.

Sure, farmers are going to find it tougher to bring goods to market. It means breaking down bigger cities into smaller ones.

It is *so* much harder to agitate for change if there isn't a place where people can easily gather, except in the capital city, where you can keep an eye on things. If most people are rural, stuck in smaller areas and towns, they'll be less likely to rebel.

A common language is pretty easy—most people in the lands that King Alfaladon take over already speak a variation of the common tongue, though with accents or local peculiarities. The wizard's language is already specific and stable, so it doesn't need any help.

Technically speaking, everyone already has a common god: Ulthir. There are numerous holidays and celebrations involving him, his spinning tops, as well as Eowin and Eomar. All the little local gods and goddesses, well, there might be a celebration or two involving them, but those traditions are easy enough to subvert.

It takes a while for The Plan to mature enough to figure out what to do with all those local deities.

Loalmane, of course, came up with the answer. His solution was elegant and resourceful.

As they conquer a territory, Loalmane and his wizards form a long line and march across the area, tugging and pushing at the surrounding magical pools. The binding spell they all do together evens out those patches where wild magic might incubate, as well as giving other places a well-deserved shot of power.

That does mean pulling at the power of the little local gods and goddesses.

But as Loalmane has already demonstrated, he's perfectly capable of dealing with *them*.

The ones who become friends with the court are allowed to keep their minuscule power bases intact. They are ranked, though, based on their willingness to work with Loalmane and the others.

Those who are more amenable retain more power. The rest don't.

Their power gets spread out evenly across the land, again through spells of Loalmane, so that many of the lesser gods and goddesses just shrink down, diminishing until they are less than ghosts in their own land.

What Loalmane and the others won't tell you, and what Brennan can't see, not really, is that those areas where Brennan thought he saw the remains of a local god or goddess are actually, in fact, the local god or goddess themselves. They've just been reduced to a bit of light in the distance.

And because the magic has been stripped from the land, they cannot reform themselves.

Not without some help.

Their pleas and offered bargains and even angry demands have all been falling flat at the feet of the Twins.

Who might only now be realizing what's been going on, how they've been fooled.

And starting to think about what might they do to fix this mess.

Before Ulthir looks over and figures it out himself.

ORLA

After the first headlong flight of soldiers coming to engage in battle with Talon's army, Orla and the others were able to regroup and push them back.

A little bit.

Then came the next line. And the next line. And the next.

Orla hacked and slashed and fought with honor. With great bravery. As well as with cunning, tricking the soldiers into overcommitting themselves, then circling them, cutting them off from their companions, then cutting them down.

She didn't bother keeping track of the number she killed. It was too many to bear.

All those lives lost. And for what?

It wasn't until Kato rescued Orla a second time that she realized those soldiers didn't want to kill her.

No, *she* was a target to be captured.

It made her even more desperate.

Finally, the number of attackers appeared to dwindle. Instead of the next line coming charging up, a new group appeared, riding up more demurely, on horseback. They had the look of generals, not the regular rabble. They started shouting orders, telling the soldiers who were still fighting to retreat.

It took some time for the troops to disengage. Mostly it was honorably done, without a lot of backstabbing.

"We have captured Talon," the group on horseback announced. They held up one of Talon's claws.

Orla wasn't Da. She couldn't judge the truth of someone's words, as she didn't hear them in her head.

She still believed them.

If Da had been capable of fighting, he would be. She kept calling out to him in her head, but heard nothing in return. Saw no sign of him in the sky.

One of the representatives of the big towns stepped forward, seeking terms. Then another. And another.

Orla ground her teeth, but wisely stayed silent, stepping back further into the crowd.

"Where do you think you're going?" someone growled in her ear, grabbing hold of her elbow.

Orla started, but then relaxed when she realized it was just Kato.

"I'm not surrendering," Orla said softly. "We have to rescue Talon."

She wouldn't let herself think how she'd failed to protect him. If only she'd been there with him, he wouldn't have been captured. Somehow, she would have saved him.

No matter how they'd been betrayed.

Had that been Brennan's plan all along? Had he been a plant, the first time he'd met them? Or had he been corrupted later? Had he *arranged* for that second battle, just so he could be there?

Orla looked up at Kato. He wasn't that much taller than she was. His black hair was just starting to come in gray along the temples, and he was starting to make noises about how he was getting too old.

Wrinkles massed across his tanned face. They hid most, but not all, of the white scars. Constantly working in sunlight had turned his skin dark brown and leather-like. He had a small nose and thin lips, all the better to hide his emotions. The top of one of his ears was missing, and his hair barely covered the scar just above it.

Though Orla had seen Kato smile, and watched his dark brown eyes grow kind, right now, they were like black iron, harsh and cold.

"And how do you propose to rescue him?" Kato asked, his tone soft, but still as hard as his eyes.

"We have to get to the coast, to the capital city. We'll need to break into the castle. Da has told me about those nets they use to hold him. They drain away his power. But it comes right back as soon as he's freed. All we have to do is to cut him loose. He can do the rest himself," Orla said quickly.

Kato's eye didn't grow any kinder. "Just break into the castle, huh?"

"I don't know any of the details of this plan," Orla said. "I've never been there. I take it you have been?"

Kato nodded. "It isn't as easy as walking into town," he warned.

"I didn't figure it would be," Orla said. "Are you with me?"

Kato stared at her, unspeaking for a short while.

Orla had learned long ago how to be still, to not fidget, even though Kato was starting to make her nervous.

What if he, too, was a traitor? Would he sell her out to the king?

"I always do a risk analysis before I take any job," Kato said. "I've never knowingly walked into a situation that's going to be deadly. It means choosing not to ride with certain caravans. Some of them were too unwieldy to be easily protected. Some refused to hire enough security. Some hired too much, and so people would be tripping over one another if an attack came."

Orla nodded. He'd told her this before, even though she'd never had a choice about the battles she'd fought in. She was at Da's side. Nothing else mattered.

"When I agreed to mentor you, I didn't see the harm in it. It had many benefits, actually. It forced me to become a better fighter, because I had to break down the things I did naturally, instinctively, and then put them into words." He shook his head. "But you're more trouble than all of the other protection jobs I've ever taken combined."

Orla looked around. The generals were still talking with the mayoral representatives. No one was paying attention to her.

Yet.

"So you won't come with me. Fine," Orla said, stepping away from Kato.

"Didn't say that," Kato said, grabbing her elbow again, turning them, and starting to walk away. "Just that you're more trouble." He sighed.

"What are the chances that we'll succeed?" Orla couldn't stop herself from asking.

"Little to none," Kato said. "But someone should be concerned about Talon. And it's right that you are. And that I accompany you."

"How are we going to get to the coast?" Orla asked, already starting to plan out what happened next.

"Oxen are too slow," Kato said. "Horses are much faster. Plus, this group are going to be moving more quickly than normal. They'll be magically assisted."

"Can we steal a horse?" Orla said.

Kato snorted. "No. They can't be controlled without magic." He glanced at her. "Brennan might be able to help with that."

Orla set her lips in a firm line, pressing them together to contain her immediate outburst of vitriol. "No, he cannot." She paused, making herself take a deep breath. "He was the one who betrayed Da."

Kato kept them walking. "I see."

Orla could hear the argument already in her head—Kato inquiring if she was really going after Da, or after Brennan.

If she was honest with herself, her desire to get to the capital quickly was a combination of both.

"That might change our plans a little," Kato said after a bit. "Though it makes our odds worse."

"I know," Orla said. They'd reached the edge of Talon's troops, where tents were already being set up to tend to the wounded. Orla couldn't let herself look at the bodies, how much they'd lost, and for what?

Had it been a lost cause from the beginning?

"We'll have to wait until tonight," Kato said quietly as he steered her toward one of the tents at the back. "We need to make ourselves useful here for now, so no one will look twice at us."

He paused, glancing at her. "Lose the armor. And the sword. And anything else that makes you recognizable. Stealth, not strength, is going to take us further for now."

Orla nodded in agreement. They were going to have to sneak into the group from Alfaladon, travel with them to the capital.

But how?

ON STORMING THE CASTLE

Quite frankly, a review of the literature should show anyone with a modicum of sense that castles are rarely ever actually "stormed." There's a reason why you build those huge edifices to defense. And no, it isn't just so that you can stand safely behind your walls and go "*neaner-neaner-neaner*" at the huge army marching toward you, though that's part of it.

It's difficult to knock down those castle walls. Particularly since the army behind those walls has a huge advantage and, if they're prepared, can spend weeks if not months shooting down at the opposing army, throwing boiling oil and dropping rocks on them.

Siege engines can help the attackers, as well as catapults to toss those rocks back. Ramming equipment to pound at the gates can never hurt.

However, the losses are going to be staggering, and in a place like Ulthir's lands, when there's no hope of reincarnation, the chances of forming such a huge army are slim.

Instead, most people trick their way into the castle. Whether it's by digging underneath (like Little Irvine's dragon) or ramming the door by surprise (like Soliki's dragon), or even by fooling the guards (as Maloneal did with the Trojan Bird). Once someone sneaks in, they then only have to figure out a way to let their friends in. And their friends. And their friends, until it's a party.

There are exceptions, of course. Like one of the empires on the east coast which claimed to be unassailable until an entire contingent of wizards working together attacked and literally brought a lightning storm down on the castle walls. Or that city-state island which not only upset the local population but also the local gods and goddesses, until *they* worked together to bring the walls down.

Mostly, though, it's a matter of getting in first.

The castle at the heart of Alfaladon where the current King Alfa Edwardo resides has more than one defense against attackers, some obvious, some not so.

For one, it lies in the center of the city of Ibramz. Which is big. Very big. The home to over 100,000 souls. The castle sits there like the pearl in the heart of all that dross, or so some of the royals would have you believe.

Any attacking army is going to have to cross a *lot* of hostile territory before they reach the castle walls.

Next, because the castle wasn't planned, but just kind of growed there, it isn't an architectural marvel. There are parts of it that are fabulous, but then there's a hallway, two staircases, and a courtyard to get through before the next showcase area.

A stranger trying to make his or her way from one end of the castle to the other is likely to die of starvation before finding a quick route. Servants are quartered in their part of the castle and unlikely to interact with the other parts. Some may know two or three areas well, but not the entire castle.

There are only a few who have The Knowing, as it's called, who can find the back passages and secret hallways and can quickly make it from one part of the castle to the other, who are familiar with both the dark dungeons as well as the lofty attics.

All the King Alfas are expected to have The Knowing. They get tested on it before their coronation. Occasionally, the ceremony has been postponed until the king can get it right. That is always a bad omen, and no one likes that kind of reputation.

Certain members of the guard have The Knowing, gradually acquired over the years and shared down the line once a guard reaches a specific rank and can be trusted.

Loalmane knows the entire castle. As do some of the wizards, who are certain that there are hidden libraries containing powerful spell books. So they search, only to find these bookshelves filled with diaries of former King Alfas as well as the original histories of the various territories before they were taken over by Alfaladon and their story completely changed. They keep sending members from the school into the castle though, telling them to look further.

However, enchantments have been laid down over the years, so finding spells don't work. Once you're lost, you stay lost.

Staircases rarely climb easily from one floor to the next, and frequently the trapdoors to either the attic or the basement are hidden. Looking out a window might give you a sense of north or west, but it's almost impossible to get to the top floor to achieve a bird's eye view of the place.

All this means is that while breaking into the castle isn't that difficult, getting to where you need to go, or to where you think you need to go, is.

Surprisingly, or perhaps not so, the tunnels under the castle where prisoners are kept are less confusing and difficult to traverse. There are very few exits from the dungeon into the upper floors of the castle and they are all heavily guarded by people as well as warded by magic.

Occasionally, people do escape from the dungeon. Of course, no one likes to talk about such things. Excuses get made. Sometimes the officer in charge lies about what actually happened to a particular prisoner, not wanting to admit their failure, and will provide a convenient corpse that's been burned beyond recognition to back up their story.

One of those dungeon exits happens to be into the antechamber of the throne room. That way political (and other) prisoners can easily be brought before the king to receive their sentence.

Was that way into the castle guarded more heavily than most?

Yes.

And no.

Of course there were guards stationed there. However, it was considered a cushy assignment. Rather stupefying, at that.

Who would break into the castle at that juncture? Everyone knew a plethora of guards would be there. No one had ever tried breaking in that way.

No one had ever been as desperate before, either.

BRENNAN

Brennan had thought that Millerstown was big.

Yet, everywhere he looked from where he was currently seated on his horse on the bluffs going down to Ibramz, were houses. And more houses. Plus, streets full of people. And more people. And carts. All up and down the bluffs, as well as extending along the coast.

He had no words for suburbs. Or exurbs. Or bedroom communities. He didn't even understand commuting.

All he knew was that there were more people there, gathered in that one place, than he'd ever imagined even existed.

He forced himself to take another deep breath while he could, certain that once they wound their way down into that moving mass of humanity all breathing his air that he'd never be able to take another deep breath again.

Sitting far in the distance, up to his right, squatted the castle, sprouting like a white tumor among all the brown and green houses and streets.

Just a bit further up stood another white monstrosity. The wizards' school, the most famous in all the lands. Supposedly the best, though Brennan had his doubts.

It was probably a fine place. Trained powerful wizards.

However, there was a sameness to their magic, to how they approached spellcasting, that Brennan didn't like. They were all so regimented. He wouldn't be welcome there, not just because he was a traitor, but because he didn't wear the appropriate clothing.

He might not have a choice about exchanging his shirts and pants for robes, eventually. It would all depend on whether or not he could free Talon and clear his name among those who mattered, or if he'd be forever known as Brennan the Traitor.

Loalmane at least had left him alone for the rest of their trip, though Brennan had felt the wizard's eyes on him now and again, studying him, as if trying to figure out the puzzle he presented.

Brennan didn't feel like a puzzle. Or even like someone involved in a grand plot. He was just trying to survive, to get through one day after the next, while feeling overwhelmed with guilt and regrets.

He had been able to spend some time studying the nets that held Talon down, unraveling the spells woven into the metal and rope. His gift for seeing magic really aided him in this, possibly giving him the slightest of edges. He'd learned that just slicing through the ropes wouldn't do the trick. No, he'd have to attack them magically first, then physically.

If he got the chance.

Talon roused a little more each day. His wounds were finally starting to heal. At first, Brennan had believed that Talon had been doing it, but no, he'd finally traced a line of magic back to Loalmane.

Why was he healing Talon? Slowly bringing the dragon back to full strength? It didn't make any sense to Brennan, who felt himself growing stupider with each passing day, the magic in the land so smooth and even and never quite enough.

"Quite a sight, eh?" Concha asked, coming up beside Brennan. He was the only one of the wizards who voluntarily talked with him. The others might deign to include him in a conversation if he was riding beside them and spoke up, but they never asked him anything.

They had their prize.

Loalmane was the one who insisted that Brennan should be there with them, as he was the one who knew Orla the best.

And Orla was the key for controlling Talon.

"It sure is something," Brennan admitted freely. "Did you grow up here?"

"Aye," Concha said, a quick smile transforming his usual dark features. "Or near enough to here to call it home. Little fishing village, down the coast. Though it isn't really there anymore."

Concha gave Brennan a second smile that wasn't quite real.

"You know how it is. Kids growing up. Leaving the homestead. Moving into the city, until the village is mostly deserted. Just old folks hanging onto a life that no longer exists."

"I see," Brennan lied. Though he really didn't.

What would have happened to Papa and Mama if none of his brothers or sisters had followed in his footsteps? Would the family have had to move from the forest, and into a town? Someone would have taken it up.

But if the god Num was gone? And there were no blessings in the trees? Would they have stayed?

Brennan gave Concha a smile in return, though he felt chilled to his soul.

He *had* to free Talon. Had to make sure that he could escape. It didn't matter if Brennan died or not.

Talon needed to live on, for the sake of all the people in his territory if nothing else.

The castle was as confusing as Brennan had heard. And then some.

Just the entrance of it was jarring. There was a hedge running all the way around the place that wasn't blackberry bramble but a close cousin. (And yes, the King Alfas had gotten the idea from Talon's hedge.) It was at least three men tall and impossible to climb, the thorns as likely to kill you as any guards who heard you trying to scramble up the bramble.

The gate they came through was wide enough for half a dozen horses to ride side by side. It all looked very fine and orderly, until you got to the other side.

Three buildings faced the gate. The middle one was three stories tall and done in a checkerboard style, with large white, black, and red tiles decorated the sides, giving it the feeling of being created for whimsy and not much else. (It actually was very practical, as the tiles were magically enhanced to prevent mold from growing, which was always a problem given the rains on the coast.) The building to the right of it was only two stories tall and appeared to be made out of gray driftwood, the walls all nobbily and weathered. It looked as though it belonged in the forest where Brennan had grown up, not part of a castle. The building on the left at least looked the part, though it, too, was a completely different style, being made out of a beautiful orange clay with smooth walls and rounded windows.

Loalmane was staring at Talon, and for the first time, Brennan saw one of the dragon's eyes open. He looked dazed, as if he couldn't believe what he was seeing either.

Then the eye snapped shut and the dragon made an effort to turn his face away, despite being held tightly by ropes.

Loalmane sniggered to himself and rode forward.

Grooms came out to take the horses. Brennan wasn't sure how they were going to get the cart with the dragon through the smaller, internal gate.

Loalmane used his magic, forcing the walls to *flex* in a way that was just unnatural and made Brennan uncomfortable to pass through afterward. (That sort of magic *will* get you into trouble eventually, as while solid structures prefer to remain solid, it also doesn't take a lot to get them to lose all coherence. Change their shape too many times and they'll turn into gelatin. Or worse.)

They wound their way through more courtyards and different styles of buildings: tall buildings that had more windows than walls; short buildings with vines lovingly carved on every wooden surface; brick buildings that looked so cold and sterile Brennan figured that it took three times as much firewood to heat the rooms (he wasn't wrong); more buildings covered in every shape, color, and style of tile than Brennan had even known existed; as well as some lovely cottages camped in the middle of courtyards, like refugees from an island paradise.

Brennan was lost after the second turn. He might have been able to trace the magic in the various buildings and build himself a map out of that, but he didn't have time, and quite frankly, hadn't consider it until after he was already completely turned around.

Finally, they came to a broad, circular courtyard surrounded by (mostly) white brick buildings. Iron gates covered the windows. Their tall, four-story roofs blocked most of the healing sunlight. Vibrant green moss crept along the corners and edges of the cobblestones.

"You will rest here," Loalmane told Talon, speaking out loud, possibly for the benefit of all. "Tomorrow, you will have your audience with the king. Then, we get to play."

Brennan didn't see Talon twitch, and he didn't open his eye again. However, he must have had some choice words for Loalmane, as the wizard threw back his head and just laughed.

"We'll see, sir beast. We'll see."

He winked at Brennan and strode off on his own, letting the servants who'd come racing into the area do their jobs with the equipment and horses.

"You're with me, for now," Concha told Brennan.

Brennan nodded, and tried, really tried, to pay attention to where they went next, through hallways and rooms and up one staircase then down another.

However, he quickly realized that he'd never be able to find his way back to the courtyard where Talon lay.

He'd just have to wait until the next day and the audience with the king, to put their paltry plan into place.

Hopefully, it would be enough.

And maybe the Twins would finally wake up enough to push a bit more luck their way.

MALONEAL AND THE TROJAN BIRD

Maloneal has heard the myths about horses being used to trick people into allowing you access to their castle.

However, the people in Ulthir's lands don't really know horses, don't understand them. Coming in with a horse honestly draws too much attention of the wrong sort.

Instead, he approaches the castle walls with a bird.

Not just any bird, no.

This is a golden bird inside a golden cage. Rubies form its eyes, and diamonds stud its beak. Gears and clockwork make up its wings, and its talons are pure onyx, blacker than the blackest night.

Did I mention that it's the size of a small cottage? Maybe bigger?

The cart groans under the weight of hauling it. Two large, stubborn oxen draw it along the rutted path leading to the castle gate.

All the time, it sings. Beautiful, clear honeyed notes that soothe like a dip in a warm lake in the summer. There's no repeatable melody, just a shapeless tune that pulls you along as surely as the oxen pull the cart.

The guards at the gate are suspicious, of course. Who has ever seen such a creation? It must be magical.

And the bullshit story that Maloneal comes up with doesn't sound right either. Who would gift King Bart with such an exquisite piece? He'd never done anything to deserve it. He is too well known as being just slightly, *barely* above the common working man, wearing regular clothes and picking his teeth (rather unpleasantly) after each meal. He'd only come to be king because of the plague that had swept through the royal family and no one else wanted the job.

(Sure, there are perks like clean sheets, servants, good food, and even better beer. On the flip side, you also have to listen to those whining courtiers all day, complaining about how you're not doing the job right. The barbarians and soldiers also whine about not enough battles. King Bart might occasionally regret allowing his wife to talk him into taking the role.)

On the other hand, King Bart also hadn't pissed anyone off recently. He'd successfully negotiated a treaty with the neighboring kingdom up north, providing better trade and fewer wars. (Another thing that his warriors complained about.)

After the court magicians (who weren't actually second rate, but this is Maloneal we're talking about, and magic is in his blood, literally) cleared the cart, it slowly comes lumbering into the castle courtyard.

The bird starts singing joyously at this, as well as flapping its wings and doing a little dance.

A victory dance, perhaps?

Maloneal and King Bart hit it off fabulously, as Maloneal has ensured that they will. They go off drinking, possibly having a contest or two about who can hold the most ale.

The bird finally quiets down as night falls, though it ends its day of song with a lovely lullaby.

A most effective lullaby, as most of the guards in the castle fall asleep.

The cage around the bird dissolves when the moonlight strikes it, revealing a large contingent of men who'd been posing as the bars of the cage.

The bird itself is quickly dismantled, the clockwork turning into many weapons.

King Bart and his men are overwhelmed and surrender in due course.

Seems that while striking a bargain with the neighbors to the north was a good idea, seeking to bargain with the neighbors to the south would have been better.

Had such an elaborate ruse been necessary to break into such a small little backwards kingdom?

No.

Maloneal had been paid fabulously to make the battle worthy of song, and the story to live forever, not just a mundane takeover, the kind that happen every day of the week. To make the conqueror's cause seem noble, or at least clever.

But beware of what you wish for. Because others will hear your tale, and decided to do one better.

ORLA

Orla had never had to be still for such long periods of time before. Had never had to ride in a wagon, hidden by blankets and other gear, curled up and unable to stretch out, for hours at a time. The air she breathed was hot and humid, and she felt so stifled sometimes she just wanted to scream.

She told herself during the worst of those times that she was doing this for Da. Da, who must be in agony, captured by his enemies, hurt and all alone.

No, wait, he wasn't all alone.

Brennan was with him. Probably torturing him further, taunting him with how *easy* it was to get both Da and Orla to trust him.

Orla grit her teeth and endured the long days.

Kato had hired on as a mercenary to protect the group they traveled with as they made their way back to the coast.

Something had happened to the majority of their original guard.

Orla didn't know for certain, hadn't asked any questions, had just trusted that Kato had taken care of it.

They were less than a day behind the group carting Talon along.

Though they'd left a few days after the original group, they'd caught up over the week, the members of the group eager to get back to the capital, to report their success to the king.

Kato helped set up camp every night, allowing Orla time to sneak out of her hiding place and disappear into the darkness. Though she'd toyed with the idea of following them on foot, she knew she couldn't. They moved too fast, and she'd never be able to keep up.

Orla endured, and would endure more, in order to save Da. Particularly to make up for her mistakes, such as letting him go off alone in the first place.

She only knew they had reached their destination by how the cart tilted as they headed down the bluffs toward the city, as well as the sounds beside her: snatches of conversation from a thousand different voices; the hawking of vendors, enticing people to come sample their wares; children screeching with laughter as they raced between the carts, some sort of game that only they knew how to play.

Finally, the noises outside the cart grew hushed and the cart drew to a stop.

Kato and Orla had made a couple of different plans at this point, as they had no way of knowing if they'd be unloading inside the castle walls, in some courtyard, or outside.

They'd hoped for the latter, but were prepared for the former.

The Twins appeared to be smiling at them, though, for the cart had been pulled into a side street, off the main drag, where a warehouse stood ready to receive all the camping goods inside, to be stashed away against further need.

Kato physically picked up the pile that hid Orla, carrying her just inside the door, then reaching down and dragging her out.

"Out the door. To your right. Along the side of the building. I'll be there shortly," Kato whispered.

Orla forced her legs to work, as she'd been practicing that every day: going from motionless for hours, then able to spring into movement.

The noise outside the warehouse was staggering, but she strode quickly away, as if she had business elsewhere.

No one stopped her, though by the time she slipped around the edge of the building, she was shaking and had sweat through her shirt.

First step down. Now, to move on.

Kato collected her shortly, taking her through the city quickly. She was grateful for his guidance as the crowds, noises, and smells overwhelmed her.

Why would so many people agree to live here, one on top of another? She didn't get it.

Then again, she'd come to love Da's mountain, with just the winds for company.

They spent the rest of the afternoon in a café, eating, drinking, and watching an amazing number of people walk by. They came in all shapes, all sizes, all colors and manner of dress: islanders wearing a single highly decorated piece of cloth wrapped in a complicated manner covering all the important bits with knots and pins; both male and female barbarians from the north who roamed (mostly) bare chested wearing badly-formed shaggy goat pelts for pants; elegant ladies in brilliantly colored brocades and silks; and just as elegant men in even brighter long robes.

It really was something to behold, and Orla was grateful for their time sitting, with her back to a wall so no one could get at her, watching this parade.

As night approached, the pair of them disappeared into the stream of people that had only thinned a little, making their way to a nearby park.

Orla at least understood the notion of adding a little greenery to the surrounding press of people, a small open space that let you see more than just a little slice of the sky. She took a deep breath there, smelling moist ground and greenery for the first time in what felt like days.

Under the trees that edged the park stood a man-sized boulder. Though Orla couldn't see it, Kato quickly found the trap door built into the side of the rock.

"Are you sure you want to do this?" Kato asked one last time. He'd checked with her on more than one occasion.

"I do," Orla said formally, feeling her very soul commit to this course of action.

Kato sighed. "There's no going back from this point," he added.

"I know," Orla said. "You could just give me a map, and let me go on my own."

Kato snorted at that. "I don't know if you'd be able to find your way. And once you did get through, then you'd have to fight half an army on your own. No, it's better for me to come with. That way, if we do succeed, I don't have to face an angry dragon alone."

"Why would Da be angry if I rescued him?" Orla asked, confused.

"Because I put you in danger," Kato pointed out.

"Oh, yeah. There's that," Orla said. "Thank you."

"You're welcome. And it's been an honor to fight beside you."

Orla gave him a bow, because she couldn't convey how much that meant to her. "It's been an honor being your student." And she meant it.

She wouldn't be there without him.

Oh, she would have gotten to the capital. Probably far too late to do anything about freeing Talon, though.

Kato took a step and the dark opening swallowed him whole.

Orla gulped, then followed.

Time to save Da.

TALON

The trip to the coast had been mostly agony. Fortunately, Talon had been able to sleep through much of it. He'd wake to pain and a longing to turn over. Even the small itches he felt along his back were torture because he couldn't move.

At the same time, he had that false Orla in his head saying soothing words, yet also harping at him to give up, stop fighting.

Laughing at his feeble attempts to break free.

Talon knew it wasn't the real Orla. She was much fiercer, much less sweet, and more likely to yell at him than to whisper honeyed words in his mind.

Still, the sound of her voice, even as false as it was, gave him hope.

He noticed that he was starting to heal after a few days, knew that it was Loalmane doing it. And while he occasionally smelled Brennan nearby, he never directed his thoughts at the boy.

The wizardling had done what he'd been asked to do.

Talon hated having to rely on the boy to free him at the end, but he didn't have a choice.

Where was the real Orla? Talon had a fantasy that she was safe, back inside his territory, that she'd gone back to hold it for him until he returned.

He knew better. He still allowed himself to think of her that way, letting his daydreams carry him away, picturing her making it up to the top of his mountain, making herself a comfortable nest in his tunnels.

It was better than imagining her dead, or trying to mount some impossible rescue that wouldn't work.

Talon felt almost fully back to strength by the time they pulled into the castle. He didn't bother trying to sense where he was, or how he'd gotten there. Given the least chance, he'd fly up and out of here.

Though he would be back to wreak his revenge later.

We're home! Came the singsong voice of the false Orla.

Home is on the other side of the black curtain of death, Talon warned. *For you, at any rate.*

Loalmane threw back his head and laughed and laughed.

No, dear beast, that is where you'll finally find your release.

Talon would have shaken his head to get those hateful words out of his ears.

However, he was still firmly attached to the cart that had dragged him there so ignobly. Those damned nets were just too hard to claw his way through, particularly since the majority of his claws had yet to grow back.

Talon spent the long night awake for once, breathing the cool air and thinking back on his long life.

Though he'd formed a safe territory, a haven for his people, he was still most proud of being Orla's Da, of raising her up to be a fierce warrior who had stood at his side until the very end.

He would gladly sacrifice himself to save her.

The morning brought cool air and no rain. Talon felt the castle waking up around him. People looked out at him from the various windows. He couldn't see them, and would only occasionally hear them, but his sense of smell had come back and he could certainly scent them. Some of the observers were poorer—servants, probably —given their natural body odor. Others were probably from the court, their perfume unsuccessfully masking the terror they felt gazing upon him.

Loalmane's scent had been the most constant during the trip, so Talon instantly recognized the magician as he approached.

He tensed, preparing himself for more mocking, but all he got was *Let's get this show on the road, shall we?*

I can show you all sorts of aerial acrobatics, Talon offered.

Not the show I had in mind, Loalmane replied with a laugh.

A group of wizards approached, working in concert to levitate Talon up, off the cart, still safely ensconced in ropes, through the gate, then, finally, into the castle itself.

Now, Talon did pay attention to where he was. He didn't bother tracking people, or corridors, or rooms.

No, he tracked windows.

Though none of them would be big enough for him to slip through, they would still provide him with easier access to outside and the freedom of the skies.

Too bad that he might leave a dragon-sized hole behind.

At least the wizard's levitation spell was more comfortable than that damned cart. He felt carried on air, not feeling any bumps, even when they went up one set of stairs, then down another.

He was glad that he didn't have to try to find his way here by scent alone. That might have been difficult, even for him.

Finally, they reached the antechamber for the throne room. Talon could sense all the guards around him, smell their hostility and fear. He was glad that Orla wasn't here to see them, or she would have tried to face them all down by herself.

Did the king really need that many guards? Was he so hated by his own people, or by those who he'd subsumed?

(Yes. And no.)

(King Alfa Edwardo tended to believe his own press releases of how mighty and how fierce he was. Just look at how much he'd accomplished!)

(Never mind that most of those victories came through due to the thorough planning of his generals and war staff, or the manipulations of his court wizard.)

(So of course, he needed to be heavily guarded at all times.)

(Particularly since he was "entertaining" foreign visitors that day, namely, the fiercest dragon of all time.)

(He might have also been fed a load of hooey when it came to Talon, backed up by the wizards' school that kept losing people in battles with him, never bothering to remember that they'd been low-level people who hadn't been properly trained.)

Talon sensed the room opening up above him. He didn't bother opening his eyes yet, but his senses told him that the throne room was at least three stories tall, with balconies up above for people to look down on the court. (Yet another security hazard that ensured even more guards, watching to make sure that the rabble in the upper tiers didn't do anything like throw things down on the nobles and the court below.)

There were windows up there as well. Windows that Talon was already planning on diving through.

Then came the acrid smell of magic. It tickled an old memory, one of his oldest, in fact: the magic in the throne room stank similarly to the spell that had originally crafted Talon into a dragon.

Talon had no idea what that meant, but he knew it wasn't good.

As Talon had never met the king, he couldn't identify him by smell. He eventually figured out that it wasn't richness or corpulence that marked the king, but smugness.

Finally, the procession came to a halt. The wizards did something to the ropes, then to Talon's prone body, as he felt himself being raised up. He still couldn't stretch his wings, tail, or arms out—he was still forced into a compact shape.

However, for the first time in a week, he was upright.

He opened his eyes and steadied himself against the onslaught of light. Sun streamed in from the windows that were shaped like tops —with a broad base leading up to a skinny, thin peak. The walls were covered in a white marble with random black streaks running through it. They reflected the light of a hundred magelights burning, along with candles. They were also hardly resistant to the corrosive acid that Talon spat out. He looked forward to marking them.

In front of Talon stood a group of people. He figured the fancy one in the center, on the throne, was probably the king, surrounded by both guards and courtiers.

Immediately in front of Talon stood a large black cauldron, bubbling with something sickly yellow-green. It was big enough to boil a half-dozen babies at the same time, an image that was both disturbing as well as highly appropriate.

That was where the scent of the magic was coming from.

Talon had a bad feeling about this.

"So, beast, you are finally here, brought as low as you deserve," King Alfa Edwardo said, addressing Talon.

Why? Talon asked plainly, addressing everyone in hearing range. *Why do I deserve to be brought low? I've done nothing against you or your people. You're the ones who attacked me.*

Several of the people in the court gasped to be addressed in their minds. They either raced from the room or reached for these bizarre silver hats that they then jammed on their heads.

"You are a beast, unfit to live," King Alfa Edwardo said, still convinced he was in the right.

I don't kill people unless they attack me first, Talon said. *I don't eat them either*, he added, having heard that rumor whispered about him on the trip there.

Everyone who listened to Talon knew he spoke the truth.

There was a rustling among the courtiers, and an uneasiness settled in the room. Even King Alfa Edwardo paled slightly.

"No matter," Loalmane said, stepping forward. "You are not as worthy as the king, and that is all that matters. You should be grateful that we are going to use you, your life, in the best way possible. Isn't that right, my lord?"

"That is correct," King Alfa Edwardo said, puffing himself back up. "You will give us your secret to living forever."

Talon couldn't help himself. He snorted in laughter. *Don't have a clue why I've lived so long*, he said. *Figure it's just an oversight on the part of Ulthir.*

Again, the truth bore out in his words.

Again, everyone grew slightly less comfortable with the whole proceeding.

"Let me show you, my lord, just how wonderful the strength from this beast will be, fed into your deserving self," Loalmane said, stepping forward, trying to take control of the situation again.

You know that this is wrong, Talon warned. *You will not succeed.*

"But I already have!" Loalmane said, turning and addressing Talon for the first time. "I have you, don't I? And soon, I will have all of you."

His greedy eyes sucked at Talon, as if through sight alone the wizard could consume him.

Talon shivered, unable to help himself.

"Let us begin."

The spell didn't take that long, as Loalmane had already set up most of the component parts.

Smoke rose up out of the cauldron, thick and dripping with yellow ichor, slowly wending its way up toward Talon's head.

While Talon had rarely struggled to get free from his net, not wanting to give Loalmane or anyone else the satisfaction of seeing him squirm, now, he couldn't help himself. He jerked his head back, or at least he tried to.

The nets held him firmly.

Kind of.

There appeared to be more slack in the nets than there had been earlier.

Just another moment. I'll have you free, came whispered words in Talon's head.

Brennan.

But Talon didn't have another moment.

The smoke grabbed him and wrapped around his head like a sickly glove.

He shuddered again, unable to think, unable to move, unable to breathe.

Though the ropes had drained him of his energy and magic, this smoke was ten thousand times worse.

It sucked away pieces of his soul.

Talon hadn't ever really believed all that talk about how Ulthir had placed a light in every person.

Watching his own light flickering made him a true believer.

Just then, a loud shout went up.

Near the doorway of the throne room.

Talon had his own battle, trying to hold onto his soul.

Still, a part of him realized that either the best thing—or the worst—had just occurred.

Orla had arrived.

"Don't kill her!" ordered Loalmane.

Talon still struggled, trapped by the sickly smoke. He still shouted out to her, *Run, daughter, run!*

It wouldn't be enough. She wouldn't go. He knew that.

The clanging of swords and the crying of dying men filled the throne room.

I'll submit if you promise to not hurt her, to let her go free, he said, switching tactics, turning his thoughts to Loalmane.

"Will you, now?" the wizard said. "What if I don't want to?"

Don't hurt her and I'll give you my soul, Talon said to the entire group who remained in the throne room.

"No! Da!" Orla cried out, having also heard his bargain.

She's my adopted daughter, Talon implored, still broadcasting his thoughts widely.

"Do not hurt the girl," the king ordered, calling out over the ruckus.

Almost have your ropes undone, Brennen promised.

Talon shook his head, grateful that he could finally make such a motion.

He'd already promised, if the wizard lived up to his side of the bargain.

It wouldn't matter if Talon was free or not.

Orla was captured in short order, quickly overwhelmed by sheer numbers, though she'd made a good standing for herself. Kato, too, was captured alive, though he looked more beaten up and ragged when the pair of them were dragged before the king.

Talon could barely see them through the yellowed haze that covered his head. He could at least scent that his daughter was hale and healthy.

Oh, Da, was all she said as she came forward.

We did our best, Talon said quietly. He didn't want to say anything more, didn't want to indicate that Brennan was still working on his netting, that there might be a chance, even at the very end, for them to all get to safety.

Somehow.

"Do you give your word, dragon, that you will submit to us, freely give us your soul, if I see that no harm comes to your daughter?" King Alfa Edwardo said from behind the plethora of guards protecting him.

Not your word. His word, Talon insisted. *Loalmane's.*

The wizard heaved a loud, put-upon sigh. "Very well. I promise to not hurt your daughter or to order another to harm her."

You will allow her to go free, wherever she chooses, Talon instructed.

"I will."

Talon knew that he couldn't make the bargain airtight. He didn't have time. But he didn't sense any falseness in Loalmane's voice. He meant what he said.

Probably would be worth it to him to see Orla's soul suffering after the death of her Da.

Hopefully her life would be long enough to make up for that.

No, Da, don't, Orla insisted.

You're the best thing that ever happened to me, Talon told her gently.

He didn't say goodbye, because those words were too final, and he didn't want for the court to find out that even dragons could cry.

The ropes fell from Talon, Brennan having finished his task.

Power, magic, and energy rushed into him.

Thank you, Talon said to everyone who could hear, though they had no idea that it wasn't Loalmane who'd freed him.

He stretched his wings out fully, the throne room being big enough to accommodate the movement. Then he turned to Loalmane. *I am ready.*

"No! Da!" Orla cried out again, struggling to free herself from the four soldiers who held her.

Kato merely bowed his head to the inevitable.

A whirlwind now spun up from the top of the cauldron. It danced there for a few moments before hopping down and speeding its way toward Talon. It engulfed the dragon, seeking to rip his soul to shreds, disperse all that he'd ever been to the undeserving fools of a court.

Talon felt himself fading. The world was growing dim. He kept his eyes on Orla, though, the one bright spot in the room, in his life.

Someone moved. It took a while later on for Talon to piece together the sequence of events.

No one was paying any attention to Brennan.

He darted forward, rushing toward Loalmane.

He didn't try to stop the spell. It was already too far along. Talon would never recover at this point—too much of his sense of self had been drained away.

Instead, Brennan pushed Loalmane from behind.

Directly into the whirling cyclone surrounding Talon.

Bright light flashed and blinded Talon. He heard as well as felt the resulting thunderbolt deep in his bones.

A ripping noise followed, as Talon felt himself torn in two.

Then there was darkness.

And cold.

Talon opened his eyes to see endless black night above him, with stars twinkling around the edges. He lay on his back, on cold snow, that he knew was never going to melt, no matter how long he laid there.

He shook his head to clear it.

His human head.

It was the wrong proportion. Felt odd and small and surprisingly flat, given the two centuries he'd spent wearing the form of a dragon.

Slowly, Talon—no, Killian, now—looked down his body. There were his original arms and hands, the fingers tipped in regular nails, not claws or talons. He had legs again. Wriggling his toes felt amazing.

He sat up and looked around. Though he tried to remember everything he saw, his poor head couldn't hold it all in, the immensity of the mountain beneath him, the unreal sky above him, the smell of the cold, the goosebumps (goosebumps!) that chased across his shoulders.

There, to his right, stood a huge throne carved out of a single piece of ice. It was both the biggest thing he'd ever seen, almost as big as the mountain itself, while still he could see the whole thing from where he sat.

Tiny crystal tops danced at the foot of the throne, throwing rainbows of light as they continually spun.

The person—god—sitting on the throne looked normal enough. At least as much as Killian could recall. Dark hair, as black as the sky above. White skin that could have been formed out of the pure snow all around him. Plain beige shirt and gray wool pants, like a farmer.

He had a plain face, somewhat stern. Killian could never say exactly what he looked like, except possibly the most ordinary man he'd ever seen, with a regular nose, mouth, forehead, cheeks, and chin.

His eyes, though, stopped Killian cold.

They were wholly black, and speckled with starlight.

Ulthir, Killian knew without a doubt.

He wasn't sure what to do next. Bow? Kneel down? Curse the god for having killed him, his daughter, and so many good people?

He settled on nodding in Ulthir's general direction.

Ulthir returned the nod.

"You have been unmade," Ulthir said, his voice a little rough, as if he hadn't used it in a while.

"And Loalmane?" Killian had to ask. While Orla was important, his destructor was top of his list at the moment.

"Maloneal? He's temporarily unmade as well," Ulthir said with smug satisfaction. "Thank you, for that. He was getting too big for his britches, and needed to be taken down a peg. Or three."

Killian had to sit for a moment to absorb that.

As a dragon, he'd always been awaiting his cause.

Had taking down Maloneal been it?

"And Orla?" Killian said, turning to his next priority.

"Hmmm," Ulthir said, looking off to the right for a moment. "She's still alive. Still fighting."

"Good," Killian said. Really, that was all that mattered.

"But what am I to do with you next?" Ulthir said, turning those disturbing eyes on Killian.

They felt cold, as if driven by ice, boring holes through his newly acquired body.

Killian faked as casual a shrug as he could. "You could send me back," he said.

"What, as a dragon?" Ulthir said.

Though he didn't narrow his eyes or peer more intently, Killian still felt the intensity of his stare increase.

"Only if that's the only form available," Killian replied. "I'd like... I'd prefer to be a person again. To live out the rest of my life that way."

"Hmmm," was all that Ulthir said as his gaze swept away and he looked to the left this time.

Killian had the impression that Ulthir was talking with someone in the distance.

Eowin? Eomar? The Twins?

"Yes," Ulthir said after an endless time. "That might do nicely."

"And what about the land? All the little local gods and goddesses? And all the people who died while under the influence of Maloneal?" Killian had to ask.

"They'll be taken care of," Ulthir said with a careless wave of his hand. "The Twins will see to that."

Killian knew, *knew* that wouldn't be good enough. Too many families had lost loved ones.

However, he had nothing to bargain with, no way to force fairness out of a god.

Even though he'd done said god a favor.

"What will happen to Maloneal now?" Killian asked as he stood up, his feet feeling foreign and small to him. He didn't tip over, though he was going to have to relearn how to walk.

"He'll regain his strength eventually," Ulthir said. "Hopefully, though, he's learned his lesson and won't try to challenge me again."

Killian shook his head. Maloneal/Loalmane would never learn.

But that was going to be someone else's problem, many, *many* years down the line. Long after Killian/Talon had become a myth on his own.

He still had so many questions of Ulthir. So much to say.

Ulthir, though, had grown tired of someone else breathing his air.

Darkness whirled around Killian again. Instead of being torn apart, he felt himself being compressed, pushed into a smaller and smaller form as he descended.

Though he couldn't say for certain, he would swear that he thought he heard Ulthir say one last thing.

"Welcome home."

EPILOGUE

FINAL WORDS ARE FINAL

Ulthir sighs when he feels that oh-so-familiar presence coming to stand next to his throne.

Again.

"Thought I'd gotten rid of you for a while," he mutters before finally turning to see Maloneal.

Except that Maloneal isn't all there. He's translucent, for a start. His white hair lies flat and dull, instead of reflecting the starlight above. Solemn gray eyes gaze at Ulthir with just the barest spark of life. He still wears the white robes he'd donned as Loalmane, the silver trim brighter than the rest of him.

"Are you happy now?" Maloneal whispers, his voice hollow and thin.

"Are you content to leave well enough alone?" Ulthir asks in return, trying to keep his temper down.

Doesn't do to kick Maloneal when he's down. Might come back more vicious next time.

Maloneal shrugs. "It is my nature," he says, as if that were enough of an excuse for Ulthir to forgive him for all the harm he'd done.

Ulthir sighs again. Though some of the myths claim that Ulthir is the father of all, including Maloneal, Ulthir knows that Maloneal came into being through his own force of will, whether Ulthir had a hand in it or not.

"Just as it is my nature to resist your chaos," Ulthir says.

"True."

They stay like that for a while, Ulthir on his chair, Maloneal standing by his side. The stars whirl and dance over their heads, like the crystal tops at their feet.

For now, Ulthir has ordered things to his liking.

The wheel would turn again, as it always does. Things will get out of hand again.

Good thing that Ulthir still has the Twins on his side, despite how Maloneal had blinded them for a while.

As well as dragons.

READ MORE!

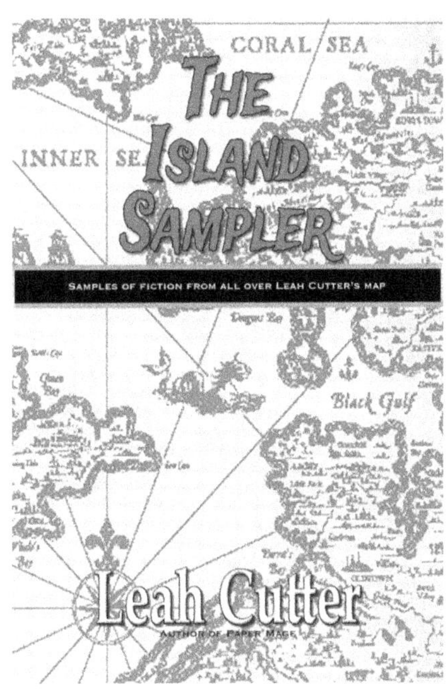

Do you enjoy exploring strange new worlds, new societies, new characters?

ABOUT THE AUTHOR

Leah Cutter writes page-turning fiction in exotic locations, such as a magical New Orleans, the ancient Orient, Hungary, the Oregon coast, rural Kentucky, Seattle, Minneapolis, and many others.

She writes literary, fantasy, mystery, science fiction, and horror fiction. Her short fiction has been published in magazines like *Alfred Hitchcock's Mystery Magazine* and *Talebones*, anthologies like Fiction River, and on the web. Her long fiction has been published both by New York publishers as well as small presses.

Find Leah's books on Knotted Road Press at (www.KnottedRoadPress.com)

Follow her blog at www.LeahCutter.com.

Reviews

It's true. Reviews help me sell more books. If you've enjoyed this story, please consider leaving a review of it on your favorite site.

Come someplace new...

Do you enjoy exploring strange new worlds, new societies, new characters?

Journey into the various lands envisioned by Leah Cutter.

Sign up for my newsletter and I'll start you on your travels with a free copy of my book, *The Island Sampler*.

http://www.LeahCutter.com/newsletter/

About Knotted Road Press

Knotted Road Press publishes dynamic fiction set in exotic locations and unique non-fiction voices in genres such as autobiography, business, cookbooks, and how-to. Our authors cover a wide range of genres including science fiction, fantasy, mystery, literary, and poetry, appealing to all readers. We offer both DRM-free ebooks and print books for a global readership.

Knotted Road Press
www.KnottedRoadPress.com
www.KnottedRoadPress.com/Shop